What the critics are saying…

4 ½ hearts "An interesting tale of old love found again, this book is intriguing and takes readers on an emotional roller coaster. Andy has to deal with past feelings in order to move forward and Jack has to show her that he always had strong feelings for her. Can this couple finally find happiness? Mlyn Hurn has created another story that will stick with readers long after it is over and is sure to go on the keeper shelf." ~ *Angel Brewer The Romance Studio*

3 "There is much more to this tale than love and sex. There is a finding of trust and self, mixed in with some truly sizzling chemistry. However, don't let the title fool you. I was expecting much more BDSM between the lead characters and found there to only be a tiny taste in comparison to the overall story. There are some exceptional scenes involving the lifestyle, but our leads are merely observers, not players. This un-met expectation is the only reason that the rating is not higher." ~ *Thia McClain The Romance Readers Connection*

Mlyn Hurn

Voyage to Submission

ELLORA'S CAVE
ROMANTICA PUBLISHING

An Ellora's Cave Romantica Publication

www.ellorascave.com

Voyage to Submission

ISBN # 141995296X
ALL RIGHTS RESERVED.
Voyage to Submission Copyright© 2005 Mlyn Hurn
Edited by: Linda Carroll-Bradd
Cover art by: Syneca

Electronic book Publication: May, 2005
Trade paperback Publication: November, 2005

Excerpt from *Submissive Passion* Copyright © Mlyn Hurn, 2003

Warning:

The following material contains graphic sexual content meant for mature readers. *Voyage to Submission* has been rated *S-ensuous* by a minimum of three independent reviewers.

Ellora's Cave Publishing offers three levels of Romantica™ reading entertainment: S (S-ensuous), E (E-rotic), and X (X-treme).

S-ensuous love scenes are explicit and leave nothing to the imagination.

E-rotic love scenes are explicit, leave nothing to the imagination, and are high in volume per the overall word count. In addition, some E-rated titles might contain fantasy material that some readers find objectionable, such as bondage, submission, same sex encounters, forced seductions, etc. E-rated titles are the most graphic titles we carry; it is common, for instance, for an author to use words such as "fucking", "cock", "pussy", etc., within their work of literature.

X-treme titles differ from E-rated titles only in plot premise and storyline execution. Unlike E-rated titles, stories designated with the letter X tend to contain controversial subject matter not for the faint of heart.

Also by Mlyn Hurn:

Voyage to Submission

Chapter One

Andrea Bond was a woman who had learned about herself the hard way...through countless hours of introspection and journaling, and visits with her therapist. She felt pretty secure in who she was, now anyway, including her strengths and her weaknesses. Certainly, she believed she was successful in her chosen profession. There was money for most things she wanted and most assuredly for all the things that were needed. At thirty, she wanted for nothing in the life she'd chosen to live.

That wasn't entirely true, she reminded herself gently while she paid the taxi driver before directing the porter regarding the luggage she'd brought. If she was truly happy and secure, then no way in hell would she be about to embark on a reunion cruise with her friends from college. Yet here she was, about to face a seven-day cruise with people, most of whom she'd not seen since college graduation. She needed to face this part of her history, come what may.

Turning, she started walking towards the check-in point at the base of the modern-day gangway. As the quiet, gray-haired couple in front of her moved along, she smiled and offered her papers to the young, handsome officer in charge of this portion of the arrival processing.

He accepted her papers without looking up, checking on several things, saying several things by rote before finally lifting his gaze as he returned the folder.

Andy was prepared for his reaction. At the moment his eyes focused on her face, she noted his whole body stance changed. He straightened his shoulders and back, sucking in his gut and then smiled. After five years, she was no longer shocked by strangers' reactions once they stopped and really looked. No mirror was necessary to know he saw a woman who was five feet, seven inches tall, and possessed a body that rivaled a *Playboy* centerfold, none of which was enhanced. She had hidden under layers of fat for the first twenty-two years of her life. But thanks to months of introspection, years of exercise and weight training, very few people who had known her before she left college would recognize her.

She was glad she didn't have a famous face as she took the folder from the officer. The attention she attracted since she'd lost all the weight was something she still had some trouble accepting without a lot of doubt as to sincerity. She made her way to the next check-in point.

Well-placed signs directed all new arrivals to a small reception area. Upon entering the room, visitors were welcomed by two women, both smiling so much Andy was sure their faces were either frozen in place or they took breaks when she blinked. Almost before she knew it, she was through the reception area, arms full of instructional handouts, one of which included a map on finding her cabin.

Luckily, she was fairly good with directions and easily found her stateroom. After the others booked the cruise, she decided to contact a different cruise agent. Even though it was expensive, she booked a stateroom on her own. Her gut instinct told her she had made the right decision and ignored the logical voice that gave her grief over the cost.

In spite of their being best friends in college, the contact since then had only been sporadic at best, with nearly all of them. Having a room to herself would allow her somewhere to escape in case they didn't get along after all these years.

The stateroom was way more than she had anticipated and wandered around, checking out the closet and drawers before she went onto the balcony. While the view wasn't great at the moment, once they were at sea, she had no doubt it would be worth the extra money. This way, if the cruise proved a total bust, she could hang out here, order room service and get some work done!

* * * * *

After an hour of checking out the stateroom, taking her time to put away her clothes and other belongings, she picked up the phone and requested the room her friends were staying in. She hoped they were not too angry with her for switching to her own cabin. "Hello?"

"Gayle, this is Andy."

"Andy!" Her friend shrieked into the phone. "Where are you? Please don't tell me you missed the boat! Hush up you guys, I can't hear her."

"I'm here, on the ship. I did run a little late. Did the others make it all right?" Andy asked the question to deliberately delay answering her friend.

"Yes, we're here, but where the devil are you?" Gayle paused.

Hearing all the chatter between the three women on the other end of the receiver, Andy wondered if the others were all talking to her as well. That was how it used to be, all of them trying to talk at the same time, even when one was on the phone.

"We are supposed to meet the guys in the lounge on…uhm, some damned deck in thirty minutes!"

"I know," Andy reassured her friend. "We're to meet outside the Constellation Lounge. I just called to promise you I'd be there." A few seconds more passed before she heard a different voice.

"Andy! Where are you? They didn't deliver any luggage for you. Don't tell me you only brought the one bag? Sweetie, you'll need more clothes than just the sweats you used to wear all the time in school."

"Liz, relax. I'm fine. The truth is — "

11

"Oh, God! Did you book a separate room? Andy, you dog, you!"

Andy smiled as she listened to her friends' chattering voices. She wasn't completely sure who said what as the voices came at her. "Stop!" she almost shouted through the phone. "And yes, I booked a suite so I could get some work done."

"Aaw, Andy! This is a pleasure cruise, not a working one. Wait a minute! What in the world could *you* be working on?"

"Liz! Look, I'll meet you guys in the lounge in five minutes. We can have a drink before the guys arrive, okay?"

She heard the frustration in her friends' voices as they agreed to her suggestion. As she hung up the phone a few moments later, she glanced down at her outfit. She didn't wear sweat suits all the time anymore, but she still preferred casual dress. Quickly, she decided to put on one of her new dresses. No doubt, her friends would be nicely dressed for the first evening of the cruise. She wanted them to be impressed the first time they saw the *new* her.

Six minutes later, she entered the lounge, looking around for her friends. She doubted they would have changed much over the years. If anyone recognized her...now, that would be impressive. The dress she had chosen was knee-length, red, sleeveless and embossed silk cheongsam-style. Her black high heels matched the woven trim around the high neck and down the off-center and the closure togs. Maybe it was silly, but she felt like a million bucks.

Taking a deep breath, Andy pushed open one of the double glass doors and entered the lounge. The place wasn't deserted, but the majority of tables were empty and several men were seated at the bar. Almost immediately, Andy recognized three of the five men who were joining them on this cruise. The closest was dressed in shorts already with a logo t-shirt in matched colors. The black curly hair was shorter than he'd worn it in college, but Andy still recognized Tony Marello. All through college, he'd dressed better than anyone else. His father could afford it, but it was based on his personal taste. She easily saw him as the successful restaurateur she'd read about in the newspaper several times over the recent years.

Seated beside him was Ray Williams who had finished medical school and then joined his father's practice. She wasn't surprised to see he already had a receding hairline. He was dressed in casual trousers and a short-sleeved shirt. His blond hair had darkened since she'd seen him last, and when he turned to look at Tony, she saw he now had a mustache.

The last guy at the bar was Mark Sherman, the brains of the group. Most likely, he traveled the tenure track at a college somewhere, working as some kind of science professor. This career choice was inevitable because both parents had been tenured science professors. His reddish-brown hair was still a little long in the back, and the fact he wore a tie with his shirt and a sweater vest would easily serve as a dead giveaway.

For a moment, Andy considered turning around and leaving. The last time she'd seen all of these guys together had been the spring break vacation their senior year. They had all worked quite hard to finish their work on Wednesday, giving them almost eleven full days of vacation time away from campus and studies. Mr. and Mrs. Riley, Jack's parents, had generously offered them the use of their house in the Keys.

Jack Riley.

Andy didn't see him at the bar. He was the one she had always had a crush on…the only who had really mattered. If she were honest with herself, he was the real reason she'd wanted to come on this cruise.

Like the other four guys in their group, he'd been nice to her. Other than a few pecks on her cheek, not counting spring break, platonic didn't even describe the relationship they didn't have. For three and a half years, she had traveled with her friends and never really given much thought to why none of the guys ever hit on her. She'd accepted her friends' belief it was because she was the youngest. On the second to last night of their spring break, Andy had been unable to sleep. Giving up finally, she had wandered soundlessly down the stairs towards the kitchen in search of a glass of milk.

Entering the kitchen, she reached for the light but stopped when she heard voices coming from the verandah just beyond the double screen doors. Obviously, the guys were still playing cards even though the girls retired to bed more than an hour ago. She opened her mouth to announce herself when she heard Jack speaking. Her breath caught in her chest, just like it did so often when she heard the deep timbres in his tone.

"Now look, guys, the girls are insisting."

She knew his voice so well because she often replayed his words over and over in her mind, rehashing what she could have said, or even should have said.

"We don't have to draw numbers, guys. I'll volunteer," Jack continued a few seconds later.

Andy smiled in the darkness, wasn't that just like Jack—he was the most generous of the five male friends. No wonder she loved him, she wrapped her arms around her waist.

"Gayle told me that unless one of us takes Andy out tomorrow night," Ray Williams pointed out. "I can forget about having sex until after graduation. You better be serious, Jack. Otherwise, she'll be with me and Gayle, and I'd planned a romantic picnic for our last night here."

"But Ray, I thought you guys were going to different med schools," Danny Fishbein interrupted.

"No shit, Danny! Keep pointing it out to make me feel even better about my sexless future."

"Hey, don't jump me, Ray! Ruthie and I have plans for the day tomorrow. What about you, Mark?"

"Liz and I made plans as well," Mark replied quickly.

"Jack and I were going to troll the local bars and maybe get lucky," Tony Marello spoke up. "It's either your turn, Mark, or Danny or Ray."

"One of you goes out with Andy. Draw straws or something and the loser must ask Andy out for dinner...and whatever," Mark interjected immediately.

"Come on, guys, that isn't fair," Danny protested. "She'd tell me no, and then we'd be right back where we started from."

"That's because all you talked about was accounting," Mark Sherman pointed out.

Tony's laugh carried through the night air.

Andy felt a chill run up and down her spine. Danny had asked her out for pizza a week or so before this trip and she'd thought it odd at the time. The whole evening he'd explained all the intricacies of a full accounting audit, besides which, she knew he was really interested in her friend Liz. Before she could ponder it further, an unfamiliar voice answered.

"Shut up, Tony. Besides, if you lose, I'd say not having sex would be a sure thing."

"Screw you!" Tony replied.

"We agreed to share the ordeal. Whenever the majority wants to divide and conquer the women, somebody has to take out the 'duffer' or we all suffer."

"Let's drop it." Jack cut off his friends' conversation.

Andy was having more trouble telling their voices apart over the roaring in her ears that had nothing to do with the ocean surf nearby.

"Come on, Jack, it was a given there would be a duffer. Every group of hot chicks always has one dumb, ugly, fat friend. It's a given if you don't occasionally take out the D-U-F-F gal pal, all the gorgeous women will join ranks to protect her and nobody gets laid. Andy's always been the 'duffer'. Deny you weren't hoping as much as the rest of us her parents would refuse to let her come along this time. We tried to find a geek or a nerd for Andy, but there were no takers. Tomorrow night is our last on break and some of us want to cut loose or have plans. It's noble of you, Jack, to offer again."

"Especially since we've all hooked up except you or Tony." Ray spoke again.

Andy barely heard him. She took a step back from the open window, dreading Jack's answer and yet still needing to hear the truth.

"I've told you before, Tony, drop the duffer thing," Jack spoke quickly.

Tony answered defensively, "The last thing I want to do is go out with the duffer. Jack has volunteered more than anyone else, so I'd say it's up to one of you three to do it."

"For the last time, just drop it, damn it! I'll ask Andy out for tomorrow. And Tony, I don't ever want to hear you discussing this again."

Hearing Jack state he'd take her out had hurt her the most. It's like he was being the noble one and sacrificing himself for the others. There was a roaring in her ears, barely registering the last words. She knew she had to get out of there before the guys realized they'd been overheard. Barely breathing, she backed out of the kitchen. Upstairs in her bed, which she shared with Gayle, she pulled up the covers and cried herself to sleep.

A voice jarred her thoughts abruptly and painfully from the past into the present.

"Excuse me, miss."

Andy turned, realizing she was blocking the entrance. Behind her stood the man she'd most dreaded seeing, Jack Riley. The quintessential successful businessman, who since taking over for his father, had advanced the company to be included in the Fortune 500. He was dressed in a suit and he looked better attired for the boardroom rather than a cruise.

"I'm sorry for blocking the road, Jack." She spoke without thinking, surprise getting the better of her. She leaned to the side, looking for her friends. When she met his gaze, she saw the curiosity and male interest. Immediately, she knew he had not recognized her. A thrill raced through her that she'd changed so much. She watched as he extended his hand, his sensuous mouth curling up on the corner in a sexy smile. God! So many times she'd wanted him to look at her just like that…ten years ago. Not taking his hand, she gestured towards the men at the bar. "Only Danny is still missing from your group, but none of mine made it here yet."

As if they realized they were being talked about, the men at the bar turned and saw Jack. "Hey, it's Jack!" Ray spoke first.

Mark grabbed his drink and started over. "Leave it to you, Jack, to find the first beautiful woman on this cruise ship! It's a pleasure to meet you, lovely lady. My name is Mark Sherman."

Andy knew Mark had had one too many drinks already to be so friendly, unless he'd radically changed. Nodding, she spoke first. "Yes, I know who you are, Mark. How is the science world these days? Are you on the tenure track?"

The surprise on his face was laughable and yet not. She opened her mouth to tell them her name.

"Andy! You look fabulous!"

She looked over her shoulder as her friend Ruthie burst through the glass doors first. Before she could reply, Ruthie hugged her tightly. Soon, she had hugged all of her female friends, but held back from getting that close to any of the men. Purposely, she avoided meeting any of their gazes either, even after they pulled two tables together and ordered drinks.

Danny Fishbein joined them a short time later. He took the empty chair beside Ruthie.

Andy refused to be maneuvered in the seating arrangements and seated herself between Ruthie and Liz. Jack sat directly across from her, but she managed to never totally look in his direction. Despite several glances at the clock over the bar, Andy realized no one remembered the welcoming lecture that was scheduled to begin soon. She had noticed the signs posted throughout the ship and finally brought it up. "The lecture begins in five minutes."

Tony grinned, shaking his head. "Who wants to listen to some stuffy lecture crap when we have the company of the four most beautiful women on board seated with us?"

Ruthie nodded. "We have ninety minutes until our dinner seating. And they have two more lectures tomorrow."

Andy shook her head and pushed back her chair. "Well, I need to attend this one, so I might see you later at dinner." Even though she knew her words were abrupt, her behavior a little rude and completely different from what she would have done in the past, she didn't succumb to their pleas to stay. Since she'd already signed for her drink, nothing delayed her departure.

* * * * *

Seated in the small lecture room, Andy had out her PDA in preparation of taking notes. At the back of the room stood two long tables of handouts and, glancing down at the overfilled folder on the chair beside her, she doubted she'd missed a single one. If anyone had been watching her, they most likely would assume she was strongly interested in the topic.

The truth of the matter was she'd had mixed feelings about coming on this reunion cruise until her publisher had learned about it. In fact, her editor, David Raymond, thought this was a great opportunity for research for a future book and took the idea to the publisher. That's when they offered to pay for the cruise, which she knew they could take as a tax deduction. Now, she found herself on a bondage and general D/s cruise. Crossing her legs, she closed her eyes still in disbelief at finding herself here. "What next?" she asked herself quietly.

"How about some dinner, followed by dancing?" Jack suggested as he picked up the folder and took the chair beside hers.

Andy was startled by his sudden appearance and jumped.

Jack caught her PDA as it began sliding from her lap.

The heat she felt from his hand immediately shocked her. Quickly, she grabbed the device. "Thanks, Jack, and I'll take the folder. I can set it next to me." She gestured to the empty chair on her other side.

"I don't mind holding it. And you never know, there may be a sudden rush and the room will fill up with last-minute attendees."

Damn it! Andy had forgotten how beguiling Jack's smile could be. She was sure she'd been cured...but now she wasn't so sure. "Okay, and uhm, thank you."

"So formal, Andy? Eight years doesn't change those kinds of things."

Andy nodded slightly. She didn't want to delve into the past with Jack, of all people. With a sigh of relief, she was grateful to see the lecture was about to start. "Oh, good," she murmured unconsciously. Quickly, she turned on her PDA, setting it up for note-taking.

* * * * *

Jack Riley sat quietly beside Andy, taking as many sidelong glances towards her as possible without actually staring directly. He was still feeling the shock from learning this was the same overweight young woman from their college days. Back then, she'd been quiet most of the time, even during their wildest of group get-togethers. Compared to the other three women, she'd been the country mouse to their city mice.

He felt uneasy as he thought back on the group dynamics that existed among this steadfast collection of friends. Somehow, the four girls had become integrated with his friends from high school, who had all attended the same college. He just remembered one night they attended a party held by a girl Ray knew. The pretty, dark-haired girl had been Gayle Green. Even now, he couldn't say for sure he'd met Andy that night. But he did recall meeting the vivacious, blonde Ruthie Silverman and the intensely pre-occupied, but gorgeous, Liz Antonelli.

He and his friends had invited the girls out for pizza a few nights later and that's when he knew for sure he met Andy. She was overweight and always wore sweat suits to cover her body.

Her soft brown hair was usually in a ponytail, but it hung halfway down her back. Looking at her hair now, he could tell it had been professionally colored, or lightened, and the cut made the hair into a silky bell shape. His fingers itched to touch it and see if it was still as soft as it had been that night at his folk's house in the Keys.

"No way!"

Startled to hear Andy speaking, he saw she wrote furiously into her PDA. Obviously she'd commented on the lecturer's words. "What?" he asked her quickly.

Andy twisted to look at him.

Jack realized that except for her beautiful hazel-colored eyes and those full lips, he found it hard to believe this was the same girl from college. He shook his head in reply to the questioning look from her, and then watched as she resumed her note-taking. For a moment, he looked at the lecturer, listening to what the man had to say.

"Rule number three for the submissive is to 'be open'. You can learn something about the D/s scene and about yourself from every person you encounter, no matter if they are dominant or submissive. Each and every activity, as well as your partner, can become an enhancing and enriching experience, if you remain open to the possibilities. Now, rule number four for the dominant is to find out all the necessary information about every person you play with. This includes experience, limits, likes and dislikes, and, of course, health information." The speaker paused to take a sip of water.

"The dominant must set down the roles, rules, limits, and contracts. Never assume the bottom knows the ground rules. Especially on a cruise such as this, you can encounter people who range from serious, long-term committed participants to newbies, who've only read about it or seen it on the Internet."

People around the room laughed at the speaker's joke, but Jack turned to look at Andy. He hadn't really given the underlying purpose of the cruise that much thought until now.

Ray had been the one to bring up the topic, and Tony had immediately jumped in to support the idea. One of his friends had brought some handouts to the monthly poker night they still had. From there, Ray had talked to Gayle, who had recently started seeing him again. After her agreement, the idea had grown to include the old group from college. None of them were married, engaged or seeing someone at the moment.

Jack suddenly smiled as he recalled Danny and Tony had tried to convince Ray he would need to dissuade Gayle from inviting Andy. He was glad he could say he had objected to their idea from the beginning. They'd been sitting around the kitchen table at his place, playing poker, when the discussion arose the second time. He recalled Ray had started it all —

"Gayle really likes the idea of the cruise, guys. She is going to ask the girls if they'd all like to go. They're all unattached at the moment, too."

"Hey!"

"I thought this was no women!"

"Of course, we want women there, Danny! I'm not going on a gay cruise, damn it!"

"Since when are you seeing Gayle?" Jack asked Ray over the din.

"Just this last month on a regular basis," Ray replied, without looking up from the cards.

Tony held up his hands to get everyone to stop talking. "Tell Gayle to invite Ruth and Liz."

"You can't tell her to deliberately not ask Andy!" Jack said to the others.

"Why not? You had the one and only date with her. Does that mean you want to give her a second chance?"

Looking at Andy's profile now, Jack remembered he had not answered the question that night while he insisted the fairness of including her in the invitation. Seeing her now, he could easily answer the question. The problem was she'd most likely never believe he'd actually been looking forward to seeing her again.

He continued to stare, marveling at the near-perfect way her lipstick highlighted her mouth.

She lowered her head enough so her hair swung forward. When she looked back up, a few strands had been caught by her lipstick.

For some reason, Jack was struck by how this made her lips looked even more kissable. Without forethought, he lifted his hand and gently brushed the hair back, freeing it.

Jack immediately noticed the softness of her skin and the silky feel of her hair. The startled look on her face told of her surprise, which she quickly suppressed and resumed her writing. He was more than a little shocked to discover her interest in this subject. His own agreement was to get away from work and spend time with his friends. The fact that this was a BDSM cruise had seemed an interesting idea. He possessed some knowledge, and a little experience, about the whole scene, but as far as participating—

Suddenly, he imagined Andy in black leather and was almost instantly aroused and rock-hard. He wondered just what kind of games she might be interested in playing while on board. He found it amazingly easy to come up with quite a few he'd enjoy.

"Dungeon parties will be held nightly, and the rules are posted in every room, as well as being available in the handouts at the back of the room. Now I will just go over a few of the more important ones. I don't want to bore you, but we've found the better informed our guests are, the better their overall experience tends to be."

Jack looked from the lecturer, who had caught his attention with saying "dungeon", back to Andy's face. She looked as serious as she used to when she'd be studying for a class. He was surprised at how quickly she could input data using that stupid two-inch keyboard and a silver-colored stick! He had nothing against the computer age and used the most current and up-to-date electronics for running the businesses he'd taken over from his father. Just personally, he hadn't made the jump from paper to electronics. When it came to handheld devices, he'd rather occupy his hands with much warmer and softer things.

Watching Andy bite her lower lip while she continued to tap furiously on the screen, he knew exactly which device of his he'd enjoy her hands on. Yes, indeed —

Something drew her attention towards Jack. Turning her head, she found he was staring. It caught her off-guard and she immediately looked down at her PDA. Damn it! Why was he looking at her? This was crazy! She should never have agreed to come on this cruise…research or not. Things were not going as she had planned. The picture in her head of how the meeting with Jack would go had rapidly disintegrated.

Jack didn't help when he leaned towards her a few seconds later. He was close enough to stir her hair and she felt it wisp across her cheek. "That's a beautiful cheongsam. It looks like the ones I saw in Hong Kong."

Andy felt Jack's fingers lightly rubbing her shoulder, back and forth across the embroidered silk material. She had to swallow before she could answer. "Yes, I got this one there."

Quickly, she looked back down at the screen, hoping it would help her return her focus onto the speaker and away from the sensual feeling Jack's light touch evoked. She was unnerved to realize the caress would be considered innocuous by most or under other circumstances. Her flesh was tingling as if little sparks of fire ignited in the aftermath.

"Female breasts and male, as well as female, genitalia must be covered."

The lecturer's words startled her. What in the world was he talking about now? Then almost as if Jack read her mind, he told her softly.

"That's rule number three, and the first part was that unless you are involved in a play activity, tempting treats must be covered."

Andy argued with her inner self — *do not turn and look at him. Don't you do it, Andy!* But she did shift slightly, and met his gaze. His eyes were just as green as they'd been in college. The same green she had used in the background on all of her books, and the source of her pen name, Emeraude. God! She was getting ridiculous and forced her gaze to the front once more.

"Whips are limited to six feet in length and are not allowed to be cracked outside of the Dungeon. This completes the rules for the parties. Every morning at breakfast, you'll find signs posted to let you know what events are going on and where. I'll let you know now, the first lecture tomorrow morning will fill up quickly, but you can sign up tonight. It's called 'Dominance and Submission'. Mistress Laurel will be covering sub-topics such as Models of Power Exchange, negotiation, contracts, slavery, punishment, and lastly, collars. Trust me that Laurel is an excellent person to speak on the topic. Thank you for coming and the sign-up sheet is up here."

Andy stood quickly but dropped her purse and the stylus. Jack spoke up quickly.

"Go sign us both up, and I'll bring your papers and pick this stuff up."

She hadn't been going to sign up, just leave. But now…she nodded and walked up to add their names to growing list. Jack already stood by the entrance when she turned around. His gaze seemed to move down her body and then slowly work its way upward. Now she knew what she'd felt in college when Jack looked in her direction was absolutely nothing compared to this.

She'd seen other men looking at her in similar ways since her dramatic image change. But not one had affected her in the same way Jack's single look did now. Her nipples were hard and she felt wetness forming at the top of her thighs. Her breathing was ragged and uneven, but it matched the racing of her heart and the somersaults her stomach seemed bent on accomplishing.

"The lecture ran over slightly, so we'd be better off going directly to the dining room, don't you think?"

Andy nodded as she accepted her purse from Jack, quickly stowing away her PDA, along with the errant stylus. This allowed him time to shift the folder to his further hand and curve the other around her upper arm.

"I'll lead the way, if you don't mind, Andy. I've got the copy of the deck plans in my pocket."

"All right, and I've got the download from the cruise lines on my PDA."

Jack led her over to the elevator, pressing the button. "I never would have figured you for going into the techno-age."

Andy turned to look at Jack. Maybe it was just her personal prejudice, but she thought he had fared much better in the battle against time. His light brown hair still looked quite full, and she saw no evidence of an early "comb-over". She'd easily noted the muscles beneath his shirt, as well as his flat stomach. In fact, he'd probably end up fighting off women on this cruise.

"You mean using past behavior as a predictor for future actions. I've changed a lot since school, not the least of which is choosing to let computers into my life." Shaking her head, finally remembering she owed him a response, she replied, "It became a huge necessity." Gratefully, she saw the elevator opening and stepped inside.

Jack followed her, as well as another couple, a man and a woman. Andy immediately moved into one of the back corners. It only took a moment to realize this wasn't her wisest option, unless her plan to put distance between herself and Jack had suddenly changed. Jack followed her and pressed close. To her further consternation, he lifted his nearest arm and wrapped it around her shoulders, pulling her in even closer to the warmth and strength which was having such an overwhelming feeling on her tonight.

"We're going to dinner. Are you two headed in that direction as well?" asked the male half of the couple who had joined them at the last minute, looking from Andy to Jack.

Jack spoke up before she could think of an answer other than "yes".

"Yes, we are. Andy insisted on attending the lecture to find out all the interesting things that would be going on here."

The man smiled, nodding. Andy noticed his black hair was slightly peppered with gray, but only on the sides, which made him look interesting, and added to his overall air of intrigue and attractiveness. She then turned to look at the woman. Andy was immediately struck by the woman's impeccable makeup and dress. Around her slender neck, accented by the upswept hairdo of her black hair, was a golden link chain, with a small gold padlock hanging in the front. The woman had not yet looked up, and Andy guessed perhaps this couple was full-time practitioners of this lifestyle, dominance and submission. Following this thought came the surprised acceptance of the arousal this had caused.

"Yes, we understood there would be quite a few people who've never experienced the whole range of BDSM lifestyles," the man replied.

Andy was still focused on the woman's necklace when Jack suddenly lifted his arm to pull her closer. As she turned to glare, he winked, grinning for a moment, and then he replied.

"We're complete newbies at this. Do you have any advice or recommendations?"

"I'm sure Margrit or I could certainly answer your questions. Would you care to join us for dinner tomorrow night? We are already committed for this evening."

Jack nodded his head before Andy could consider a proper response. "That sounds fantastic."

"Here is my card." The man pulled a white business card from his suit pocket, as well as a very expensive pen Andy recognized because she'd shopped for one of them to give her editor for Christmas last year. "How is eight-thirty, tentatively, and if you'd like to join us in our suite, we'll have cocktails first? I've written our suite number and deck on the card."

Jack accepted the card, tucking it into his pocket. "By the way, I'm Jack Riley and this is Andy Bond."

"It is nice to meet you both. My name is Ethan Williams and this is my wife, Margrit."

Andy glanced at Margrit and caught her glancing up for a brief moment, smiling at her and just as quickly looking away. There was no doubt in her mind just who the sub was in their relationship.

"It's been a pleasure meeting you both, as well." He stopped as the elevator came to a halt.

Andy glanced at the panel of lights and realized they were stopped one level above her deck.

Ethan nodded, placing his hand beneath Margrit's elbow as they stepped forward to exit. "Are you two dining in the Queen's Grill?"

Andy shook her head, speaking quickly. "No, we're dining with friends in the Britannia room. But I've already reserved an early table for breakfast in the Queen's."

Ethan directed his wife off the elevator, but stopped the doors from closing. "Well, if you two oversleep, join us for lunch there at two. Enjoy your first evening on board."

Chapter Two

No sooner had the elevator doors closed than Andy stepped several feet away from Jack. Even though it was unnecessary, she pushed the button, which was already lit.

"You can't just make reservations at the Queen's Grill, Andy. I might not have the ship's deck plan memorized, but I do know you have to be in a certain cabin category to eat there. Same thing with the Princess' barbecue, too."

Andy looked forward, ignoring his attempt at humor because she still stung from the remark about the cruise's blueprints. She had gone further than just getting the information into her PDA for reference...she'd printed off blow-ups of the decks, studying where certain things were so she wouldn't get lost. Knowing where things were located was something she'd always done even if it was kind of obsessive-compulsive. Staring at the buttons on the panel, she mumbled her reply, half-hoping he wouldn't hear her and shrug it off. "I'm in a Q-category cabin."

Suddenly, an arm appeared in front of her, blocking her vision as its palm rested on the wall beside her. In her ear, she heard Jack's voice whispering, "When it comes to that level, sweetheart, it's against the law to even mention the word 'cabin'. I've heard the Captain has the Queen's approval to dump them in the brig to await transport to the Tower of London."

Andy glanced sideways, met Jack's piercing green gaze, and looked away just as quickly. "There haven't been any prisoners kept there for a very long time, not to mention how silly it would be to put thieves in the place you keep the Crown Jewels."

"I thought you ladies were sharing two cabins."

"Yes, well…an opportunity came up and I took it." Andy breathed a sigh of relief as the elevator doors opened. She took advantage of Jack turning to duck beneath his arm and walk into the entranceway for the restaurant.

"It's about time!"

Andy and Jack both turned at hearing a voice they recognized.

Gayle came towards them, smiling. "Andy, you just have to visit the little girls' room later. Just follow me, and I'll lead the way to our table. Can you believe this place? I feel like I've died and gone to heaven."

"I should be wearing a long designer satin gown, glittering jewels dangling from my ears, draping along my neck, and elbow-length white gloves. In the background is the sound of a string quartet playing beautiful chamber music." Andy stopped and found both Jack and Gayle staring. Laughing quickly, she shrugged. "Silly me, rambling on there. Let's get seated. I'm getting hungry."

Gayle nodded and started leading the way to the table.

Andy took a step forward to follow when Jack stopped her by curving his hand around her elbow, the same way Ethan had with Margrit.

"I can imagine you'd look quite spectacular, and I wouldn't mind putting on a white tie and tails to accompany you."

Andy pressed her free hand to her stomach. It didn't do any good because her stomach had already jumped into her throat! To discover Jack still had such an effect over her was daunting. She needed to say something to break the spell he seemed to have over her.

"I can't wait to see what you come up for the Disguise Party in a couple of days." Jack interjected quickly. "We better go or Gayle will be coming back to find us."

* * * * *

If she had hoped her appearance change might have already been dismissed as a topic, she was quickly dissuaded as Tony, seated across the table, commented, "Damn Andy, you look hot!"

Liz must have kicked him because a second later he said ouch and shot her a dirty look. But she was undaunted, smiling at Andy. "You look really wonderful, Andy. Now answer the important question. Why aren't you sharing the cabins with us?"

Danny Fishbein, the accountant, cut in before Andy could reply. "Do the girls have to pay for the single supplement on the one cabin?"

Tony grinned, leaning forward to look at Gayle, Liz and then Ruthie. "Well, ladies, since we have five guys in our two adjoining cabins, I'd be happy to move in with you, just to even things up and all."

Ruthie was vigorously shaking her head. "Maybe one of us will get lucky and finally trip over Mr. Right. This gives us a room to…well, I remember how you guys would always act on spring breaks."

Liz laughed and patted Tony's hand. "That's right, and now *we* have reached our sexual peaks—"

Gayle, the doctor, interrupted the others to interject. "We're at the beginning of our peak. The best is still to come…in more ways than one, for us."

Ray shifted in his chair to look at Gayle. "Uh, honey…I thought—"

Gayle leaned over and kissed his cheek. "I was talking about the other girls, sweetheart. I've found my slave in you."

Danny flushed as he spoke. "Don't you mean Master, Gayle?"

Andy spoke without thinking, her hours of Internet research revealing itself. "Not all tops are male, Danny."

Immediately, she was aware of her friends all turning to look. She started to speak when a handsome young waiter interrupted them by clearing his throat. He looked at her, rather than at the whole table.

"Excuse me, ma'am. Are you Ms. Andrea Bond, from the Balmoral Suite?"

Andy nodded, embarrassed at being singled out like this, before she'd gotten a chance to explain about her accommodations.

"We have champagne reserved for you, ma'am, compliments of Mr. Edwards. Shall I serve it now, or perhaps later in your suite? Your butler informed us he missed your arrival and sends his apology."

Andy had thought she was embarrassed, now she had no doubt she was! Nodding, she spoke quickly. "I'm not sure how large the bottle is, but perhaps we could share it and just pass it until all the glasses are filled."

The waiter nodded and departed immediately. Andy wished she could do the same until Danny broke the silence.

"Hot damn, Andy! What have you been up to since college? Here I thought Jack was the successful one amongst this crowd of lay-abouts. Or at least that is what my dad used to call us all when I went home over the holidays."

Andy listened as the others laughed, but she was intensely aware of Jack, who was still staring at her. When more conversation broke out, he leaned closer to whisper. "Who is Mr. Edwards? I assume he isn't your talking horse."

Andy couldn't help but laugh. Unfortunately the sweet and elderly Emerson Edwards had a long face. "He is my next-door neighbor. I will need to make a note." She paused to open her purse and pull out her PDA. "I will email him a quick thank you before I go to bed tonight."

Jack watched as Andy wrote the message on the small screen. The flush on her cheeks made him want to caress her skin and see if it was warmer there, or on the paler skin of her upper arms. He was intensely aware that very little other skin

31

was available due to the discreet cheongsam she'd chosen to wear. At this point he wasn't sure if her choice was deliberate, but it was directly opposite to the outfits the other women had worn tonight. None of them had been naked, or dressed inappropriately, yet the dresses had been short and showed cleavage. Andy's cleavage was something he'd definitely looked forward to seeing.

Her hair fell forward, and just as she had many times before Jack watched as she artlessly tucked it behind her ear without more than a second's pause. Suddenly he recalled the way he'd begun to stare at her after their last spring break, scrutinizing and studying her every move. Instead of trying to sit beside her, as he had in the past, he now deliberately sat away, so he could see her face.

Like now, he realized, as she caught her lower lip with her teeth. At first he had thought it was a cute, most likely nervous gesture she had when she was thinking and didn't want to be distracted. But then he saw her tongue come out, and slowly rub across the spot for a moment or two, almost but not every single time after biting her lip. That was the day he discovered gut-wrenching desire.

Sure he'd been attracted to women, and began his sexual life in high school. He'd never lacked for dates throughout college, but since senior spring break, things had been different, at least for him. For a long time he'd thought the change had been inside, and happened suddenly. No longer did he find himself feeling the same pull and attraction to every attractive woman he passed on campus. Now he compared them to Andy. Finally, he acknowledged he only wanted Andy's kisses. If her tongue was to lick anything, it should be him!

As graduation neared, with everyone talking about where they were going after college, either for the summer, more school or just life, Andy never volunteered what she was doing. Jack found his need to get close to her growing, but his every advance was met with her erecting more barriers and retreating.

At first, he'd prodded her with teasing questions with the others around. But nothing would drag the answer out of her. Finally, the night before their graduation ceremony, he'd cornered her at the party they were having at the double apartment the guys had been sharing their senior year. Without undue effort, he maneuvered her into his bedroom, closing the door. He'd switched her iced tea with a Long Island Iced Tea.

"I feel dizzy, Jack," Andy murmured moments later.

"Just sit for a couple of minutes," he told her quickly, surprised at how quickly the liquor had taken effect. "I'm sure you'll feel better. Maybe if you drink the rest, it would help. You could be dehydrated," he added, appealing to her logical side.

"Thank you, Jack." She drank down the rest of the potent disguised liquid.

"Tomorrow's the big day for us all, Andy. You haven't said if your parents are coming." He realized in their entire group, she never complained about her folks, or any sibling problems. Now he wondered why. "Mine are arriving early tomorrow morning and staying at the airport Hilton. Ray's are flying in with them."

Jack waited, watching Andy, but she didn't answer him. He considered asking her more directly again, but decided to change tactics. "What are your plans, Andy? Everyone else has talked like crazy about their future. I can't remember hearing you say where you head from here?"

Andy nodded and turned to look at him. "That's right." A second later she flopped back onto the bed, grinning up at him. "You're going to Harvard for your Master's in business."

Jack smiled, speaking quickly. "So, what will *you* be doing? Gayle said something about getting accepted several places, didn't she?" He stretched out along side her, lying on his side.

"It doesn't matter," she muttered.

"Of course it matters, Andy." While it hadn't been his intention, he couldn't resist the need. Reaching out, he lightly touched the side of her face, curving his hand to her neck and caressing his way down onto her shoulder. He rubbed lightly. "Are you still dizzy? Does it help, lying back?" he added. His good intentions were finding it hard to resist the desire he felt.

Andy melted under his hand and wriggled around on the bed, smiling. "Jack," she murmured softly.

Jack's argument over why this was a bad idea got lost in his need. Leaning over her, he lightly caressed her shoulder, moving down, just a little. "God! I wish I had more time," he muttered even as he lowered his hand towards his goal.

"Time?" Andy asked. "I'm hot!" A second later, she tried to tug off her sweatshirt. Since she was lying on it, all she managed was to tug up the front part.

Jack groaned. He realized he'd given her too much to drink, and way too fast. Her one arm was tangled in the sweatshirt, while the other had shimmied free to reach up towards him. Knowing he needed to be careful how he handled the situation, he couldn't resist the temptation. His hand curved over her large breast, savoring the feel of her hard nipple. He moved his palm back and forth, so the firm, rubbery tip dragged against it.

It must have worked because Andy groaned and Jack knew he was dead meat if he didn't stop right now! "I'm interested and I want to know what will you be doing while I'm in boring classes all day," he asked her quickly.

Looking into her eyes, Jack had seen something change.

Her eyes had filled with tears.

The door to his room banged open and Gayle had stormed in. Without asking, she came over and took the empty glass that had rolled from Andy's hand to the floor.

Sniffing it, Gayle glared at Jack, ignoring Ray, who had followed her into the room. "What the hell do you think you are doing? You know Andy doesn't drink? Is this some kind of sick 'last hurrah' joke you guys are playing?" That's when she noticed her friend's state of partial undress. Gayle jerked down Andy's shirt even as she shoved Jack away.

Unresisting, he fell back on the bed and looked to Ray, who flushed a guilty red color. He didn't know for sure what Gayle talked about, but she had acted quickly, pulling Andy off the bed.

"Ray!" Gayle had practically shouted at his friend. "Help me get her home. I will talk to you later, Riley!" At the door, Gayle had turned to glare at him. "Of all the guys, Jack, I had really thought you were better than this."

Jack had sat back down on the bed as Andy was helped out of his room. Her step was a little unsteady. He was angry at being interrupted. He'd been positive Andy had been only seconds away from telling him something about her past, or even her future.

A little less than twenty minutes later, Ray had returned alone. Not looking the least bit happy, Ray sat on the sofa next to Jack, leaving the end cushion free.

"What's wrong, Ray?" he asked after a few moments of silence.

Ray groaned before he answered. "Gayle's pissed at me because of you. The last thing she said to me was *Jack just ruined your chance of a graduation fuck*. She said she probably wasn't come back here tonight."

"I wasn't doing anything to Andy. Gayle has no reason to be upset."

"You gave her the drink!"

"I wanted to loosen her tongue up so she'd talk to me."

"She was on your bed," Ray pointed out instantly.

"Sitting, since I don't have decent chairs in here."

"Andy was lying down and you were leaning over her." Ray countered once more.

"Look, pseudo-Gayle, I've been trying to get out of her what her graduation plans are. It's harder than pulling teeth to get information out of Andy."

"Damn it, Jack! Who cares what she'll be doing? You're heading to Harvard, man! With a Harvard MBA you can go anywhere!"

Jack had to hold back his anger at Ray for the offhand way he was dealing with a friend's future. Hell! They'd known the girls for close to four years. Of course he cared what they'd be doing. Before he could yell at Ray, Gayle reentered the living room, calling out his name.

Jack remembered the look of happiness on his friend's face at Gayle's appearance and Ray had run across the room to meet her. Glancing at Gayle, he recalled she never had talked to him that night, or the next day. Of course, it wasn't until after graduation, with everyone milling around before he could get close enough to her to ask where Andy was. They had skipped her name during the callout for diplomas. He'd been watching for her quite closely.

"She left this morning, before the rest of us got up." Anger blazed in Gayle's gaze. "All she left was a short note saying she didn't like ceremonies or long goodbyes." Her voice had cracked for a moment, but she'd straightened her back. "She also wrote it had nothing to do with you or last night. I didn't believe it until now."

Hearing Ray and Gayle laughing over something, usually a medical joke, drew him back to the present. Every time he thought about that brief conversation, he recalled he had not asked why she changed her mind. Somehow he was pretty sure her answer would have been it was look on his face. Abruptly, he felt the need for some space and stood. Realizing he'd drawn almost everyone's attention, he muttered briefly. "Just heading to the gents' and you can start the champagne without me."

Jack ignored the sign directing to the right for the men's restroom and kept on walking. Seeing the sign for the Golden Lion Pub on the right, he entered the darkened room. It was partially filled and he easily found a seat at the bar. As the bartender wiped off the gleaming bar top in front of him, Jack noticed the guy was in his early twenties, tanned and obviously worked out, when he wasn't tending bar. For the first time in his life, he questioned his own appeal to a woman. He wasn't in his twenties anymore.

It had begun with the comment about sexual peak for a woman starting now. He'd noticed the way the swarthy waiter's eyes had lit up when Andy replied she was the lady he'd sought. Then there had the extra glances Tony kept shooting towards her. He'd not once considered facing competition on this cruise for Andy's attention. Not that he couldn't face it because he could, he argued silently. If she rejected him—

"What would you like to drink tonight, sir?"

Jack looked at the younger man, shrugging. "Whisky on the rocks."

"Make that two," Ray said as he sat beside him. "Thanks to you I've just embarrassed myself in the men's room." Quickly he held his hand up. "No, I won't tell you how. Just tell me why you are holed up in here instead of drinking the included booze at the table and enjoying all those lovely ladies."

"I was coming straight back. I just needed to get away for a second."

"Then tell me why you were staring at Gayle so hard."

Jack glanced at his friend. "Relax, Ray, I'm not going to put the moves on your lovely lady."

"I wasn't thinking that at all." Ray accepted the drink and passed the barkeeper his keycard for charging the drinks. Sipping his drink, he turned slightly to look at Jack. "Not that you could," he chuckled. "Instead I wondered how you were going to tell Tony he's out of the running."

Jack took a long swallow of whiskey before he glanced at Ray. "Are you turning into the man with a riddle for every occasion?"

Ray shook his head, drained his glass and stood up. "Keep on lying to yourself, buddy, but I know what you're denying."

Jack pushed his glass away and stood as well. "Let's go before Gayle comes looking for you."

* * * * *

Returning to the table, the first thing Jack noticed was Gayle had moved into his seat. The second was that she was determined to stay in this particular chair.

"I switched chairs so I can catch up with Andy. Jack, you and Ray can sit together and talk sports or whatever," Gayle said without a smile.

Jack glanced from the set look upon the dark-haired emergency room resident's face to Ray. Obviously, his friend had gotten some unspoken message because he was already walking to his chair. Before stepping away, he glanced at Andy, but she had her face down. He'd forgotten the trait she did whenever she chose to opt out of a decision-making process. It was clear she accepted Gayle's action.

"Sure thing, Gayle, enjoy your girl talk. Just don't hog all the champagne." Shrugging, he smiled at Gayle.

Andy gave a quick sidelong glance as Jack moved around the table. She could have protested and insisted, but she liked to avoid drawing attention to herself. And to be honest, she'd be more relaxed with Gayle beside her than dealing with the onslaught of emotions being close to Jack was causing.

For the next several minutes, she just listened to the others talking back and forth across the table. She laughed when required until she realized Jack was staring. Quickly, she lowered her gaze to the table, aware of a flush now covering her cheeks. Feeling overheated, she blew little puffs of air upwards, slightly fluffing her soft bangs across her forehead.

"Shall I pour the champagne, ma'am? Do you want all the bottles opened at once?"

Andy jumped at the waiter's voice. Looking up at the young, dark-haired man, she asked, "Uhm, how many are there?"

"Four, ma'am, and I have them all on ice."

Andy turned to look at Gayle and then at the others. "Do you want to drink it all now?"

She couldn't make out who said what, but the overall answer was yes. Except for Jack who suggested she keep one for herself, for another time. Avoiding Jack's gaze, she told the waiter her decision. "We'll have three and could I have the other bottle delivered to my suite?"

"Of course, ma'am, we'll have it placed in the refrigerator of the downstairs bar."

Tony leaned forward. "I'll be happy to pop that cork for you later, Andy. I'm getting very curious to see this *little cabin* you've got for the trip."

Everyone laughed and the champagne was poured into everyone's glass. Lifting their glasses, they toasted their trip.

"Here's to a successful cruise!" Ray pronounced the first toast.

"How do you define a successful one, Ray?" Andy questioned him a few seconds later, waiting until everyone had sipped at least once.

Ray shook his slightly balding, blond head. "Still getting into the psychological mojo, aren't you, Andy?"

Shrugging, she replied, "Yes, I guess I always have and not really thought about it. I just squirrel all of it away for later." She jested, hoping to make light of the situation.

Ruthie smiled. "Other than Andy and Jack's secrets, what's been going on with the rest of you?"

Jack knew he stared at Andy, and suddenly he didn't give a damn what the others thought. One way or another, he had to make sure the two of them got time together tonight! Accepting more champagne, he listened as the conversation moved back and forth across the table.

Danny took on the duties of adding champagne to each person's glass. When he reached Ruth, he leaned down to kiss the side of her neck. "What happened to that schmuck I saw you with at lunch last week?"

Ruthie shook her pale blonde head, lifting one hand to tuck loose strands of hair behind her ear. She looked so cool and polished with her hair pulled into a roll at the back of her head. Jack saw the nervous tremors, even though they were minimal. As she opened her mouth to reply, he wondered whether Danny's words or his gesture upset the usually reserved attorney.

"Just a guy I work with, Danny, nothing more. I've been too busy to date," Ruth murmured.

Gayle leaned forward to get a better look at Ruthie. "Any idea when you'll find out if you're making junior partner or not?"

Ruthie shook her head. "The decision is all based on billable hours and the clients you bring to the firm. Thanks to Jack and one other, I know I at least have a good chance."

Jack shrugged, not liking to draw the attention his way. "I needed a good attorney and luckily, I knew one."

Ray laughed. "Did you ever realize we have the perfect little society here? We'll have two doctors if anyone gets sick, a businessman to organize our shipwrecked bunch, and Danny will be our accountant to organize our riches in case we need to buy our way off the island."

"Or dole out the sheets of toilet paper," Danny quipped self-deprecatingly.

Ray laughed and finished his explanation. "Tony can hopefully whip up some good food to eat. Ruthie can set up a fair judicial system for our disputes so we avoid any hostile coups. Liz and Mark will serve as the brains of the outfit and will make us a phone or a hot-air balloon to get off the island."

Everyone laughed.

"What about Andy?" Jack asked softly.

Ray turned and looked at her before he replied to Jack.

Jack felt sure he knew what his friend was thinking, especially with his added attention to her.

Interrupting, Danny asked another question. "What do you do, Andy?"

"Well, for one thing, I type."

"Super! You can work for Jack and be our chronicler," Ray suggested quickly. "When we are rescued, you can publish your journals and become a famous writer."

Ruthie coughed suddenly, choking slightly on her champagne.

Jack leaned forward, looking at Andy. If he had to guess, he'd have said she deliberately avoided looking in his direction. Perhaps if he spoke provocatively enough to catch her attention, she'd have to look towards him. "Without a proper desk, you can take dictation sitting on my lap."

"Perhaps I'll be the one casualty at sea, you know, shark food, never to be seen again."

His ploy worked, but only for a few seconds. Her words, though, took him by surprise. Hearing her casually refer to herself coming to such a tragic end didn't sound at all humorous to him.

Mark Sherman, usually quiet and fulfilling people's expectation as a college professor of science, sat beside Andy. He reached over and lightly patted Andy's hand. "You can be our mascot, our Gilligan!"

Andy laughed, smiling at Mark. "I've heard it said if it had been real life—Gilligan would have been murdered by day two and served on a platter for the castaways that night."

Jack spoke, knowing his words would get her attention. "Since I'm the organizer and the boss, that makes me the skipper and Andy can share my grass shack."

Liz shook her head. "If the skipper had looked as handsome as Jack, he could have been sharing with someone besides Gilligan."

Jack laughed with everyone else, but he kept his gaze on Andy. Following his comment she had glanced at him, but almost the very next second after their gazes met, she turned away. He had to wonder why she acted so skittish. He definitely needed to talk to her privately.

* * * * *

Following dinner, they couldn't decide as a group what they should do. The women were leaning towards strolling on deck, or perhaps adjourning somewhere quiet where they could talk. Four out of the five guys were in favor of checking out the different bars or the casino.

Andy listened to the suggestions and when they had finally decided, she spoke quietly. "I'll say good night here. I have a few things I need to do tonight."

Before she could leave, everyone seemed to be speaking at once, vying for attention. Voices and sentences ran together.

"Aww, Andy, don't be a sleepyhead. We're here for fun," Danny jested quickly.

"Do you feel okay, Andy?" Ruthie reached out, touching her arm.

"I suggest you don't drink any more champagne, or you'll have one hell of a headache," Ray offered in his most official tone.

"I'll walk you back to your cabin and meet up with you guys later," Jack spoke softly.

"We plan on sleeping in tomorrow and ordering room service, Andy. Do want to join us?" Gayle asked finally.

Andy couldn't remember whom she answered but in less than a minute, she stood once again in the elevator, alone with Jack. She pressed the button for deck ten and then stepped back to the far corner. Since they were alone, there would be no reason for Jack to stand so close. When he didn't say anything, her nervousness drove her to speak. "You can get off on your deck, or just go straight back. I don't need to be escorted."

Jack turned and nodded. "I know, but I'll walk with you anyway."

"All right, I guess." She looked around the elevator, anywhere but at Jack. She was surprised they rode all the way up without any other passengers joining them. Finally the doors slid soundlessly open.

Andy bolted forward. The soft shush-shush of his feet along the plush carpet intensified her awareness of Jack walking a few steps behind her. At the double doors of the suite, she fumbled in her purse, juggling the folder with the papers, before she finally found her keycard. Gratefully, after several curse words, she reached out to insert the card.

The carved double doors swung open a second later and she stared at the handsome face of a tall, good-looking man dressed impeccably in a black three-piece suit and dark silk tie.

"Welcome to the Balmoral Suite, Ms. Bond. I apologize for not being here earlier to expedite your arrival. I am Henderson, your butler for this voyage."

Andy knew her mouth gaped open. Amidst her surprise, she dropped the folder and her purse. "Wow! You even have a British accent."

"Allow me to pick all this up, ma'am. If you and your guest would like to be seated in the main lounge, I'll be with you in a moment to fix drinks, if you'd like." Henderson bowed just slightly, and quite correctly.

Andy had already started to bend down and realized how silly she must have looked with her mouth open and half crouched. A moment later, Jack took her upper arm in his grip and steered her into the room.

As they entered the sunken living room, Jack released her arm. A large semi-circular sofa partially faced the large bank of windows. Beyond the glass, he could see a deck with chairs and table. At the moment, he had some trouble dealing with the impressiveness of this place, let alone the damned butler who'd opened her door. He sure as hell didn't like the idea of this guy drawing her bath, bringing her breakfast in bed or anything else for that matter. Hearing the footfalls signaling the butler's approach, he turned and saw Andy seated on the sofa, still not moving. He'd seen the look on her face when she'd first looked upon *her* perfect butler.

Looking at her, Jack could see how beautiful she'd become, and he could easily imagine any man being attracted to her. He couldn't say for sure what he'd wanted to happen aboard this cruise, but he'd hoped to talk with her privately before the onslaught from outsiders encroached on their time. Perhaps more than an iota of hope existed that something would come from their time together. Maybe he sought to discover whether a future with Andy was possible.

"I finished your unpacking, Ms. Bond." Henderson spoke just loud enough to get their attention. "I wasn't sure when you would be retiring so I've turned down the bed and set out your nightclothes. I've also prepared a light snack for you in the refrigerator of the wet bar in the master bedroom. Would you like me to mix cocktails for you and your guest? Or if you prefer, I could set out your clothes for tomorrow and take care of any pressing they might need."

Jack turned from Henderson to Andy and saw she still stood with her mouth open. He moved forward as he spoke. "I'll have some brandy and the lady would like some iced tea."

"Excellent, sir. Shall I arrange for breakfast?"

Andy shook her head, standing to take her belongings from Henderson. "I made reservations already."

"You don't need reservations for the Queen's settings, miss, which includes the Queen's Grill Lounge, as well as the private sun terrace."

"Thank you, Mr. Henderson." Andy smiled at the handsome butler.

Jack watched and felt his teeth grating angrily together.

"Just Henderson, ma'am," her butler clarified.

Andy shrugged but grinned as she replied, "Okay, but I'll probably forget."

Henderson returned the smile. "I'll return with your drinks in a few moments. If you should need anything, including in the night hours, there is a call button for me beside your bed, as well as in the master bathroom and in all the rooms down here. I plugged in your laptop to recharge the battery."

"Wow! Thanks. I'm always letting it get so low it's screaming at me to plug it in or face dire consequences."

Jack smiled at Andy's jesting, but stopped when he saw Henderson had broken his stiff manner enough to smile. Telling himself to stop worrying about the butler, he crossed back towards Andy. "Have a seat, Andy. We can relax and chat for a while."

She didn't say anything as she sat, but he was sure she'd choose to be alone. Usually he wasn't like this, which unsettled him. He never bothered a woman who wasn't interested in him equally as well. So, this persistence with Andy was completely abnormal. To say it bugged him would be an understatement. He watched as Andy sat once more, carefully pulling down her skirt as far as it would go. Jack waited until Henderson returned with the drinks so he could sit close to Andy without her putting more distance between them.

As soon as the butler returned, Jack met him partway and accepted the drinks. "Thank you, Henderson. Good night." Jack didn't like the way the other man looked at Andy.

Henderson nodded his head. "You're welcome, sir. Once again, Ms. Bond, please feel free to ring at any time."

Andy shook her head. "I wouldn't want to disturb your sleep."

"That's what I am here for, Miss, to service your every need."

The words hung in the air for a few seconds and then Andy coughed slightly. "Thank you, Henderson."

The butler turned and walked over to another set of double doors.

Hell! The damned place had a private elevator. As the doors closed behind the butler, Jack walked to the plush off-white sofa, piled high with thick, silk-covered pillows in golden colors to match the lush décor. Holding out the tea to Andy, he waited until she took it. He sat sideways so he could look at her. He sipped the brandy, finally realizing just how good, and expensive, it was.

"I could've peed my pants when he opened the door," Andy spoke quickly. "I didn't know this suite came with a freaking, honest-to-God British butler. Now, I'll be scared I'll do something stupid and he'll wonder how the *poor white trash* girl snuck on board."

That sounded like the Andy he used to know. Jack shook his head, letting his gaze rove over Andy's face and upper body. "Trust me, sweetheart, you could pick your teeth and scratch and no man is going to think that about you. Didn't you look in the mirror when you got dressed?"

Jack savored the way her red silk dress fit closely, clearly outlining her shape without being flashy or flaunting her attributes. He wondered if her breasts still felt as soft as they had on the last night of spring break. Just remembering the night and he always got hard—

Chapter Three

Andy sipped her tea, and then kicked off her shoes. She wished she could get comfortable. This was a dress for making impressions and dancing, and it kept her from eating too much. Suddenly, she leaned forward and set her glass on the dark wooden coffee table. "I'm going to look around. Do you want to come?"

Jack frowned. "You haven't seen the whole thing yet?"

Andy shook her head and stood. "No. I arrived so close to sailing, and then it was too late to linger. I had to rush to be on time for drinks."

"Sure, let's see what there is to the place. I noticed the complete bar setup." Jack walked over and found an electronic panel. "Watch this, Andy." He pressed one button, and the glass mirror behind the bar slid sideways and revealed a wine rack. It held a few bottles of wine. "You should keep this a secret or Tony will be up here all the time."

Andy nodded. "I feel self-conscious already. I wanted to upgrade to have a cabin by myself, and then things got out of hand."

"Why did you feel the need to be alone? I thought the four of you girls have always gotten along."

"We do," she answered, turning away to explore more of the suite. Just inside the double entryway, there was a small closet on one side, and a guest bathroom on the other. She peered in.

"Two toilets," Jack joined her. "That's convenient if you have guests. They can go through here like Noah's Ark," he joked with a smile.

Andy laughed, shaking her head. "One toilet and one bidet. I'll have to try that. I've never used one before."

She turned away as Jack replied with a chuckle. "Tell you what, you test it and submit a written report."

"Very funny." Andy laughed, amazed at how relaxed she felt once again. This was more the way she used to feel when it had been just the two of them. They had enjoyed a camaraderie she'd never felt with any of the other guys. "I wonder if people actually dine in their cabins much. I'm going upstairs."

Jack followed her. "I'm sure they do, Andy. Sometimes you just don't want be around people, let alone a crowd. I like spending time by myself or with one other person."

Andy stopped at the top of the stairs. She wondered who was the person that he liked spending time with. She had learned from Ruthie he wasn't married, or engaged, but that didn't mean he wasn't dating someone. It just might not be serious enough for him to skip the reunion, or bring her along. Still the little voice in her head asked whether he might be attracted to her now. And, if he were, would he pursue the attraction, in some way. Immediately following the thought, she always reminded herself she was still undecided about what she wanted. She was single, and spent a lot of time telling herself and others, she was quite happy staying that way.

"Hey! You're not supposed to come to a complete halt without blowing your horn," Jack protested as he stopped behind her. His next words reminded her he was taller than she and could most likely see over her shoulder. "Wow! Is that the queen's bed? Do you think she knows it's missing?"

Andy laughed and stepped into the wide-open bedroom. The bed sat on a platform a few inches off the floor. Heavy, silken curtains surrounding the bed made it appear so royal. "I think this bed will kick me out as an imposter."

Jack moved around her walking into the room, looking around. "Did you see the bathroom?"

"Just as far as the sink." Andy moved the rest of the way in. "Calling this a master bathroom doesn't give it credit. Two sinks, two toilets—"

"Shower big enough for two," Jack said.

Andy walked over towards the circular tub. Her breath caught when she saw the walls around the tub were glass. "Jack? Look at this."

The night was clear beyond the glass wall and easily gave the impression of bathing outdoors. She'd never imagined something like this, and she should have! It was so romantic and sexy. She would have to use this in one of her stories, she was thinking. Then she realized Jack stood behind her, leaning close to look over her shoulder.

"This makes me think about champagne, bubbling water and the night sky, the perfect combination for romance."

Andy felt the butterflies go wild in her stomach and forced her breathing to slow down. "You forgot something," she whispered. For a moment, she thought she dreamed it, but it was real. Jack's hand moved gently around her waist, until he pressed his palm flat to her stomach, pulling her back. She felt his heat immediately. Suddenly, it felt as if her heart was going to pound its way out of her chest.

Jack's voice stirred the hair beside her cheek as he replied. "Hmm. I thought I had everything. Champagne should be chilling, and the tub can easily be turned on…and the sky has graciously been provided. I wish I had roses to give you—"

He hadn't said it straight out she was the one he wanted in the tub. The logical corner of her brain quickly pointed out it was *her* tub, after all. Usually she made jokes to shrug these things off. She opened her mouth, hoping something clever would come out. The words never materialized, and then she felt his fingers moving her hair. She knew in her erotic books, the hero always did this so he could kiss heroine's neck.

"Andy, I don't want to pressure you. The only reason I agreed to come on this reunion cruise was after I found out you had promised to join the trip."

She gasped in surprise and his hand tightened at her waist, keeping her close. Almost immediately warmth swelled, buried deep inside the place she held most secret and protected. She knew she should say something.

Jack tightened his hand once again. "Nothing I can think of would make me happier than to join you for a nice, long soak, sip champagne and share kisses in this tub. Drying off, we'd go in and sample your incredible bed."

Andy closed her eyes, but was still compelled to ask. "You mean, like we used to do with me under the covers and you on top when the others were sharing beds."

"No, Andrea. I want you naked, with me, under the covers. Neither sleep, nor conversation, are my number-one priority, honey."

Andy started to say something when she felt Jack's fingers on the back zipper of the dress. He pulled it down a few inches very slowly and when she didn't stop him, he pulled it all the way to the bottom. As he began pushing the dress forward, Andy panicked and spun to face him. She had to lift one hand to maintain her decency in the brightly lit bathroom.

"Could we go into the bedroom with the lights out?" she asked quietly, not quite meeting his normally intense and too all-seeing gaze.

"Sure, Andy," he replied, stepping aside to allow her into the bedroom first.

Andy moved quickly, turning off the lights as she went to the bed. When she turned so her back was towards the bed, Jack was already coming towards her. She gasped to see he'd removed his clothes so quickly without mishap. Then she allowed herself to really look at him, the way she used to do when she was sure no one was watching her at the beach. His shoulders seemed a little broader, but his waist was still flat.

And lowering her gaze…oh yeah! Things were just as she remembered the one and only time—

She stopped thinking as Jack's hands came up to her shoulders. The only light was coming from the bathroom and with it being behind him, Andy relaxed because she was sure Jack's ability to see her would be diminished. Lowering her hands, she let the dress fall to the floor at her feet. Suddenly she wondered what he was thinking as he saw her. Nervousness forced her to speak.

"I should imagine I look a lot different from the other time." Immediately, she thought how needy and insecure her words must sound.

Jack slowly looked up from the amazing display her red bra made of her breasts. Pushed up and together, he was tempted to pull those straps down now. Taking a deep breath, he lifted his head to look directly at her. "I wasn't thinking that, Andy. If I was thinking at all, it was about how beautiful your skin looks, or how much I want to hold your breasts."

Her hands lifted and released the bra's clasp. It sprang open and she caught the red silky garment with one hand pressed to her chest.

Jack lifted his hands to her shoulders, shaking his head. "Allow me, sweetheart." He slid the narrow straps down her shoulders. When he moved his hands to hover above the silken cups, Andy dropped her hand. He watched as the sexy bra fell to the floor. He heard Andy's breath catching, but he was more concerned with his ability to keep air flowing in and out of his lungs. Now would not be a good time to pass out! A second later, either his hands moved forward or Andy leaned towards him because he was holding her full breasts. "God, honey, you feel so wonderful."

Jack was careful as he held her breasts, feeling hard nipples pressing into his palms. He looked down at her high-cut red silk panties, topped with a red and black garter belt holding up her stockings. There was a good chance if he didn't hurry things along, he could end up embarrassing himself. His hands slid down and began tugging at her underwear. He released it to fall to the floor once he reached her knees.

"Let's get horizontal, Andy." Resting his knee on the bed, he gently eased their bodies back. "You look beautiful, honey," he added and lowered his mouth to press kisses across her chest. With his hand pushing beneath one breast, he slid her taut nipple inside the wet heat, wanting to suckle her.

"Oh God, Jack!"

Continuing to pull and tug on her nipple, he slipped his hand down her tummy. He paused when he didn't feel the lush pussy fur which he'd only had the pleasure of running his fingers through just once before. This time, her pussy was smooth as his fingers eased down. Her thighs fell apart even as he felt the wetness flowing forth to welcome him. Damn! He got hotter with each passing second. Easily he found her clit, and the clever dance his finger performed with the bud of flesh was powerful.

Andy cried out again, and then her body jerked against his spasmodically.

Jack lifted his mouth from her breast and reached his hand out to grab the packet he'd tossed onto the bed.

The tear of foil sounded like thunder cracking in her ears. It brought home what truly was about to happen. She'd wanted Jack for twelve years and other than the senior year spring break when they came so close—

She shifted her legs, watching his face. There were no doubts in her head. This had to happen...it went beyond fate, kismet or destiny. He was the man she dreamed about. Only his face had ever filled her sexual fantasies, and too many times to count he had served as the hero for a story.

Andy tilted her hips, moved her hands and pulled him towards her. It was all the encouragement Jack needed and he started to move when the phone started ringing beside the bed. Neither of them moved for a few seconds as their gazes met, both just listening to the phone ring.

Finally, Jack rolled away, grabbing the receiver off the phone's cradle as he came to his feet. A second later, he growled into the mouthpiece impatiently. "Yeah?"

The phone was then held out towards her and Jack walked towards the bathroom. Lifting the receiver to her ear, Andy spoke softly, "Hello." She couldn't see what Jack was doing as she came to sit on the side of the bed.

"Andy! Come and join us in the bar. Bring Jack with you."

Taking a deep breath first, Andy still tried to decide if the phone call interrupting them was a good thing or not. Everything had certainly spiraled way beyond her control. Ten seconds later and she would have been...her mind rebelled at the words. Her stomach clamped down painfully in response. Was she upset because they'd stopped, and now she could reconsider?

"Where are you?" she asked instead.

"Ray says to tell Jack it is The Golden Lion Pub. He will remember where it is, according to Ray anyway. Hurry up, sweetie, you don't want to sleep this cruise away."

The receiver went dead as Gayle hung up. A noise caused her to turn her head as she reached over to replace the phone to the cradle. Jack stood in the doorway and he had replaced his trousers. Immediately she knew he had realized they had almost made a huge mistake. She jerked one of the pillows forward, holding it the long way on her lap. Her arms came up to clasp it tightly in place.

"That was Gayle, and the others. They want us to join them. Uhm, Ray said you'd know the way...a place called The Golden Lion Pub." Nervously she shifted her hands, freeing one to push the hair back off her face. "I think you should join them, Jack. I don't want to get all dressed up again. I'll just go on to bed."

Andy held her breath, waiting and half-scared as to what Jack would decide. She wanted him to go, right? What had almost happened would have been a mistake, so it was good Gayle had interrupted them. Anyone and everyone would agree. Obviously, Jack thought so, too, or he wouldn't have started to redress. Looking around the room to avoid meeting his gaze, she saw her negligee had been laid out across the stool which stretched almost the full width at the foot of the bed. Without thinking first, she leaned sideways to grab the robe. Only as she fell onto the bed did she realize how silly she would look. Now she was stuck in this position unless she released the pillow and wiggled around to stretch the last few inches.

Her opinion was confirmed when she heard Jack clear his throat before he spoke and it sounded like he was covering a laugh. "Need some help?"

"I wouldn't want to delay you if you are in a hurry," she added, thinking if he left now, she might still keep some level of dignity.

Jack grinned and walked around the foot of the bed. He didn't have to be hit over the head to know the mood had been lost for tonight. While he'd prefer staying here with Andy, even if they sat on the sofa downstairs and watched television, it was obvious she would prefer to be alone. He wasn't a fool and he wasn't going to press forward too soon, hoping to God he had not just screwed up everything. Picking up the filmy soft negligee, he carried it back around to the side of the bed.

It took him a moment to realize Andy wasn't reaching for the negligee or sitting back up. Watching her lying on her side with the one arm stretched above her, he wondered if she was comfortable. Still, something about her didn't look like she was relaxed.

"Is there a problem, Andy?" he asked finally, still holding the negligee.

"Uhm, sort of, I can't get back up."

"Okay, just give me your hands —"

The shaking of her head told him his suggestion was useless. The fact she was being modest seemed beyond logical since he was the kind of guy who felt comfortable walking around in his underwear or less, if need be.

"If you just let go of the pillow —"

Once again the negative movements of her head told him this idea was equally useless. "Andy, I'd like to help you, but I think the only way is for you to let go of the pillow. I could pull the bottom of the blankets up for you to hold instead."

As if she realized she was being unreasonable, she pushed the pillow away and lifted her hand towards him. Easily, Jack pulled her upright, holding out the negligee. He argued for a moment a gentleman would turn away, but he still looked. In the dim light, he could easily see her upper body. As she pulled on the thin, multi-layered garment, Jack enjoyed the bouncing movements of her breasts since she hurried. Regretfully, he saw her close the robe, tying the belt to hold it closed. Turning, he walked back to the bathroom, picking up the clothes he'd dropped earlier.

When he exited a few minutes later, completely dressed, he was surprised to find the bedroom empty. He wasn't sure leaving was a good idea. Maybe he should insist on staying to iron out some issues between them. Considering how skittish Andy still seemed to be, despite their history, plus what had just happened, would he find himself back at the starting point? As he descended the stairs, he saw Andy behind the bar. The clattering and clinking of glass against crystal forewarned her activities.

* * * * *

Part of her wished he'd leave so she could write this off as closure and nothing else. Doing it and planning in advance to have sex with Jack were two completely different beasts she was discovering. She wanted to lock away her emotions —

"Look at the time!" she said, deliberately forcing a bright tone to her voice. "You could probably still meet the others in the casino if you want, if they've left the pub already."

Moving about behind the bar, Andy busied herself with moving glasses and looking everywhere but at Jack. Gratefully, she found the bottle and started looking for a glass. She knew there had to be another one like the one Henderson had served it in earlier. Aware that Jack watched her, she suddenly became all thumbs.

"Does it matter what kind of glass?" she asked, breathlessly a few seconds after she knocked over a second glass.

"Forget the drink, Andy."

Setting down the bottle, she came from behind the bar. Since Jack had not yet taken a seat, she figured she could sit on the sofa. But he surprised her by grabbing her wrist and stopping her. Looking over her shoulder, she was intently aware of how attractive Jack was. If only circumstances could be different. Quickly, she spoke, her nerves becoming more intense with each passing moment. "The casino is on deck two."

"Yeah, I remember. Why are you in such an all-fired hurry to get rid of me?"

"I'm not in a hurry...I did offer you a drink," she reminded him, lifting her chin.

"True," Jack told her as he pulled on her wrist, turning her to face him. His hands lifted to catch her upper arms. "But usually when two people almost make love then some conversation is called for. I think we should talk about this tonight."

"Uhm, normally I would defer to your greater experience with situations like this. But I figured you'd want to get back with *your* friends and have a good time." It wasn't easy, but Andy kept the tears from breaking forth and choking her words. She was torn, but still felt obligated to point out the barriers between them.

"They are *our* friends, damn it! I don't want to argue over this, Andy." He released her arms. "I wanted us to talk, sweetheart. I really didn't plan on any of this happening."

Andy wasn't sure if he was saying sleeping with her…not that there'd been any sleeping involved as of yet, but the fact he considered sleeping with her the furthest thing from his mind when they started could mean something. Was he thinking this had been a mistake? Undoubtedly, he regretted his impetuous behavior.

"You don't need to apologize, Jack."

"Apologize! Of course, I'm not going to say I'm sorry. I have no reason to apologize. Maybe it's you who feels a need to do so," he shot back.

Andy felt her chin drop in surprise. "What? Do you regret what happened?"

"I didn't say that, Andy. Look, all I wanted to do was get the chance to talk with you in private. But having you prance up those stairs, wiggling your cute ass and then showing me your bed, I made the natural assumption you wanted to have sex."

Andy was hurt and angry. Pushing away the pain, she let the anger bubble up. The heartache she'd deal with later. "If I wanted to have sex, I would say so. I was merely being friendly, considering the way you'd glommed onto me from the moment you saw me."

A second later, she saw the fire blaze up in Jack's eyes. The stiffening of his body followed the glare darkening his face. She bit her lower lip and knew she shouldn't have used the word "glommed". It sounded as if he was something nasty she'd discovered on her shoe. He turned away and stomped several steps towards the door. She saw his shoulders lift and fall and she guessed he took some deep breaths. Reluctantly, she acknowledged she should have taken a few seconds to calm herself before she'd answered.

It had not been an accurate description. He had been polite and attentive from the first moment. Not once had he done anything she had not wanted…even longed for, so why had she accused him? Her heart told her to speak up and tell him what she desired…him.

Jack turned and nodded his head once. "I'll go for now, Andy. We can talk at breakfast." He walked to the double doors. Opening one side, he stopped in the doorway. "Don't forget to lock up, even though you're in the high-rent district. I'll stand out here until I hear the bolt click."

Andy stared at the closed doors. Feeling as if she carried the world on her shoulders, she crossed to the entryway. For a moment, she leaned against the heavy doors, pressing her cheek to cool wood. Nothing was going as she'd fantasized and hoped for in her daydreams. Lifting her hand, she slowly turned the latch for the deadbolt. She listened closely, knowing she couldn't really hear Jack walking away. Only silence both inside and out.

Then she remembered the peephole. Quickly, she rose on tiptoe, looking through the tiny magnifying glass. She could see Jack had reached the elevators and was pressing the button. If only this was one of her books, she could be the heroine who threw open the double doors and ran down the hall, crying out her lover's name. He'd turn, see her and open his arms. Pressing against him, their lips would meet to kiss passionately. And when their lips finally parted, driven only by the desperate need to breathe, he'd tell her, "I love you." Then he would make the grand gesture and sweep her into his arms, carrying her back to bed for a night of wild and erotic lovemaking.

Andy straightened and moved away from the door. A half smile curving her lips, she lifted her hand to brush back her hair. She was surprised to feel the tears on her cheeks. Using both hands, she rubbed away the tears. For some time, she wandered about the first level of the suite, picking up little knickknacks, checking them out. Three different times, she walked out onto the deck before trudging back inside. Suddenly, she decided she needed something she'd not had in a very, very long time. Looking around, she saw the panel on the wall to ring for

Henderson. It didn't seem fair to drag him out this late so she went to the phone and found the number for room service.

She knew it was not a wise choice, but old habits die hard. In times of stress, she usually started writing. Only this time...maybe it was being in a strange place, or facing old friends—she wasn't sure why her usual methods weren't working. Of course, she could have puttered about, tried writing or even sleeping to stop the desire. But she knew just as surely as she recognized her face when she saw it reflected in the reflective glass behind the bar, nothing else would work tonight. A few minutes later, she hung up the phone and settled back on the sofa to wait.

* * * * *

Jack opened the door to his side of the double cabin. According to the travel agent, it was really a "deluxe balcony" not a cabin. And there certainly was a lot more glass to look out of than just a porthole. Stepping into the room, he realized he wasn't alone. At the far end of the room, sitting on the small sofa, Ray watched television. From the look on his friend's face, Jack figured his friend's evening hadn't gone as he'd hoped either. "Hey, Ray. I thought you'd be across the hallway, sharing that half-empty cabin with Gayle."

Ray glared at Jack, took another sip of beer, and then turned back to the screen. "So did I."

"You fought?" Jack tossed his suit jacket on the nearest twin bed. As Ray nodded, Jack asked him another question. "Got any more of those?"

Ray lifted the hand holding the beer and pointed to the refrigerator on the other side of the television stand. Jack pulled out one and twisted off the cap. Taking two long swigs, he sat beside Ray because other than the desk chair, there wasn't any place left to sit. Immediately he compared the room to Andy's suite. God! They were as different as night and day.

"Everything seemed great at dinner. What did you guys fight about?" Jack asked after a few more swallows of cold lager.

"You and Andy, and before you say anything else, damn it all, it was my fault. I was being Mr. Sensitive and listening to Gayle prattle on and on about Andy this and so on…well, I screwed up. I brought up the night in your room as a sign of your concern for her baby pigeon."

"So? You said she was fine with it once you explained everything," Jack shook his head and took another deep swallow of the cold beer. This evening just wasn't going the way he'd planned in the least.

"Well, thinking it would help, I told her something else…and she, uhm, didn't follow my logic."

"What did you tell her, Ray?"

"Remember how we used to joke about our nicknames? I was *doc* and Mark was the *professor*."

"Sure. Danny was *bean-counter* and Tony called himself *playboy*." Jack chuckled softly. "He didn't like the name we gave him."

"Maybe, but more likely Tony didn't like it was you we called playboy."

Jack shook his head. "You never called me that."

"We did." Ray shrugged. "We knew you wouldn't like it so we would call you J.D."

"Just when I was around, otherwise it was playboy? Great!" Jack leaned his head back against the wall behind the small sofa. "So finish the story."

"All right. I finally told Gayle to quit worrying because playboy would never hurt anyone deliberately, let alone—"

Ray's voice trailed away so Jack turned to look at his friend. The truth was written on doc's face.

"You didn't Ray, did you? Remember I made you all swear to never use that term again after spring break. You promised me, Ray, as my best friend since grade school."

Ray stood and walked to the far end of the stateroom, standing in front of the entrance. "I'm sorry, damn it! It slipped out. I had too damned much champagne. God, I don't know. So, now I'm cast out and I'll probably end up sharing the queen-size bed with Danny."

Jack watched as his friend turned and lightly banged his head against the wall. Damn! Nothing about the first night aboard this so-called pleasure cruise of their lifetime was going very well. Standing, he went to the refrigerator again and pulled out two beers. He held one out to Ray as he walked towards him. The room was small enough for Ray to reach out and grab it as Jack sat on the edge of the first twin bed. He watched as his friend twisted off the cap and took a sip. Shaking his head, he dropped back to lie on the bed.

"Why are we drinking alone in this tiny room?" Ray asked a few seconds later.

Jack lifted his head to look at his friend. Had he gone crazy? Early "old-timers"? "Because you opened your big mouth to Gayle. Did you at least get her to promise she wouldn't tell the others?"

"She laughed in my face and gave me the speech about how she thought she *knew* me, but now that I've kept a secret from her for all these years…yada yada yada." Ray stood and began walking the short distance between the door and balcony. He paced a few times as he continued speaking. "That's when I left. Why are you here? How come you aren't down winning another fortune in the casino or looking for a sweet companion in the bar?"

Jack opened his mouth to reply when a tapping at the door stopped him.

Ray turned and opened the door.

A second later, he saw Ray fall back against the wall as Gayle sailed in right past him. Her gaze landed on him. She tilted her head slightly, looking down her nose. He was pretty damned sure it was contempt he saw in her expression. Once again, he felt like he was the dog shit on another unhappy person's shoes. Hell!

Sitting up slowly, he lifted his bottle towards Gayle. "Salute, Gayle. Did you come for some more sharing with Ray? He's pretty bummed at having to sleep with Danny tonight."

Gayle folded her arms, looking at Jack and then Ray. "Yes, well…stop distracting me. Where is Andy?"

"She's in her suite. I assumed she went to bed."

"Take me to her then. I want to talk to her."

Ray came to stand beside Gayle. "Why don't we call her, sweetheart? You can use the phone here."

Jack watched as Gayle glared at her lover. The two of them had been off and on since college. He had little doubt this minor disagreement would blow over like all their tiffs. "Sure, Gayle, call her," he added a moment later.

"I tried already. Her phone is on 'no-call' until morning. I must speak to her as soon as possible."

"I doubt she is in the mood to hear any of this crap tonight," Jack muttered softly.

"I would never tell her what creeps you guys were in college. It's bad enough I've had to learn what complete assholes you all were. How dare you call her that?" Gayle asked, nearly shouting, disbelief evident in her tone. After a short pause, she asked Jack a question. "What did you do to her?"

"I didn't do anything, as you are implying. I'm sure she was going to bed after I escorted her back to her cabin."

Gayle flopped down on the other bed. "Why are you back here then? I thought the goal for you guys was to 'bag as many babes' as possible."

Jack lifted his gaze towards Ray. "Good Lord, Ray, is there anything you haven't told her?"

Gayle smiled and patted the mattress beside her.

Ray sat, gratitude to be back in her good graces evident on his face.

"Pillow talk, Jack. Now, I've got an idea. You two put on your pajamas—" She stopped at the appalled look on the men's faces. "Geez, you guys! Pretend and just put on something that will pass as pjs and a robe. If anyone asks, we're just taking a last-minute stroll. Well, what are you waiting for? Change!"

Jack stood. "At least turn around, Madam Dictator. I don't want you telling everyone I'm fast and loose."

Gayle stood and walked over to the glass door leading to the small balcony. "Wouldn't you like to boast on your first night of the cruise a woman saw you naked?"

Jack groaned as he started to move off the bed. "Why haven't you drowned her yet?"

"Because he loves me, Jack."

She started to turn to add something when both men yelled. "Hey! Eyes front!"

Twenty minutes later, they stood outside the impressive double doors to the Balmoral suite. Gayle rapped her knuckles on the door loudly.

"If these doors are any indication, this must be some cabin." Ray looked around them, and then down the long hallway.

"We have staterooms, darling," Gayle reminded him gently.

As the door opened, all three turned to smile at Andy. Instead, there was a tall, dark-haired man dressed in silk pajamas, slippers and a monogrammed robe, all in deep, rich burgundy and hunter green. From head to toe, he looked like the gentleman's magazine ideal for a pajama model that was worth a million bucks.

Gayle was the first to speak, a grin spreading across her face. "Wow! Talk about trading up."

Chapter Four

Not too much earlier, in the crew's quarters —

The phone rang twice before it was answered.

"Hey, Rick, good buddy, did you forget to sign out?" The voice on the phone asked, more joking than serious.

Richard Henderson the fourth closed the leather-bound book he'd been reading. "I haven't signed off, David. What are you talking about?"

"The kitchen called the night-duty desk to see what the problem was."

"David, stop stringing this out and just tell me what you need." Rick made no effort to keep his frustration out of his tone.

"You must have pissed off the ritzy lady paying for your lone ranger ride in the Balmoral, friend. She just called room service, instead of ringing the night desk."

Rick came to his feet immediately. Once he'd left Ms. Bond, he had assumed she retired for the night. He'd also gotten the distinct impression the gentleman with her planned on sharing her bed. Over the last fourteen years, he'd seen all kinds of wealthy people occupying the largest and most expensive suites on this cruise line. None of his passengers had ever complained about his work service, which was one of the main reasons he'd been promoted when this newest ship had come off the production line last year.

He was fourth-generation English butler and very proud of his history and his work. After attending the prestigious school in London, he could have had any number of posts considering whom his father worked for. Instead he'd decided to travel and see the world. The money was good, he had a bed at his parents' house for vacations if need be and he enjoyed what he did. David's voice caught his attention again.

"So I'll deliver this but I'll need you to turn your call button over to the night desk now."

"No thanks, David. Tell the kitchen to prepare whatever it is, and I'll be down in less than five minutes to pick it up."

Seven minutes later, Rick waited quietly for the elevator doors to slide open for the Balmoral Suite. A soft, deliberate ding sounded. Alerting guests of the suite that the elevator was arriving, it could be turned off. Stepping into the living room of the suite, he was surprised to find it partially lit.

"Oh! Hello!" A soft feminine voice called out.

Immediately, he recognized the voice as belonging to Ms. Bond. Rick's head turned and he saw her seated on a chair she'd pulled to a few feet in front of the double doors, which led into the suite. She stood though, as soon as she saw him.

"I called room service because I didn't want to disturb you." Andy smiled. "I figured you'd be sound asleep."

Rick smiled in return, shaking his head. "I knew there was the logical reason," he spoke half under his breath. Talking louder, he continued. "Aboard ship your butler service, namely me, or the night staff if I sign out to them, takes care of these things for you. I serve as your link to the other services."

"Damn and I'm sorry. I hope I didn't get anyone in trouble."

"Not at all, Ms. Bond. Leave the chair, miss and I'll get it. Where would you like to eat this?"

Andy sighed and crossed to the deep, rounded sofa. She plopped down in the middle, crossing her legs Indian-style, and then rearranging her robe to cover her legs.

Rick set down the sterling silver tray and then spread a large, crisply ironed and folded white linen napkin across her lap. "I apologize we were unable to fulfill your request exactly, but I had them put three large scoops of the best kinds of chocolate ice creams we have into this bowl." He handed her a shining silver bowl piled high, with one spoon. "I'll be happy to go back for more if you wish."

There was no missing the flush that flooded the lovely woman's cheeks. Dressed in the golden peignoir set, she was very attractive. Straightening, he stepped a foot backwards, moving to the shorter side of the coffee table. He was too much of a professional to ever become involved with a passenger, but there was something about this one that was different. The fact she so obviously was not used to this kind of living, endeared her to him. She seemed fragile—

"Why don't you join me, Mr. Henderson? I see you brought another spoon."

"I always bring an extra, in case the first one is dropped."

Andy took a bite of the ice cream.

He watched as she closed her eyes for a moment, obviously savoring the taste.

She then pointed the spoon at him. It moved slightly with each word, as if to further enunciate her words. "Smart thinking, Mr. Hen...uhm, Henderson. Can I call you by your first name, since I'm not supposed to use mister?"

"If you prefer, miss. My first name is Richard, but I tend to answer better to Rick."

"Nice name and totally British. Actually, I think it's a good name for a hero. A good name is strong, short...two syllables or less is preferred, with one being best and it should have a strong masculine tone. So, you see Rick is good, as are John, Robert, or Mike." She stopped and pointed at the extra spoon. "Please join me or I'll feel like such a glutton."

Reluctantly, Rick picked up the spoon and took a small bite of the ice cream. Surprisingly, he found it pretty tasty. When Andy patted the sofa, he perched on the edge and joined her in a second spoonful.

"Are you married? I didn't see a ring."

He was swallowing when she spoke again. Coughing, Rick recovered quickly. He'd never had a passenger inquire about his personal life. Shaking his head a little, hopefully to get some sense into it, he then answered. "No, I'm not married."

"You've got a fiancée, or you're very close to popping the question."

Rick sputtered this time. "How did you know that?"

Andy grinned and pointed the spoon again. "Simple." She passed the bowl to him to hold. One finger popped up as she spoke. "You are a good-looking man. In most circles, I bet you'd pass for buff and stud."

Rick watched as she wiggled her eyebrows at him. He barely contained his laughter.

"Two is you're straight," she finished.

"Wait, how do you know that?"

"Women know...unless they lie to themselves. And I picked up a definite heterosexual vibe from you earlier."

"I apologize if you feel that—" he said quickly.

"It's nothing you did towards me. Let me see...two was straight. Three is that you appear to be fastidious so I doubt you are a cruising Casanova."

Rick handed her the bowl and then reached over for another spoonful as he considered her words. "You seem pretty good at this. Are you a private detective?"

Andy laughed. "No, but if I tell you what I do, you'll have to promise to keep it a secret."

"Of course," he said, straightening his spine. "I give you the word of an English butler, ma'am."

"You know what would be good with this?" Andy asked quickly.

She surprised him by the change in subject so abruptly.

"What?" Rick asked, thinking this was definitely one of the oddest things he'd ever done at a passenger's request. It would definitely go down as one of his top ten oddest passenger encounters.

Andy was already pushing the bowl at him once more before she scrambled to her feet. Behind the bar, she began opening cabinets.

A knock at the suite's front door stopped them both for a second.

"It's probably David checking up on me." Rick spoke as he set down the bowl and crossed to the front doors. "He is the guy serving the night shift." Holding the spoon in one hand, he opened the door.

Andy nodded as she continued looking for something she'd seen earlier. Most likely, the people who usually stayed in a suite like this would be interested in champagne and unpronounceable wines. Then she spied the squat black glass bottle with the signature gold paper. Jumping up, she spun and danced her way to the entryway. "I found it!"

Immediately, she saw his fellow butler had not joined Rick. Rather Jack had returned, bringing Gayle and Ray with him. And quite amazingly she noted lastly, they were all dressed in their pajamas and robes. She met Rick's gaze and saw his concern there. Instinctively, she shrugged and lowered the bottle. Taking a deep breath, Andy realized that everyone had gone from looking at Rick, to staring at her. As a person who always avoided being the center of attention, she felt a heated flush cover her cheeks. With false bravado to disguise the sudden rush of insecurity, she spoke loudly. "I see we have guests, Henderson. We're going to need more spoons!"

* * * * *

Andy cursed loudly as she turned over in bed. She realized the curtains had been opened and the gentle breeze blew in. Rolling over, she saw Rick, once again perfectly attired in his black suit, carrying a tray in her direction.

"Good morning, Miss. I've brought you some tea. Would you care to have breakfast on the upper deck or the lower?"

Andy pulled up the sheet over her head. "What time is it?"

"It's nearly noon."

"Noon! Oh shit...crap. Sorry. I had things I wanted to do this morning."

"Did Madam use all of the liqueur on her ice cream after we left?"

"Not all, but enough to make this unpleasant. Did I apologize for last night? I don't know why my friends all showed up like that."

"Your friend, Miss—"

"Gayle."

"Yes, she kept talking about a slumber party, but your male friends didn't seem in the party mood."

"I noticed that, too. Thanks for shepherding everyone to the elevator."

"I sensed they wouldn't leave until I did."

Andy sat up and pushed the hair out of her face. "Yeah, well they aren't sophisticated like I am and used to having a butler about the place." She waited to see if Henderson responded to her little joke, but he was in perfect form.

"Shall I run a bath for madam?"

Andy drew up her knees and wrapped her arms around them. "Okay, and I'll sip the tea. I must skip breakfast because I have to get to work." Seeing the frown of disapproval on her butler's face, she smiled. "I'll explain later. Thanks."

* * * * *

Dressed casually, Andy watched as Jack came towards her. After her bath, she'd called his stateroom. The phone was answered on the second ring. She recognized the voice on the other end immediately.

"Hi, Danny, it's Andy. Is Jack around?"

"Good afternoon, Andy! We missed you at breakfast. Ruthie visited the purser this morning and got us all these cool pagers. We can message each other and stay in touch, make plans and stuff."

Danny was ever the techno-geek, same as Ruthie. If it was new, electronic and promised bells and whistles, either Danny or Ruthie would have it first. Hearing the excitement in his voice was no surprise.

"She passed them out at breakfast. Jack has yours because he said you both were attending something at two today."

Andy breathed a sigh of relief. She really wanted to explore the whole BDSM scene after listening to the lecture…partly for research and the other because it did excite her somewhat, maybe even a little more than what she wanted to admit. After last night, she was feeling off-center, and hopefully, once she saw Jack again, everything could go back to normal. Of course, defining just what normal constituted at this point was the problem.

Standing opposite the elevators just outside the Queen's Grill on deck seven, she'd waited nervously for Jack to show up. Watching him as he walked off the elevator, she felt a shiver of desire travel through her body. She was worried her behavior last night, in the effort to maintain her dignity, might have damaged his. She had pretty much kicked him out of her bed. And truthfully, she believed he'd mainly wanted to talk. But their emotions had gotten out of hand. For her, she'd waited too many years.

"Hi, Jack, thanks for meeting me," she spoke quickly, greeting him with a half-smile.

"I was looking forward to learning a little more myself. Oh, here's your beeper." He pulled it from his pocket, passing it to her. "Between your PDA and this, you're wired for contact."

Andy smiled because it was expected, but she felt the coolness in his reception. As he turned to start for the Queen's Grill, she grabbed his arm. "Jack, about last night—"

Jack smiled and pressed his finger against her lips. "Shh, sweetheart, we'll talk later. No interruptions or getting off-track this time."

He reached and took her hand.

With a sigh, she followed him.

Andy knew her mouth kept dropping open as she listened to Ethan Williams and Jack talk. Occasionally, Margrit spoke but she never initiated conversation. Unsure whether she felt more surprised at learning the Williams had a 24/7 Master/submissive relationship, or the fact Jack might not be as much of a novice as she certainly was, all she could do was listen. On many topics, Jack discussed the subject intelligently and asked succinct questions.

"As today progresses, you should begin to see more people appearing in their clothing of choice. The first night is usually quiet. Tonight is the first Dungeon Party. It should be interesting from what I saw scheduled before we sailed."

"Like what?" Andy asked, unable to keep the excitement from her voice.

Ethan smiled. "As usual with the first party, there will be a lot of demonstrations going on. Normally, there would be role-playing going on at the assigned stations and rooms, but since they anticipated a large number of first-timers, I expect mostly demos tonight."

"People walk around and watch?" she asked.

"Yes, and once the role-playing games begin, you'll find people signing up in advance and often just volunteering when something catches their eye. The organizational committee arranged to have a number of devices available also."

Andy could feel Jack watching her, but she didn't dare meet his gaze. She had little doubt that if she did, what she saw there would have her blushing until tomorrow. "What kind of devices?" she asked, hoping she didn't sound as naïve as she was.

"Chairs, torture and bondage devices. Some are serious and others are just for play."

"Do people get hurt?"

Jack's hand covered hers where it rested on the table between them. "There is always a safe word, Andy, which stops everything the second it is said. Trust is foremost in situations like these."

Andy looked into Jack's eyes. She trusted Jack, in spite of what she'd told him last night. The thought of playing a sexual game, or scene as Ethan referred to it, was exciting her, especially if she played it with Jack.

"I was thinking Andy might enjoy spending some time with Margrit this afternoon. I know Margrit made double appointments at the spa, just in case." Ethan smiled, looking from his wife to Andy.

Andy looked at the quiet woman, who had nodded her head, smiling back at her. "All right, that sounds like fun."

* * * * *

Fun didn't cover what happened that afternoon Andy decided much later, as she dressed for the party. The spa provided quite a few services. She got massaged, wrapped like a package and lastly she splurged.

Following the massage and moisture wrap, she sat, watching as Margrit finished her treatment when she noticed the tattoo the other woman had. "I like your tat," she said, enjoying the intricate design at the base of the other woman's spine.

"Thank you. Do you have one?"

Andy shook her head. "I've never had the courage…well, that's not completely true."

Margrit turned to look at her. "What keeps stopping you? To me, it's not a sign of protest or exhibitionism. Ethan kept telling me I was beautiful all over, so one day I said what if I had a tattoo?"

Andy smiled. "What did he say?"

Margrit thanked the woman who'd just finished and wrapped the thick towel around her trunk. "Well, we had not known one another too long, perhaps a little over a year, and I assumed that he would forbid it or beg me not to do it. We weren't living the lifestyle 24/7, but I had been aware of his interest."

"Did he do it?"

"No, he surprised me. He offered to make me an appointment and go with me. I was more than a little shocked because I had been speaking offhand, uhm…testing the waters, so to speak."

Andy grinned, knowing exactly what the beautiful woman meant.

"I was startled and still sure he kidded and teased me. That's when I said I'd have it done on my breast, for all the world to see." She paused and gestured to the upper curve. "As if he could read my mind, he tells me get it on my ass. I came back with it two inches above my butt crack because Ethan liked it when I wore low, backless gowns. I took the unspoken dare, half-sure he'd reject me afterwards. Instead, he spent all night and the next day kissing it, doing all the necessary aftercare and applying ice."

"Wow."

"Why don't you get one? They do it here, you know."

Andy shook her head. "I don't like to draw attention—"

"My stuffed-shirt, snobbish uncle would reply all women love drawing attention to themselves." Margrit laughed lightly.

"I was quite a bit overweight for most of my life. I didn't need a tattoo to draw more attention to my body."

Margrit shrugged. "That was then, and this is now. Think of it this way. What one part of your body do you consider most improved? With diet and exercise."

"I never thought of it like that. My butt is what I concentrated on after I lost the weight."

"Then maybe accent one cheek with a small, sassy statement, something that says 'this is one damned fine ass!' You could even just do your initials, like an artist who has made a beautiful work of art. God gave you a body, and you sculpted it."

"I'll chicken out by the time we get back home."

Margrit had hopped up and grabbed her hand. "Maybe not."

Thinking back about it now, things had happened pretty quickly. The big surprise had been that she could get small tattoos and even piercing, if she wanted. Margrit had helped her pick out a design and even squeezed her hand while it was done. But twisting around to see it now, she did wonder if she'd done the right thing or not. She acknowledged no matter how long she stared at it in the mirror, it was not going away.

The doorbell ringing made her turn from the three-way mirror, pulling closed her white terrycloth robe. Henderson was off on an errand, so she ran down the curved stairs. Without thinking, she yanked open the door rather than glance through the peephole.

"Well, hello to you, too," Jack told her as he walked past her into the suite.

Andy closed her mouth and the door, in that order. She saw him set down a bag he'd been carrying and was now standing behind the bar. "I didn't think I'd see you until it was time for dinner," she told him, folding her arms across her chest.

"You wouldn't, except Ethan and I ran into Margrit. She dragged us back to their suite for me to bring you something to wear tonight." Jack opened the can of soda and drank several long swallows.

Andy could see he'd not yet showered after his planned afternoon of working out with Ethan. As she continued watching him, he pressed the can to his forehead. When he saw her looking, he shrugged. "I know Ethan is at least ten years older than I am, but that guy must work out all the fucking time!

74

We ran into Tony and Danny." He paused to take a couple more swallows.

Andy nodded, easing onto one of the padded barstools. "That would have been enlightening."

Jack gave her a funny look, but went on. "We decided to play some basketball and drew straws. I drew Tony and he shot me one of his 'this is in the bag' looks, you know."

"Oh, yeah, he'd always give you guys that look when he was sure a girl was his for the taking. Once we started keeping track, I ran a statistical analysis —"

"You did what? Who kept track of what?" Jack sputtered on the last swallow of his pop.

"I shouldn't have interrupted you, Jack, please go on," she told him in a placating tone.

Jack frowned in her direction as he reached for another soda, easily popping the tab.

"You should probably drink water rather than soda. If he wore you out this much, you'll be dehydrated and the soda —" Andy spoke again.

"He didn't wear me out, damn it!" Jack said tersely.

Andy held up her hands, palms towards Jack in a conciliatory manner. Obviously, his masculinity had taken a hit this afternoon. Undoubtedly, so had Tony and Danny, she just hoped they weren't in this sort of mood when they all met later. After dinner with Ethan and Margrit, they were all attending the Dungeon Party together. Ethan had suggested it over lunch, and while the two men played with the electronic pager, they slowly received everyone's agreement.

Standing, Andy walked over and eased down onto the sofa, stretching out to lie on her side. Once she was comfortable, she glanced back and saw Jack drinking some water rather quickly. He then turned to offer her a soda.

"No, thank you, Jack. Henderson is bringing me fresh iced tea when he returns."

Jack walked towards her. "I thought you'd switched to calling him Rick."

Andy couldn't resist teasing him, in spite of the little voice in charge of her wiser judgment. "We decided to keep it professional, except for the wild sex orgies."

The glare she received was deflected because the private elevator doors slid open. Turning her head, she was sure Rick's step faltered for a split second under Jack's look. Still he kept on walking, carrying the tray over to the coffee table. She'd definitely award him points for bravery.

"Your tea, miss, and your ice bag."

Andy reached for the ice first without realizing she'd not yet told Jack about her little adventure.

"Do you need help applying the ice, miss?"

Bad timing was how she'd describe the fact that she placed the ice on her ass just as Rick offered. She couldn't say for sure, but it sounded like Jack actually growled. Quickly, she replied, "No, thanks, Henderson."

"Would you like me to put your shopping bag upstairs, Ms. Bond?"

Andy still tried to hide her smile at Jack's bulldog attitude, so she just nodded. Once the butler was upstairs, she teased Jack a little more. She knew it was a little foolish to tempt a stubborn dog who guarded his bone. The fact she was the *bone* was something she refused to think about just yet. "I didn't need Henderson's help because he'd already given it his visual inspection for correct placement of the ice."

Jack moved so fast that Andy barely managed to grab a fistful of his shirt to stop him. Her thoughtless hold onto his t-shirt caused her to be pulled partly off the sofa, spreading the edges of her terrycloth robe. She spoke quickly, knowing her hand wouldn't restrain him for long.

"I'm teasing, Jack. I am sorry, but I couldn't resist. You've been in a pissy mood ever since you almost knocked down my door. I'm sorry for antagonizing you."

Jack looked down at Andy, taking in the disheveled appearance she now presented on the sofa. He hadn't realized she was naked beneath the soft material, but the naked breast, which in his opinion cried out for his hand, was proof enough. As he took a step towards her, he heard footfalls on the stairs. His reaction was instinctive, he told himself later, not protective. Being protective towards her was emotion he wasn't quite ready to deal with just yet. He'd felt like that once before with Andy, and this time he wanted to play it smarter. With one naked tit, and two long thighs revealed, he covered it all as best he could…with his body.

One of them moved and their mouths came together. Immediately, he knew it was the kiss that should have happened last night. The kiss was sweet, hot and passionate, all at the same time. He sought her tongue as he heard the elevator doors swish closed. Releasing her lips, he shifted their bodies slightly on the sofa, which positioned him between her now widespread thighs and further parted the top of her robe. Looking down, his gaze caught upon her breasts.

"What little sleep I got last night was filled with dreams about making love to you. Seeing you half-naked…and I get hard and want to be inside of you."

Andy's gasp didn't stop him.

He pulled back to look into her eyes. "Are you hurt? Do you feel good enough to sit up?" When she shook her head, he eased to the floor even as he brought her to a sitting position. Straightening, Jack kneeled between her legs. He saw her hands had been busy trying to conceal her body. Pausing in his plan, still foggy in his brain due to his growing lust, he pulled free the tie for her robe.

"Andy?" He waited until she met his gaze before he went on. "Do you trust me, based on what you know of me? I mean who we were, and I swear I never intentionally did anything at all to hurt you."

She didn't do anything at first, but finally she nodded.

Jack took each of her hands and placed it at her side. He took the edges of the robe and slowly pulled apart the sides to reveal her body. The scent of soap, lotion and female musk filled his nostrils as he inhaled deeply. "You are beautiful, Andy."

"Stretch marks—"

"Shh, give me your hands," he asked and then he lightly wrapped the tie around her wrists. "Do you think you can keep them behind your head? Okay. If there is anything I do that you don't like, just say…uh, I know—Bridget."

"Your mother's name?"

"Yeah, that should cool my jets," he shrugged. Then he noticed the small smile curving her lips. "Is something funny?"

"No, but I'll tell you later."

Jack decided not to press her. Instead, he leaned towards her, bringing his hand to cup the side of her face. Using one thumb, he rubbed it back and forth along her lower lip. "You have sexy lips. Do you ever wear deep red lipstick?"

Andy shook her head. "With the dress yesterday, that's the darkest color I've ever owned. It was brand-new and I wasn't sure—"

Jack's thumb pressed against her lips, stopping her. "You were the quintessential femme fatale in that dress, Andy. All evening long, I kept thinking about how to unfasten it and what you might be wearing under it."

"A lot of my clothes are new, for the cruise, like the dress and the lingerie, too."

"Andy?"

"What?"

"Tell me how to touch you. What ways of kissing or positions do you like the best? Shall I praise your breasts, which overflow my eager hands? Full, firm and luscious boobs with lovely long nipples."

Jack rubbed his thumbs around the taut nubs that poked outwards three-fourths of an inch. "They are a pretty soft pink in color, but hard, too. Do you like having your nipples sucked?"

Jack paused to look into her eyes, all the while moving his thumbs, taunting her budding points until the surrounding flesh wrinkled tightly. Holding her gaze, he kissed her mouth lightly. "I dreamed about sucking your nipples last night. At first, I wondered if I should suckle you like a baby does, and tug your tit as deeply inside my mouth as possible. Ray, ever the doctor, said the nerves in a woman's nipple are connected through some neural pathway to her womb. The harder the sucking, more stimuli to her womanly flesh—"

He paused to watch her reaction as he said the next word in a few seconds. "So, if I suck your tit just right, your cunt should contract, or spasm. And if I were inside you at the time—"

"Oh God!"

Andy cried out as her body reacted. Her hips jerked and she was suddenly moving them, and the whole time her pussy lips eagerly sought to pull something deep into her heat. She closed her eyes. She was coming and he had done nothing except speak to her and hold her breasts. Then she took a breath, thinking it was almost over.

Jack's mouth lowered to take her right nipple while she felt his fingers easing inside her body. Impossible to say which happened first, or whether it even mattered, but between his sucking and the fingers probing forward, when he touched her clit with the thumb on his other hand, she convulsed again. She thought she cried out, or said something, but it didn't matter.

For the first time, she discovered the power of an orgasm that didn't involve her hand or batteries. She lost track of time until her arms ached and she lowered them to rest on Jack's shoulders. Slowly, she became aware he had not yet released her nipple, although he no longer sucked. As she savored the feel of his wet warmth, his fingers started to wiggle around again. A corner of her brain told her she should stop him, but the rest of it stifled the niggling voice and reason quickly.

There was no pushing him away, but her tied hands, which had moved from behind her head to the back of his, only pulled them closer. She noticed the crisp, short hairs at the back rubbing her forearms, she jerked on the tie and it came free. Quickly, she rubbed her fingers up and down the back of Jack's head, ruffling the velvety pelt. An almost instantaneous stiffening moved through Jack's body. If his fingers paused, she wasn't aware of it. After that, the only thing she really noticed was the second, and then the third, orgasm she enjoyed swamping all of her senses.

At some point, Jack pulled away from her hands and moved her body to lie on the sofa. He pulled her robe closed and then eased a blanket over her legs, tucking her feet in. She thought he mentioned a wake-up call before she fell asleep. Last night's sleepless hours, plus the previous week's restlessness and nervousness caught up with her and she drifted to sleep.

Chapter Five

Jack knocked on the door to Andy's suite about ten minutes earlier than planned. Following Ethan's suggestion, he wore a tuxedo. As he waited, he recalled their earlier conversation.

"The parties at the Dungeon can exist on many different levels. If things progress as I anticipate, once we've given your friends a tour, we'll be invited to attend a private session. You and Andy are welcome to come with Margrit and I. Dress for this is usually black tie, for male Doms, and will vary for females, both Dominatrix and subs. Any idea what Andy is planning to wear?"

"None at all."

"Margrit is planning on talking with her so she'll be dressed appropriately."

Waiting for the door to be opened by Henderson, he did wonder whether Andy had taken kindly to Margrit's suggestions. His curiosity had made him want to look into the sack he'd delivered earlier. Now he wished he had given into it. Seconds later, the door opened and Henderson bowed slightly to welcome him.

"Good evening, sir. I'm afraid we're running a little late. Would you like a drink while you wait?"

Jack shook his head as he walked past the other man. "Do you know how long she's going to be? I should probably let our hosts know."

"At last estimate, twenty minutes. If you will tell me the name of your host, or the stateroom number, I'd be happy to contact them."

"All right," he replied. "Ethan Williams and they are staying in the Queen Victoria suite."

A second later, Jack was surprised to see Henderson smile. "I'm familiar with Mr. and Mrs. Williams. My fiancée is working as their butler for this cruise. It doesn't happen often, but we were both reserved exclusively for this sailing."

"You're engaged to a guy?" Jack couldn't keep the surprise from his voice. He'd met a few guys in the past that he never would have guessed they were gay, and if Henderson was...well then, he was surprised.

"This is the new millennium and women are in every field these days." Richard shook his head. "We met on board several years ago. Luckily, my seniority and the fact women in the profession are still scarce but in demand, allowed her an assignment to this ship as well."

For the first time since he'd initially seen the other man, he relaxed and grinned. Offering his hand, he congratulated him. "Good luck! Any wedding plans? I should imagine with you both stuck to a suite it limits your time together."

"Thank you, but we don't have any definite plans for a wedding yet. We knew this cruise would be restricted. Well, I'll make the call and then I'll return."

With a decidedly perkier step, Jack walked to the staircase and up a few steps. "Do you need any help, Andy?" he called out.

Andy's hand jerked slightly. Looking into the mirror, she was glad to see she hadn't smeared her lipstick. Running behind always made her more nervous and ham-handed. She'd slept through the wake-up call and luckily the switchboard had alerted Rick. He'd brought a pot of hot tea to help her wake up while he went upstairs to turn on the shower.

Setting down her lipstick, she walked from the bathroom into the bedroom. Her dress lay on the bed and she gratefully found a note had been tucked into the sack from Margrit. A quick read-through explained the garments, including tips on wearing. A white satin, merry widow, adorned by golden embroidery and with attached garters, was the star piece of the ensemble. White silk stockings came three-quarters up her thighs. The actual dress was white, tulle material, which draped, swathed and clipped about her torso into a fashion dream. A rhinestone clip at her hip held the tissue-thin cloth and allowed it to appear as if it then fell in draped layer upon layer to her knees.

Picking up the dress, she saw Jack's reflection in the mirror on the far wall. She could feel a blush rapidly staining her cheeks.

"You didn't answer, so I came on up."

"Hello, Jack. I was in the bathroom, adding the last of the war paint."

"Looks like you did a good job," Jack complimented her, smiling gently.

"Now, I just need my war pony and I'm all set," she joked back, without thinking.

"You can ride me anytime you like, Andy."

Wow! Andy had to take a deep breath at the erotic thoughts and emotions that flooded her body at his words. Trying to think quickly, she jested. "You might not like my riding crop."

Jack shook his head and started walking towards her, their gazes still meeting through the reflection. "We can try out different ones until you find the right crop to tame your stallion."

Andy closed her eyes at his words and a moment later she felt his hands sliding around her waist. She sighed when he lowered his lips to her shoulder, bare because she'd pulled her hair back into a waterfall of curls.

"You look beautiful, Andy."

"Thank you," she whispered, keeping her eyes shut for one more second and then looked into the mirror. "You look pretty dandy as well. This doesn't look like a 'for-hire' tux." She ran her hand down the satiny lapel.

"It's not, but was a good investment, considering the use I'll be getting out of it this trip."

Andy sat on the bed and stepped into the dress. Standing, she pulled it up and then looked at Jack, silently asking him to fasten it. She was considering a suggestion that they stay here.

"All done. Shoes?" he asked.

"There on the bench." She gestured to the cushioned seat at the foot of the bed. Leaning over, she took her keycard from the small purse she'd been using, to transfer it to the tiny, perfect little white bag Margrit had included with the dress.

"Want me to carry that for you? Lipstick?"

"Thanks," she said as she handed him the card. "I hadn't thought about lipstick."

"I might grab you in the hall and kiss all that pretty color from your lips."

Andy almost quipped back something about not letting him. Instead, she turned and skipped into the bathroom and grabbed the gold tube. At least she'd splurged on a fancy tube so it wouldn't be a scratched plastic one she pulled from the fancy purse, which also held a micro-recorder for her thoughts on story ideas. She accepted her shoes before she led the way downstairs.

Henderson stood behind the bar as they came down. "May I say that you clean up quite nicely, Ms. Bond?"

"Thank you, Henderson." She crossed to the small table and sat to slip on her heels.

Jack spoke from behind her where he had perched on one of the barstools. "We'll get to meet Henderson's fiancée tonight, sweetheart."

"I knew it!" Andy hopped up, pointing her finger straight at Rick.

"Amalie is working in your friends' suite on this sailing," Rick added with a smile.

"How exciting! Will it be all right if I say something? Introduce myself?"

"If you're alone with her, then it would be okay."

"I promise I won't do anything to embarrass her." Andy crossed her heart with one finger. "Or I'll try, at least. As you've already seen, I'm a bit of a hick when it comes to this level of posh."

"Well, we better get going, Andy. We're already almost late beyond what is socially acceptable." Jack stood and started for the front door.

"I have no class, I'm afraid." Andy shrugged. She picked up the small handbag and popped in the lipstick, quickly looking inside for the few things she'd put into it earlier. Satisfied, she nodded before adding with a grin, "You can blame it all on me."

"Have a good time," Henderson wished them as he closed the door behind them. He moved around the room, tidying up. He had no doubt Andrea Bond would be something of a surprise to his sedate Amalie. A grin started as he wondered what it might have been like if they'd been switched. He loved his perfectly impeccable Amalie, but it would be interesting to see if she got ruffled tonight when Andy spoke to her directly. Chuckling quietly, he finished up and made his way to the crew quarters to enjoy his dinner.

* * * * *

Amalie St. Jacques had been busy all day getting ready for this dinner party. She was used to her passengers' entertaining, and she'd quite successfully managed three parties in one day on one particular sailing. The last one had been for eight people and had five full courses. But hearing Rick's voice telling her *his* "Ms. Bond" had run a little late served to stress her out. She'd called the kitchen, moving everything back, and then informed the Williams.

Ethan and Margrit Williams had come as something of a surprise, as well. They were obviously used to six-star service, yet they were two of the nicest people she'd ever had on a cruise. Shortly after introductions, Ethan had told her they were part of the BDSM cruising group. She had yet to see anything out of the ordinary going on. Even if she did, Amalie had spent hours working on not showing shock, surprise or any other emotion.

Walking into the small kitchenette, she saw Margrit stood at the sink, washing a few of the dishes they'd used earlier. Amalie had already tried to convince her to leave them, but the petite woman had laughed and continued washing. Giving up, she picked up a towel and started drying.

The doorbell rang.

"Oh, dear," Amalie murmured softly.

Margrit reached out with one wet hand to stop her. "Don't fret, dear." She turned her head and shouted towards the living room. "Ethan darling, could you get the door? We're tied up in the kitchen."

"Mrs. Williams, as your butler, it is my responsibility to do these types of things." Amalie quickly pointed out to her boss.

"I understand, Jackie. But we're happy, so there is nothing to worry over." Margrit turned her attention to the last glass.

Amalie winced at Margrit's name for her. Upon meeting the Williams and requesting they call her Jacques or St. Jacques, Margrit had merely shrugged. Two seconds later, Margrit was calling her Jackie. The nickname was said with such respect and care, Amalie just accepted it.

Amalie learned that even though this couple was in a male Dom relationship, Margrit appeared to be in charge a lot of the time. It was a subtle sort of thing, but she often saw Mr. Williams deferring to his wife's decision or choice. Of course,

Amalie knew very little to nothing about the lifestyle, but these people seemed pretty normal from what she'd seen so far.

Margrit untied the shirt belonging to her husband, which she'd used as an apron, as the sounds of Ethan greeting the guests drifted into the kitchenette.

Amalie looked at the expensively perfect little black dress. She was skillful at guessing the price of something, and Margrit's deceptively plain dress was undoubtedly designer and in the four-digit range. Yet, the woman had given it little thought before she started mucking about in the kitchen.

Margrit spoke, "I'll take in the ice so you can call the kitchen. Why don't you have them deliver dinner as soon as it's ready? We'll cut short the leisurely pre-dinner drinks and hors d'oeuvres part so we'll have plenty of time for the party. Thanks for your help, Jackie."

Alone in the small room again, Amalie shook her head. The personnel managers had discussed possible problems they might encounter on this particular cruise, including ways to handle certain situations. But those had all been about the BDSM scene and refusing undesirable sexual advances. Nothing had covered excessive friendliness. And when she'd told Rick of the Williams' relaxed manner, he'd merely smiled and shrugged. Then he'd recounted a few stories regarding his lady passenger.

For the first time ever since she'd met and fallen head over heals in love with Richard Henderson the fourth, she'd been jealous. Never before, despite the constant exposure to beautiful women, had Amalie felt the tiniest bit of insecurity. She trusted Rick implicitly, but she also had seen how some women could work a situation. Hearing Rick speaking so fondly of Ms. Bond normally would not bother her. But this time it felt different, and she had no real idea why. Making the call to the kitchen, she took a moment to make sure she looked perfect in her white blouse, black slacks and discretely pinstriped burgundy and hunter green vest.

One deep breath and she walked to the living room. Upon entering the room, it took her a few seconds to see Ethan and

Margrit. She then saw the tall, very attractive man in a tuxedo standing by the sliding glass door leading onto the deck. Ms. Bond must be exploring the deck, Amalie realized. The deck was in sections unlike the long continuous one in the Balmoral suite. A moment later, Amalie felt her stomach sink as she saw the beautiful woman in white reenter the living room. Immediately, she noted the other woman's full curves, comparing her own slight and slender form less favorably. In her mind, this wealthy, gorgeous woman had it all. Hopefully, the man she was with tonight would occupy her hours completely even though they were not sharing the suite.

A moment later she saw Ms. Bond look in her direction. Her prior expectations about the other woman took a nosedive when she saw how lovely Rick's boss for this trip truly was. She stiffened her spine even as her heart sank.

Andy saw Amalie and was bowled over by the tall, slender woman's delicateness of features and form. If ever she'd imagined a perfect heroine, this was its human embodiment. The way she stood reminded Andy of a graceful swan, moving and yet barely disturbing the world around her. Forgetting her promise to Rick, Andy teetered across the room as quickly as she could on her high heels.

"Hello, Amalie!" She reached the taller woman and threw her arms around her. "You are absolutely gorgeous! I bet the two of you together make the cutest couple ever. He kept you a secret until before we came this evening." Andy stepped back a little. Immediately, she noticed that in her rush to hug Amalie, she smeared some of her makeup on her shirt. "Oh, shoot! Look Margrit, I've gone and mussed Amalie's perfect shirt. I am so sorry."

She brushed her hand over the spot a little, fearful of making it worse. "Margrit, help?" She turned, hoping her new friend could help.

Amalie spoke quickly, "It's all right, really."

Margrit looked at the smudge. "I'm afraid if we try anything with her still wearing it, we'll only make it worse. We could go into the bedroom—"

Amalie wiggled her hands, palms facing the other two women, back and forth while she shook her head, very decisively. "No, really, I can run downstairs and change if you wish and let the staff waiters begin dinner."

Ethan shrugged. "I can mix drinks, with Jack's help, so whatever works for you ladies." He paused and glanced at Jack, raising his eyebrows to question his approval.

Jack nodded.

Ethan continued. "Will be fine for us. We can always skip a course if we need to be on time to meet your friends, Jack."

"That is fine with me, Ethan." Jack nodded, patting his flat stomach as he went on. "A few uneaten calories are only going to work to my advantage when it comes time to work off all these rich dinners back home."

Margrit groaned. "We don't mention calories until the ship disembarks at the end of the cruise. It's a rule, isn't it, Jackie?"

Amalie nodded.

Andy could see the confusion, or maybe it was consternation at the loss of control. From what she had seen of the young woman so far, Andy had no doubt she was even more of a stickler for rules than Rick. Clearing her throat, she reached out to pat Amalie's upper arm.

"I can run down and help you change, if that would help. I'd have to slip off these darn shoes because I'm not used to walking, let alone running, in heels this high. I told Rick I wouldn't embarrass you and I have. I've also mucked up your shirt, ruined your perfectly planned dinner plans and now I'll probably sink the *Titanic*!"

Even Amalie smiled at Andy's self-deprecation. When Amalie stated she'd stay and work if they didn't mind, Andy felt a little better. Soon, they were seated and enjoying pre-dinner drinks.

The rest of the evening was uneventful, and they were in time to meet up with the others before the party doors opened.

Andy began to think she couldn't be shocked any more. The Dungeon party went on in the center of the room in addition to circulating around the perimeter. That's where the individual scenarios had been staged. Some were quite small, and people would stand and watch for a few moments before moving on to the next.

A few of the exhibitions had chairs set in a few rows, inviting passersby to sit and observe for longer periods. One very elaborate play lasted about twenty minutes. By the time she came upon this, their group had splintered completely. She was actually by herself. Jack had been pulled off somewhere by Tony and Danny in response to "you just gotta see this!"

An hour remained before the private party was to start, and getting off her feet sounded like a spectacular idea. She chose a seat from the mostly empty chairs, seeing the next showing began in thirty minutes. Hopefully, there wouldn't be anything else which caught her off-guard. Several times, she had barely stopped the "oh my God" from popping out.

Once she'd agreed to the cruise with her publisher footing the bill, she had done some Internet research. Yet reading, even looking at pictures could not prepare her enough to hide her naïveté. She didn't feel quite so bad when she heard a few other women gasping. Everywhere she looked men could be seen nearly tripping over their lolling tongues, but otherwise it was a controlled party atmosphere.

The guidelines had been clearly posted outside the party area, and Ethan had reviewed them again before they went in. He'd also pointed out the bouncers, all big, muscular guys, dressed in black leather vests with masks obscuring the upper portion of their heads, leaving only peepholes for their eyes. She had little doubt those men could quickly remove someone not observing the rules.

She tried to file away things she saw into separate files in her brain, but with so many different scenes she'd observed it was confusing to keep them all straight. She wished her purse had been big enough to hold her PDA. She did have a small recording device, but it wouldn't hold as much. Pulling it from the white bag, she lifted it to only a few inches from her mouth.

"Separate areas for each display. The torture things are the ones I just don't get the appeal. I can understand the prolonged sexual stimulation. But how can pain be enjoyed?" She paused, thinking about it for a moment. "Maybe it is only people who have never truly experienced real physical pain, either from disease, injury, or at the evil hands of another that can derive pleasure from pain."

"Perhaps it is because their emotional pain is buried so deeply inside this is the only way they can find peace, or arousal." A deep husky voice spoke from directly behind her chair.

Andy gasped and twisted around. She saw the sensual sound belonged to a slender man dressed in a tuxedo. Unlike many of the others in the room, this man looked as if he were perfectly at ease in these expensive clothes the same as he'd be in jeans. He had longish black hair, blue eyes and that sexy one-to-two-day growth of beard. She didn't know who this guy was, but he looked European and perfect to star as her next heroic vampire!

"I apologize for eavesdropping, but it is so rare to find an unattached beautiful woman at one of these things I had to discover if you truly are by yourself, or merely been misplaced temporarily."

Andy had to smile as the stranger's mouth turned up seductively at one corner. "That implies I belong to someone who could then lose me," she pointed out, in an exaggerated patient tone.

"Precisely." The man nodded. He pulled the chair next to her back a foot or so, and then stepped through and sat sideways on the next chair. This allowed him to look right at her, she realized. Immediately, a blush began moving up her neck. "While these things are not exclusive to the BDSM lifestyle, it has been my experience the majority of couples contain a male Dom. Most of the women at these things are subs, even if they don't yet know it."

Andy bristled at his words, but stopped as she saw the twinkle in his eyes. "I've met people like you before." She pointed her index finger at him. "You like to stir up trouble. You deliberately espouse what you believe to be incendiary thoughts. I bet you then like to sit back and watch the verbal and emotional fireworks."

The stranger smiled, pressing his palm flat over his heart. "Guilty as charged, but it isn't trouble I seek." He leaned forward, resting his forearms on his thighs. He clasped his hands, interlacing his fingers. "Sometimes it is good to nudge people, and play the devil's advocate."

"You are probably one of those 'out of the box' types. You love change, being on edge and the adrenaline surge you get from the emotional brouhaha is your drug," Andy replied succinctly. "Sir, you are a bad boy. Or that is what my best friend's mama called the boys who were always in trouble and one step ahead of the law."

"Madam, do you accuse me of being an outlaw?"

Andy blushed even brighter. That's pretty much precisely what she'd just done. "I am sorry. I don't even know you and here I go accusing you—"

Immediately, the stranger stood, bowed slightly at the waist and offered his hand to her. "Allow me to introduce myself. I am Peter Waldron."

Andy put her hand out to shake his, but was taken aback as he turned it, and then leaned over further to press a light kiss to her knuckles. As he straightened, she realized why she had thought he looked familiar. "You're that duke guy!"

Peter sat back down, nodding. "Guilty as charged, but I don't use the title much, when I'm traveling. It tends to draw too much attention."

Andy nodded. She decided not to sympathize verbally because she didn't want him asking why she chose to avoid notoriety. Instead, she changed the topic. "Are you a Dom on this cruise with a sub?" The minute the words left her mouth, she realized how impertinent the question sounded.

Peter nodded. "I tend to the dominant choice, but I'm woefully all alone on this cruise. Or rather I'm here with friends from London. Now, back to you. Are you alone and why are you talking into a micro-recorder?"

"I am on this cruise with friends from my college days. It's kind of a reunion, I guess. One of them suggested the cruise instead of just meeting at some hotel or going to the infamous mouse park."

"Hmm," Peter paused, staring at her.

Andy fidgeted under his intentness.

"I should imagine visiting Mickey and Donald would be rather fun with you," he finally said. "Anyway, why the recorder?"

Andy frowned. "I hoped you'd forget that part."

"Not likely. Also recording equipment is not allowed in these things."

"I know, but I figured since I wasn't recording the actual displays—"

Peter shrugged. "I won't tell those big guys in leather if you tell me why."

"You wouldn't really turn me in. I'm sure you are too nice—"

Peter stood, craning his neck as he looked around the immediate area.

Andy reached out and tugged on his sleeve. "Okay, okay, I'll confess." She tucked the recorder back inside her purse. "I'm taking notes so I can write a book."

"Damn!" Peter had already resumed his seat, but now he leaned forward. "Are you going to write one of those exposé books that tell all and embarrass people, using their real names?"

Andy shook her head. "No, I write romance novels."

"I wouldn't have thought the American housewife was into BDSM."

"That is the second time you've made an assumption. Anyway, once my editor heard I was going on this cruise, he talked to the publisher. They paid for me to have a better cabin so I could work."

"How much working have you managed so far? Wait! I told you my name, but you managed to skip telling me yours."

"Sorry. Andrea Bond. Unfortunately, I haven't done anything concrete, which is why I thought if I recorded some first impressions here tonight I might get a germ of an idea."

"How about you and I work on a story together? I bet between us we could come up with a few steamy scenes."

Andy blushed as his words evoked a rush of nervousness. Writing about sexual situations alone in her apartment was definitely a different set of circumstances than talking about it with an attractive stranger. Feeling on edge and too warm, she blew a puff of hair upwards into her bangs. "What if I decide I need to be the one in charge? Could you handle that?"

Peter shrugged. "I've wondered about that myself. I think if it is the right woman, it will feel right."

"Andy! I couldn't figure out where you'd disappeared to!"

Andy shifted on her chair and saw Jack had indeed found her. His all-American appearance was almost the exact opposite of the bad boy look Peter had. "Hello, Jack. I had to sit down and slip these darn shoes off. I saw this show didn't start for thirty minutes so I took advantage."

As Jack neared, Peter stood.

Andy introduced the two men. "Peter, this is Jack Riley. He is part of the group I am traveling with. Jack, this is Peter Waldron."

She watched as the two men shook hands.

Peter turned to her a moment later. He pulled a business card from his pocket, holding it out. As she accepted it, Peter smiled. "Call me if you'd like to learn some facts from a pro."

Andy watched as the smooth British lord of the realm departed. She sat, aware of Jack straightening the chairs and then sitting in the one right next to her. Opening her small bag, she tucked the card inside.

"What's he a pro at?" Jack's voice caused her to look up.

She told herself not to read too much into his question or his tone. Undoubtedly, he was merely curious about a stranger. "I think he referred to this lifestyle. He said he was a Dom, but has no sub with him on this cruise." Andy was sure she heard Jack growl low in his throat before he spoke a second later.

"Was he hitting on you to be his sub?"

Andy shook her head, glancing sideways for a second. She hated sitting like this because you always got a crick in your neck trying to look at the other person. Instead, she faced straight ahead. "English dukes don't hit on women. And he certainly doesn't look like he has to *hit* on any woman. I'm sure they are lining up wherever he slows down long enough for a line to form."

"Damn! Peter Waldron. I thought he looked familiar. And any man, who isn't gasping his last breath, will hit on a beautiful woman."

Andy had shaken her head before she realized what Jack said. Was he saying she was beautiful? That certainly wasn't a way she'd ever felt comfortable thinking about herself. Most definitely her friends would all be considered pretty or beautiful.

"How much longer do you want to stay at this party?" Jack interrupted her thoughts.

"You want to leave?" Andy knew she didn't keep the surprise from her voice. She would have thought the guys would really be enjoying this kinky kind of stuff. "I thought men enjoyed this kind of thing."

Jack shifted around in his chair so he could look at her. The intentness of his gaze unnerved her somewhat. She wondered if she should have just kept her last opinion to herself. Had she insulted him?

"I was just asking a question. I didn't say I wasn't enjoying this," he replied tersely.

There was something in his voice, which went up slightly at the end, revealing he'd been emotionally affected by her remarks and questions.

"I keep imagining unwrapping you from that dress."

His words caught her off-guard.

Andy gasped in surprise, while her heart sped up and her breath came in short, staccato puffs.

"You remind me of a perfectly wrapped present," he went on. "While I can see how lovely and sweet you are all wrapped and tied up with white and gold, I have no doubt what I find inside will be amazing."

Andy told herself to look away. Yup, that was precisely what she must do. Don't believe his sweet talk. It will only break your heart. Instead, she felt her heart trip up to triple speed. Her breath became uneven and the butterflies in her stomach suddenly developed attention deficit with hyperactivity. Damn!

"Hey, you two!"

Gayle sat in the seat directly in front of Andy. Ray looked sheepish as he flopped into the chair beside her.

Gayle twisted around to smile at Andy and Jack. "Oh, my God! Andy, can you believe this stuff? I know my mouth keeps falling open as I gape from one shocking display to the next."

Ray glanced back over his shoulder. "Tell me about it! I'm the one who has to keep closing it for her."

Andy smiled, shaking her head. "You aren't alone. I came over here because the chairs were empty, and there wasn't a show scheduled for half an hour. I figured I could get some respite from being embarrassed and startled, not to mention giving my feet a break from these heels."

"I'm glad I'm not alone in that, at least. Medical school didn't prepare me for this, but Ray is beyond being shocked," Gayle added, chuckling.

"He's already seen it all," Jack murmured a moment later.

Ray reacted immediately. "I have not!"

Gayle winked at Andy. "Hmm, I think I'll not comment further."

Andy smiled, truly enjoying the warm feeling of camaraderie she experienced with these people who had been her friends a long time ago. What surprised her was it had been so long since she'd felt like this and she'd forgotten how special it was to share moments like this with people you cared about, and had a common history with as well. Feeling like her old self, she replied, "Sounds like he'll be having a tame bachelor party!"

As she and Gayle laughed, she saw the affronted looks on not just Ray's face but Jack's as well.

"I'm in charge of the party and I think I've just been insulted." Jack scowled, looking from Ray to Andy.

Andy laughed. "Perhaps you could borrow a piece of paper and pencil and make some notes."

Ray guffawed loudly, turning enough to punch Jack on his arm. "Dang! She got you with that one, dude!"

"Shh!" Gayle shushed her fiancé. "The show is going to start."

Andy settled into her seat, quietly pulling out her small recorder. She didn't know what she might see, but she didn't want to take the chance of missing or forgetting something.

Beside her she was aware of Jack moving on his chair, scooting it a little bit closer, and then putting his arm along the back of her chair. When she looked sideways at him, he merely gave her a small smile and then turned his attention back to the stage. Doing the same and stop trying to second-guess everything would be her wisest course of action.

Looking forward as the curtains swept open, she saw a tall, gray-haired man come onto the small stage —

Chapter Six

"Welcome, Masters and Mistresses, ladies and gentlemen! I'm sure you will enjoy this little scenario. We now enter *The Castle of Dark Pleasure* run by Mistress Danica. Enjoy!"

A tall, raven-haired woman walked onto the small stage a moment after the gentleman left. She was dressed in black, covered from the base of her throat to her toes, which were encased in black boots. Other than the pale skin of her face and neck, she was black. Her hair was back in an elaborate chignon. Her makeup was perfect, highlighting her dark eyes and bright red lips. Moving to the center of the acting area, she removed her gloves.

"Pierre!" the woman called out.

She was joined a few seconds later by a tall, quite muscular—as evidenced by his bare chest—blond-haired man. He wore black leather pants, white cuffs and white collar, with a black silken bow tie. When he stopped a few feet from Mistress Danica, he stood with his hands behind his back.

"Yes, Mistress Danica?"

She walked around him slowly, looking his body over, up and down. "It appears you've forgotten I was to be greeted with my preferred evening cocktail."

Pierre lowered his head as he replied, "I'm sorry, Mistress Danica. I was in the kitchen and didn't hear you enter until you called. I was preparing your cocktail when you sent for me."

"Very well, but when you return, I want you to also bring me your favorite whip."

Pierre jerked in surprise, but nodded and left quickly.

Mistress Danica turned to face the audience. Sighing loudly, she spoke as if she were speaking to herself. "Sometimes I think he deliberately disobeys just so he can feel the heat of the tails across that fine ass of his."

A short spate of tittering laughter went through the audience.

A doorbell rang, and then a few seconds later a redheaded woman entered. This woman was dressed in the traditional French maid's outfit. Her hair seemed to be pulled up and back, covered by a frilly white cap. Stiff black bombazine material concealed her arms, from shoulder to wrist, which was more of her body concealed than any place else. The bodice dipped low in front so that nearly the entire top half of her breasts were displayed surrounded by a one-inch frill of lace. The waist was tight and flared into a short skirt, which ended at the top of her thighs. There was a miniscule white apron, and beneath it all were several layers of equally short white crinoline. Black thigh-high stockings and four-inch heels completed the ensemble.

Jack leaned close to Andy and whispered. "I'd like to see you dressed in that little getup."

Andy stiffened in her chair. Unnerving how close Jack's words mirrored her own thoughts seconds earlier. She wanted to dress up to please, and certainly arouse, him! Without commenting, she stared at the stage.

"Mistress Danica?"

Danica turned to look at the maid. "Yes, Madeleine?"

"Monsieur Lascaux has arrived."

"How delightful! Come in, Francois. You are just in time for Pierre's disciplining. Would you like to assist me?"

The dark-haired man bowed low over Mistress Danica's hand, kissing it lightly. "That sounds delightful. May I enjoy the lovely Madeleine, as well?"

Danica lightly slapped Francois' cheek. "You devil, you! Very well, I know you won't be happy until you've sampled her wares. Would you care for a drink?"

"Scotch and soda, my dear." Francois moved over to sit on the small loveseat on the far left of the stage.

Mistress Danica directed the maid. "Prepare Monsieur Lascaux's drink, Madeleine. You may return with Pierre." She turned to look at her guest.

"Did you have something in particular in mind for the girl?"

Francois smiled. "Don't worry. I'll be extra gentle. Are you saving her for someone else?"

"What makes you think she isn't for me?"

"Because she looks like you've been training her. Is she a present for someone? Anyone I know?"

Danica shook her head. "You shouldn't pry, my friend. Just be grateful you arrived before he has. Madeleine is wearing one of my newest designs, by the way. You must let me know what you think of it."

"Now you intrigue me even more."

Pierre and Madeleine entered onto the stage once more. Madeleine carried Francois' drink on a small silver tray, which was identical to the one Pierre held in one hand.

"Madeleine, please serve Master Francois his drink. From this point on and until I say so, you are to serve him in any way he desires. Is that clear?"

The redheaded woman gulped loudly, her gaze darted from Danica to Francois and back. "Y-y-yes, Mistress Danica." The quiver in her voice as she replied sounded real.

Danica paused as Madeleine walked over to Francois. She offered him the drink, which he accepted.

"Kneel down, next to the sofa, and face me," Francois commanded sternly.

The young woman hastened to obey, staggering a little on her heels.

"Very good. Now assume the submissive posture," he added a moment later.

Madeleine crossed her arms behind her, one hand clasping the opposite elbow. It bowed the body slightly backwards, thereby thrusting her breasts out and up.

With his drink in one hand, Francois reached forward with the other. He hooked three fingers into her cleavage and pulled. The tearing of the sticky fastener sounded and the top part of Madeleine's costume came away in his hand. Immediately, her breasts were revealed. He wasted no time in reaching out and cupping one breast, squeezing and molding it. "Delightful design, Danica."

Andy gasped as the fabric pulled away to expose the actress' breasts. In her mind, she'd been imagining herself kneeling before Jack. Now, she wondered how it would feel to have his hands so blatantly exploring her body?

Mistress Danica smiled and gestured for Pierre to approach. She accepted her cocktail and sipped it slowly. "Delicious, Pierre. Are you trying to earn fewer lashes by pleasing me?"

"No, mistress."

"Hmm, very well. Hand me the whip." With her drink in one hand, she lightly flicked the leather flogger.

As it cracked, several people in the audience gasped and jumped in their seats. This was followed by some nervous laughter.

Mistress Danica finished her drink and returned it to Pierre's tray. "Now, Pierre. I want you to face the far wall and hold the tray with my glass. If you drop the glass, you earn five more lashes."

She moved around his body and repeated Francois' gesture of hooking the fingers. Only hers went into the back of Pierre's leather trousers. She pulled and the same sound that revealed Madeleine's pert bosom now heralded the appearance of Pierre's very tight ass cheeks. Very lightly, so it echoed throughout the small area, she slapped his right butt. His muscles tensed, which only made his taut ass more impressive.

Gayle turned and looked at Andy. "I wonder if he's booked up the whole cruise."

Ray glared at his fiancée and pulled her back around in her chair.

Andy, still grinning and hoping her excitement over what she'd seen didn't show on her face, glanced sideways and found Jack was glaring at her. Feeling a little chastised, she turned her attention back to the stage. A moment later she turned back, whispering to Jack. "What would you do if I slapped your bottom?"

She wasn't prepared for the way Jack's gaze met hers. Flames seemed to burst forth and then his mouth barely curved up.

"I'd kiss your breath away!" he murmured quickly.

Andy stared as he looked towards the stage again. Suddenly it was hard to breathe. It felt like he had done precisely that as she gasped for air. Jerkily, she shifted forward as well.

Mistress Danica had Pierre move closer to the rear of the stage. "I want you to count the lashes, Madeleine."

"Yes, Mistress Danica," Madeleine replied. "Excuse me, monsieur, but I will need to turn around."

"Party pooper," Francois murmured, but suddenly smiled. He pulled Madeleine to her feet and had her sit astride his lap. As soon as she was settled, both his hands cupped her breasts, once again squeezing and pinching away.

The first lash came and struck right across Pierre's ass.

"One, Mistress Danica."

"Very good, Madeleine. Don't distract her too much, Francois. I don't want to give Pierre more than he deserves."

The whip continued at a fairly steady rhythm, continuing to raise a few red welts. Madeleine kept count until Francois deserted one breast and slid that hand between her thighs. She gasped and lost track of the number as he teased her clit to a quick response.

"Oh! Mistress Danica, I am so sorry!"

Danica turned to shake her finger at Francois, who still had one hand between the maid's thighs.

He merely shrugged.

The doorbell rang, interrupting Mistress Danica's next swing. She stopped abruptly. "Oh, dear. Playtime is over, Francois. Quickly, Madeleine, up to your room and change into the outfit we picked out for you to wear."

Danica coiled the rope and set it aside. "We'll have to continue later, Pierre. Please let Monsieur le Comte D'Orsi in." She lightly slapped his butt as he walked by.

Walking over to Francois, she kissed him on the cheek. "I am sorry for the interruption, my dear friend, but business calls. Now, I will introduce you, but then you must leave. You may return tomorrow if you wish."

"I'll always wish to return here, my lovely Danica."

Danica threaded her hand through his arm and walked with him off the stage.

The lights came up and the audience applauded.

The gentleman who had first appeared on the stage came back. "Thank you for your appreciation. We will be performing the second act tomorrow evening, if you wish to see what happens to the lovely Madeleine. Good night!"

Gayle stood and looked at Andy. "I know what I'm going to dream about tonight."

Ray got to his feet slowly. "Hey! I'm standing right here."

Gayle giggled, looping her hand through his arm, pulling him close. "I know, darling. I'm just teasing."

"Let's go back to the cabin," Ray said, trying to pull Gayle along. "I'm so horny right now I could burst."

Gayle rolled her eyes, but she didn't resist.

Andy turned to look at Jack.

He grinned.

She spoke quickly to defuse the heat she was still feeling after watching the little sex opera. "It's really great to see them still so much in love, even after all these years."

"Yeah," Jack murmured, but his eyes she saw dropped down to settle on her chest. Her breath caught even before he went on. "I know what Ray means. Watching that guy fondle the maid made me wonder what you might look like in that kind of outfit."

Andy jumped to her feet. She couldn't believe he'd put into words her own thoughts, which she did not have the courage to express. It shocked her, but she wasn't sure whether it was because he echoed her own imaginings. Or was it because she found herself aroused and she had not considered that a possibility. It was scary to think she might harbor such dark longings. Was it possible she wasn't as white bread in her view of sex as she'd always thought? Coming on this cruise, she'd assumed she would learn new things, but she had assumed it would be in a removed, educational venue. Now she could see how foolish she'd been. Maybe she was about to open herself to things she'd thought of as play, only to discover it went much deeper.

Jack stood and took her hand. He didn't say a word, but started leading her towards the exit doors. There was no doubt what he had on his mind, she realized, but not altogether surprised. She finally managed to stop him a few feet from the exit. "We shouldn't leave without talking to Ethan and Margrit."

* * * * *

Her logic was undeniable but this didn't make him any happier. He nodded in agreement, realizing how tense he was by the jerking movement.

"We could split up to look for them," Andy suggested a moment later.

Jack couldn't stop the bubble of jealousy that rose up immediately. Perhaps she only wanted to separate so she could go off and find that Duke guy. He spoke without thinking. "The duke has probably already hitched up for the evening."

Regret filled him even before he saw her back stiffen. She had turned her face away, but he knew he'd hurt her by the tensing of the little jaw muscle at the side of her lower cheek. He tried to think fast, but nothing good was coming into his head. "Andy, I'm sorry—"

A moment later, she stepped away from his hand.

Jack tried again. "That was a stupid thing to say and I'm really sorry. Kick me, if you want."

He paused, hoping she'd respond to his humor. The Andy of old would agree and try to kick him. But this new Andy was mysterious and, at times, he didn't know how to act towards her. "Let's go together to find Ethan and Margrit. I just remembered they had mentioned another party they were attending." He waited until Andy nodded before he gently took her hand and led the way back into the crowd.

* * * * *

When it was time to continue to the next party with Jack and the Williams, Andy was ready to come up with a good excuse to miss it. Her nerves were feeling frayed and she was tired after her sleepless night. Instead, she'd stayed silent, merely nodding. Now that she was at the party, she couldn't decide if she was glad she'd come or not.

Before entering, Margrit had taken her aside to show her how the women were expected to dress inside. Andy could decide if she wished to comply, and no one would think less if she chose not to participate.

"This is a very exclusive group of Doms—Masters and Mistresses—who throw the party. They are in attendance with their subs. Also present this evening are some slaves, who you will notice are scattered around, or they might be tethered to a pole. These people volunteer to be slaves, and some are paid to do it. Nonetheless, all are willing."

Andy watched and listened as Margrit began removing parts of her dress. Before long the dark-haired woman was dressed in a black bustier, silky black tap pants, garter belt, stockings and high heels. The bustier ended below her breasts, but had a small shelf for each globe to rest upon. The padded shelf actually pushed up her boobs and together, and they were swathed in super-thin black tulle. She did look the epitome of submissive, packaged beauty.

Andy wasn't completely sure, but agreed to see how her dress broke down. If she felt uncomfortable she would replace the last piece removed until she was covered once more and hastily retreat.

Slowly, Margrit helped her until she stood in front of the bathroom mirror. The skirt had come right off, which left her white merry widow, which she wore with a white thong. No garter belt, but she did have on thigh-high, white silky stockings with lace stretch tops. Also, the white tulle of the skirt separated to form several petal-like layers making a short skirt, coming to the top of her stockings. The big shocker was the removable bodice, just like the one the maid in the play had been wearing.

She had trouble turning away from the sight of her naked breasts, so blatantly offered on display. But Margrit's hand, pointing at Andy's nipple first and then at her own, caught her attention.

"If you were pierced, you might feel more comfortable going without the attachment in the bodice. I know it helped me. After my nipples were pierced, I carried myself more proudly, like I was shouting at the world—'hey, look at me! I can do anything I want'. And it was my idea, not Ethan's."

Andy stared at the small gold rings in each of Margrit's nipples, thinly veiled by the tulle. "Did it hurt?"

"A little, but they have specialists on board who can numb the area. If you like, tomorrow we can go on a fact-finding mission."

Andy laughed. That was the very phrase she had used several times during the hours spent with Margrit earlier, as she talked about researching different subjects for her books. "Deal!"

"So, in or out?"

"In, for tonight," Andy decided with a quick nod.

Finally ready, Margrit gave their belongings to one of the female attendants. She explained to Andy, "They will send our things to my suite. When we are done, just stop by here, and see these." She gestured to several stacks of white robes. "Take one for the walk back to your room." Margrit winked as she added, "That way, decorum is always maintained in the central parts of the ship."

Jack and Ethan walked around for a few minutes after each got a drink at the bar. About half the people here were in costume. A lot of the men wore leather pants, vests and even masks. The ones who were slaves wore leather G-strings, the men anyway, and quite a few were gagged.

"Can you explain some of this to me, Ethan? I am a little familiar with some of this stuff. Masters, slaves, Doms, submissives and Dominatrix... Are they all different names for the same thing?"

Ethan laughed softly. "Not at all, Jack. Let's start with Margrit and myself. She is a submissive, which is a lifestyle, a way of thinking and she has chosen it. What she is doing is giving up control, and that is her precious gift to her Master. His responsibility is to be clear in his needs, desires and commands. The sub is not expected to read her Master's mind. He demands total obedience and her compliance at all times. Slaves thrive on rigidity, and discipline is always meted out consistently and fairly."

Ethan took a sip of his drink. "Of course, it is much more complicated but this is the basics. I got involved in college and had a few D/s relationships before I met Margrit. But almost from the first instant I saw her, I knew she was the one."

"Really? May I ask how the two of you met?" Jack asked the older man with true interest.

"We met at a party. She came with a friend because she was curious. I was attracted to her instantly and I had no idea if she had any inkling about submissiveness or not."

"Did you ask her out the first time?"

"Of course. I wasn't letting her get away from me until I knew more about her. We dated about three weeks...three dates actually because she was hard to pin down to a time to get together. She was working and caring for her elderly mother."

"Did you swoop in and rescue her on your white charger?" Jack asked with a smile.

Ethan responded with a sheepish grin before he sipped his drink. "I tried to, but she wouldn't let me. To Margrit, she took her commitments seriously and she'd made one to her mother."

"What was that?"

"To not let her die in a nursing home."

"Damn! So, what happened?"

"I finally convinced Margrit that I loved her and her mother, and I wanted them both to live with me." He paused for a moment. "Margrit said she could easily understand my passion for her, but for a man to take on a commitment like that—"

Ethan stopped abruptly as if his memories were painful. "What I did was make all the necessary modifications to my home, including hiring the additional house staff we'd need to provide good care."

"And that convinced her? She agreed to marry you then?" Jack asked.

Ethan shook his head. "Not quite. I finally caught her while she visited her mother, who was in the hospital for an illness. I ignored Margrit and proceeded to present my plan, including the changes I'd made to the house already." He chuckled quietly as he spoke. "I even had my advertising department work up storyboards, with pictures and care plans. I outlined our marriage, and how I would help in Katrina's care each day. I then proposed to Katrina, asking her to come and live with me, and bring Margrit with her."

Jack laughed out loud. "Obviously, it worked."

"Katrina loved it, but Margrit was a harder nut to crack. I proved my diligence by visiting her mother in the hospital, and then continuing for the short time Margrit was forced to have her mother in a nursing home. She had no other options."

"That's when she agreed?"

"Sort of. I came to the nursing home near the end of the second week Katrina was there. Margrit was in a chair by the bed, asleep. Katrina was awake. She patted the side of her bed for me to sit down. After a few seconds, she told me she was accepting my proposal, and giving Margrit to me in acceptance of a small dowry."

"Good Lord! A dowry? What did she want?"

"I thought she would say something like 'make her daughter happy' or 'give her a grandchild'. Instead, she said she wanted a whomping big diamond cocktail ring, something she could show off to the remaining friends she still had."

Jack laughed again. "She sounds quite the character."

"She was one in a million. The reason for the ring was to convince Margrit that she'd really given her to me. It would fit with the old-country ways she'd described to her daughter, of how it had been for her grandparents. Margrit accepted it, although I think it was partly she was just worn out. I didn't care. I was taking her any way I could. She quit her job and we got in some part-time nursing help. I will never regret helping Margrit fulfill her mother's wish. It wasn't easy, sitting with her the last few days of her life, but it changed and deepened my relationship with Margrit in ways that nothing else could have. In a short period of time, we shared things that would take other couples years to achieve."

"How long ago was that?" Jack asked softly.

"Katrina passed away about five years ago. It's been a long road back for Margrit, grief-wise. She still felt a lot of guilt. She doesn't have a single reason to be, but sometimes there is just no talking logically to a woman."

"Tell me about it!" Jack muttered under his breath, all the while scanning the partygoers for Andy or Margrit.

A moment later, Ethan grinned. "Wow!"

Jack turned his head and immediately saw the reason for the older man's surprise. Walking towards them were two of the sexiest women he'd ever seen, both scantily clad. It shocked him to realize it was Margrit, whose breasts were barely concealed, and then it dawned on him that the other woman had to be Andy.

Andy!

His eyes registered the white dress, or rather what was left of it. Her legs were gorgeous, he decided, especially when he noted the lacy garter on one thigh. He was glad that Andy's breasts weren't naked, like so many of the other women in the room. He'd have a hell of a time concentrating then!

"It's a good thing you kept this little outfit of yours a secret, my sweet," Ethan murmured as he leaned forward and kissed his wife's cheek.

"I know, my love. Now, don't you think Andy looks lovely?"

Ethan nodded. "Yes, Andy, you look gorgeous."

Jack watched as Andy's gaze turned in his direction. He smiled when their eyes met. "I agree. She looks amazing."

Andy wouldn't have thought she could flush any hotter but she did. The look in Jack's eyes was hot, and undeniable. He wanted her, and it thrilled her clean through to her toes. This was exactly what she'd always wanted—knowing Jack desired her, physically. One part of her brain was telling her that her mission was now accomplished and she could back off—

She was breathless as she considered taking him back to the suite and making love. Suddenly she wondered what Jack would look like dressed up in those breakaway leather pants Pierre in the play had worn. What had been her plans and what she wanted now were two distinctly different things. There could be no denying she desired Jack. Hell! She downright had the "hots" for him.

Ethan's voice drew her attention back a few seconds later. She only hoped she'd not been caught staring at Jack the whole time.

"Would either of you lovely ladies like something to drink?"

Andy looked at Margrit, not completely sure if they were supposed to act in character, or just what. Margrit smiled back and nodded.

"Yes, I think that would be lovely. Why don't we have Cosmopolitans just like the four women in the television show?"

Andy laughed and nodded. "The ones who have more sex in any city I've ever heard of?"

Ethan spoke. "I'll leave you here, Jack, to protect our beautiful ladies from intruders and marauders." With a wink, he was gone.

"Margrit?" Andy asked a moment later.

"Yes, Andy. Did you have a question?"

"Are we, or really I guess it is just me...am I expected to act a particular way?"

Margrit shook her head. "Not tonight. If we attend a role-playing party, then yes, people are expected to stay in character. Unless, of course, a safe word is used. There is another private party tomorrow night, and Ethan and I were going to ask if you two wished to join us."

"Another party like this?" Jack asked, sipping his drink.

"This one will be more traditional, so you will see many people behaving as they would back in their own world. There will undoubtedly be a number of Masters and slaves here, along with Mistresses."

"Sounds interesting, doesn't it, Andy?" Jack spoke, looking directly at her, grinning.

She swallowed hard, and then turned to look at her new friend. "It does sound intriguing. If Jack and I came, would we be expected to be a couple?"

Margrit laughed. "No, you can come as our friends and not participate."

Jack leaned over and pressed a kiss to Andy's temple. "Not participate? Won't that take some of the fun out of it?"

Andy suddenly decided to get back a little bit at Jack. "I wondered about getting you a pair of those breakaway leather pants, like we saw in the play. I'll be Mistress Danica."

Ethan returned just in time to hear Andy, and he laughed loudly. "I see you two saw the play then. We must attend the Dungeon tomorrow night, for act two." He passed the women their glasses and then sipped from his own. "I don't know, Jack. Would you let Andy crack the whip over you?"

Andy held her breath, wishing Ethan had not been quite so bold about the question.

It didn't get better when Jack looked towards her as he spoke. "If her heart were involved, I would."

Andy buried her face in the glass, sipping the drink and hoping the flush would fade quickly.

* * * * *

Andy was feeling even more dazed and confused the next afternoon. She was enjoying the massage, even with the masseuse making a wide path around her newly tattooed area, but it was almost impossible to calm her thoughts. Last night, Jack had surprised her by kissing her cheek at the door and bid her good night.

This morning she had slept in. She was meeting Margrit at the spa for one o'clock appointments. After a light breakfast, she made herself work on her book. She turned off her beeper and hunkered down to work until twelve-thirty, when Henderson brought her a salad to chow down just in time to leave and meet Margrit.

The surprising thing was even though her emotions were churning and going crazy, her mind was clear once her fingers touched the keys of her laptop computer. The story began slowly just a word or two, and then it flowed. In fact, she hadn't moved until Henderson arrived. Her stiff back was finally responding to the clever hands of the masseuse.

Margrit's voice caught her attention. "Are we going shopping for an outfit for you to wear tonight?"

"I'd like to, if you have the time."

"We should be fine. While I'm getting my body scrub and wrap, you are set for the piercing, if you still want to proceed."

Andy took a deep breath. The idea had been something she couldn't shake and at three this morning, she had decided. "I am going ahead with it."

"Super. Then we have our hair appointments. I thought I might surprise Ethan and get it cut short and spiky."

Andy looked over at the other woman. "Does Ethan like short hair?"

"Well, one time I let the stylist use the clippers on the back of my head, from the nape up about three inches. Ethan touched it and I felt him freeze, and then he started rubbing his fingers back and forth, across the super-short ends. With the right kind of encouragement, I bet he would have come right then and there."

Margrit smiled when Andy gasped. "You should try it. I have to admit it feels really terrific when they do it, and everything that brushes against the hair kind of touches some nerve endings, deep down inside of you."

Andy continued to lie there, thinking about it. Finally, it was time for the piercing. Following the earlier perusal, Andy had narrowed her choices down to two rings. Wearing a white terrycloth robe, she approached this and wanted to run. But once the two women who did the procedure came in, it all seemed to flow forward. Each woman had a soft, soothing and calming voice. Before she knew it, one woman tugged on her right nipple elongating it and then, whoosh!

She resisted lifting her head to look until she was done. The other nipple was done almost as quickly. Andy surprised herself by asking about multiple ear piercings. By the time she joined Margrit in the hair salon, she had three new holes in each ear besides gold nipple rings. The hair stylist talked with her about possible new styles and finally Andy mentioned the part about the clipper cutting her nape. The stylist smiled and agreed she could do that.

Excited almost beyond belief, Andy waited for Jack to arrive. Her new haircut had been artfully disguised by the stylist with a fall of hair dyed the same color as her own, and none of her friends had noticed her additional earrings by the way the hair was arranged and pinned into place. She had returned to her suite to dress for the Dungeon party, and more importantly, for the private party to follow.

After returning from shopping with Margrit later in the afternoon, Andy had beeped Jack, hoping he'd respond. When the suite phone rang, she picked it up after the first ring. "Hello?"

"Andy? This is Jack. Did you need something?"

Andy curled up on her bed, holding the phone to her ear gingerly. "Are you in the middle of something? Am I interrupting?"

"No, it's cool. We had just finished playing tennis and we're having a drink before heading down to dress for dinner."

"Ah, okay. I wondered if you wanted to go the Dungeon and then the other party, with Ethan and Margrit?"

"I thought it would be fun to go again. Did you want to go?"

"Well, yes…that's why I called. I know we're having dinner with the group, but I thought you might want to call for me here. We could go together to the Dungeon." She waited. Deliberately she'd not said as a "couple" even though it was what she meant. Silently, she hoped Jack would make the suggestion.

"You mean like a role-playing couple?" Jack asked her a few seconds later.

"Well, uh, yes. I wondered if you would care to go as my Master." Andy held her breath, waiting tensely for Jack's answer. It had taken her an hour to build her courage up to ask.

Jack slowly turned away so his friends would no longer be able to see his face. He was stunned at how vulnerable and yet aroused Andy's question made him feel. All day long, lurking in the back of his mind had been this very question, in one form or another. It had been harder than hell to leave Andy alone at the front door last evening. He had gone back to toss and turn most of the long, lonely night. Ray had gotten lucky and was sharing the room with Gayle. Tony had jumped at the opportunity to share the room with Jack, instead of the other two guys.

Today, he had been distant and his friends had all noted something was wrong, but he had just laughed off their comments. Ethan joined the five of them and they had gone from one sport to another all afternoon. Again, he and his buddies had all remarked on Ethan's stamina. And just as he got beeped, they had been bemoaning the fact they needed a nap before an evening of partying.

Hearing Andy's voice, something was different. It felt new...and he didn't know why, but he liked the heightened feelings he was experiencing with Andy Bond. The last few years, his life had been pretty boring. His dealings with Andy were like a shot in the arm of pure energy and zest. He had found himself looking forward to the cruise. Even though he told himself it was because of the chance for them all to be together once more, he knew it was the opportunity to see Andy again that pleased him. And so far, so good—

"All right, Andy. We can set a time when I see you at dinner."

Hanging up the phone, he stood for a moment, just thinking. He had to wonder what had prompted this invitation. In the back of his mind, he had been sure she wanted to switch places and play the dominant role. Perhaps she was doing this to pique his interest. She certainly had accomplished that. He turned and started back to join the others when another possibility occurred. What if she was hoping to catch the eye of a certain duke, which she knew was in search of a new submissive? He almost growled in anger when he returned to the table.

Tony grinned. "So, who was that? Did you find a lady fair to keep you company after we lost touch last night?"

Jack ignored their comments and leaned back in his chair, speaking in a low voice to Ethan, who he was seated next to. "What kind of outfit will you be wearing tonight, Ethan? To the private party, that is?"

Jack watched as the older man set down his beer on the table before crossing his arms across his chest. He knew the older couple had to wonder about his and Andy's relationship, but so far Ethan had not asked any questions.

"As Margrit's Master, I shall wear a tuxedo to both parties. If we were to attend a smaller affair, then I'd probably do a role-playing getup. I'll be honest with you, though. Margrit tends to take care of that for me." Ethan shrugged, looking a little guilty.

Jack laughed. "That helps, anyway. At least, it will get me through tonight!"

Ray interrupted with a question and soon after the group broke up until later.

* * * * *

Finally, she heard the knock at the front door. She had sent Henderson away before she started dressing because she didn't want an audience. Breathless, she walked over and opened the door.

Jack looked as handsome and debonair as he usually did in his tuxedo. Staying still as his eyes traveled over her, she knew exactly what he saw. After staring at herself in the mirror, arguing over her decisions, she could close her eyes and describe her outfit, or at least what Jack could see so far.

A long cape, with hood, covered her quite nicely, including her hair. Once she deposited her cape in the cloakroom for the ladies, then she'd be able to see his face as he got the full effect. She just hoped she didn't shock him too much with her unexpected touch of boldness.

"Don't I get an advance preview?" Jack asked, once his gaze returned to hers.

Andy shook her head carefully. "You'll have to wait. I'm ready, if you are."

They walked slowly to the Dungeon Party due to her high heels. Inside the cloakroom, she quickly turned her cape over to the attendant and accepted the small slip to get it back later. Shaking her head, she watched her new, bouncy bob fall automatically into place. With a deep breath, she walked out to meet Jack.

Jack stood alone, having told Tony, Danny and Ruthie to go in and they'd join them in a few minutes. He happened to turn around just as Andy began walking towards him. The words "struck dumb" and "frozen in time" suddenly seemed quite appropriate to describe how he felt.

The first thing he noticed was that Andy seemed to be dressed predominantly in leather. It covered her from neck to crotch, which consisted of a pair of very short shorts. Her thighs were bare down to where the over-the-knee boots ended. He was glad she was covered. Ever since last night, he'd been worried she might show up at one of these parties with her breasts exposed. At this point, he wasn't sure he wanted anyone else looking at her body.

Only when she stopped in front of him did he realize she'd cut her hair. It was smooth and curved in towards her lips. There was a fringe cut a little above her eyebrows.

God! Andy looked sexier than he would have imagined possible, considering what he knew about her. He shook his head and realized he had a lot to learn about this new Andrea Bond. "Wow!" he muttered, taking a step closer.

Andy felt her stomach settle a little when Jack finally spoke. She'd been worried the leather and her radical haircut might turn him off. Then Jack started to walk around her and she couldn't shake the thrill that went through her. She felt as if she'd dressed to please him and now she was waiting for his acceptance and approval.

When he stopped behind her, she knew without doubt he was looking at the back of her head. The stylist had given her an inverted bob, with the cut angled up in the back several inches, which exposed the buzzed nape, extending upwards about three inches. She was proven correct a moment later when she felt his fingers lift and ever so lightly rub up and down the crisp, super-short hairs.

Andy couldn't stop the gasp that escaped her throat, the catch in her chest, or clenching of her pussy muscles. Immediately followed by the wetness across her lips, and the slight buckling of her knees. "Oh, God!" she murmured in surprise.

Luckily, Jack had been watching her reaction. He stepped close and his arm encircled her waist. Holding her securely, he spoke quietly. "Sorry if I startled you, but I couldn't resist feeling it. Not only does it look as soft as velvet, it feels like it, too."

Andy closed her eyes as she felt Jack's warm breath across her newly exposed and extremely sensitive nape. At this moment, the only thing she wanted was to curl into Jack's heat. But they couldn't as they both heard their friends' voices calling.

"Hey, you two!"

"Good! I'm glad we caught up with you. Andy, I want to go with you and watch the next act in the play we saw yesterday." Gayle grinned as she spoke.

Andy smiled at Gayle and Ray as they approached. She wished for a moment they had not interrupted, but she pushed away the thought.

"Yeah," Ray added. "I want to see what happens to the busty maid."

Jack grinned and slowly released Andy. He reached out and tapped his friend's upper chest. "Ray, Ray, Ray. How many times do I have to tell you...don't speak the thought out loud until you sound it out in your head first?" Jack lightly tapped the side of Ray's head. They all laughed and then headed into the party.

At first, Andy noted many things were similar. But then she noticed many of the attendees were not in formal attire as they had been the previous evening. Instead, many were dressed in different styles that ranged from completely covered in leather, or PVC, to just straps of it here and there. But also, according to the rules, no breasts or sex organs were exposed.

Still, as they moved through the crowd, Andy became uncomfortably aware over the amount of skin visible tonight than last. As they entered the Dungeon Party, Gayle commented, leaning over to whisper in Andy's ear. "I wish I had the courage to wear something like that!"

Andy smiled back, shaking her head. "I was scared, but after I'd spent the money on it, I sure as hell wasn't going to waste it."

Gayle laughed, shrugging. "You'll have to tell me, when it's quieter, where you got it. I might drag Liz and Ruthie there as well."

Her words reminded Andy she had not spent much time with her gal pals from college, which had been the whole reason for the cruise. "I'm sorry I haven't been hanging out with you guys. I didn't realize how much not sharing a cabin would make a difference."

Gayle glanced behind them where Jack and Ray walked together, the same as Andy and she. Gayle took her wrist and dragged her several yards ahead of the guys. She spoke conspiratorially as she released her. "Okay, so what's the deal with the fancy suite?"

Andy smiled, shrugging. "Remember the champagne we received at the table the first night?"

"Sure. I meant to ask you who that guy was."

"Mr. Edwards. He is my next-door neighbor, and I guess he is more than that."

"What do you mean?" Gayle prodded.

Andy laughed at her friend's expression. "I'll have to tell Mr. Edwards about your suspicions. He is seventy years old, Gayle, and a dear, sweet man. Ever since I moved into my apartment, which I got through nefarious means, he has been kind to me. In return, I started doing little things for him. I was home a lot, so I began running errands, buying his groceries, and so on. When he found out about the cruise, and that the publisher was upgrading my cabin, he contacted a booking agent and paid for the suite I am in."

"Holy crap, girlfriend! Is he Daddy Warbucks?"

Andy laughed, shaking her head. "No, but I did learn he isn't just a tenant in the building. He owns it and about ten others. I asked him why he stays there and he told me it was his home." She paused to sniffle. "Sorry, but he is the dearest man. He's become the family I never had. When I first got to New York, I felt lost. I didn't know what to do with my degree. I started with the want ads and by accident stumbled across an advertisement for a companion to an elderly woman."

Gayle touched her arm. "Let's go over there." She pointed to the chairs in front of the stage for the play. "Did you say publisher? Why do you have a publisher? What's going on?"

Andy nodded and they walked over and sat in the front row, away from the crowd. They had about twenty minutes until the next show.

Gayle moved her chair around so the two women looked directly at one another. "Is this what you've been doing since college? I know you said something about typing. Ruthie seemed to know—"

"I began as Mrs. Winterpool's companion. It certainly was easy work, and she was a very sweet person. Her son was busy with his life and family, but once I moved in, I made it possible for her to travel to see him. Anyway, to make a long story short, if that's possible any longer." Andy grinned. "She encouraged me to write—"

Gayle interrupted her. "I remember you were always writing in your journal books or some kind of paper for your classes."

Andy shrugged as she continued answering her friend's questions. "Eventually I submitted to a publisher. I got lucky, even without an agent. With Mr. Edwards and Mrs. Winterpool to guide me, I made it through my first publication. When it came time for the second, I contacted Ruthie to serve as my attorney."

"That sneak! She never said a word."

"I know, Gayle, but that was my fault. I'd asked her to keep it confidential. You see—" Andy paused to glance around and make sure they were still alone. "I'm sure you don't remember ever seeing a book by Andrea Bond, do you?"

"No, but that doesn't mean anything. Not everyone can be a Stephen King, or John Grisham, or even—" Gayle paused as she obviously searched for the name of another famous author.

"Emeraude," Andy offered a second later, pretty sure her friend would recognize that name.

"Exactly!" Gayle said, snapping her fingers. "Like her! Ray and I went to see the movie her last book was made into...damn! The boy was randy for a week afterwards!"

Andy smiled. "Thank you, I guess that is a compliment. When I started, I never expected to sell one book, let alone have three picked up for films."

"Son of a bitch!" Gayle shouted. She immediately covered her mouth with her hand, looking around as well. "Oh my God! No way! I saw her on television once—"

"With long, black hair and wearing lots of emerald jewelry, right?

"Thanks to a professional makeup artist Mrs. Winterpool knew, that was the new me, for the book jacket and interviews. Because of my commitment to her, I was able to limit a lot of the traveling for promotions. I'm going to have to come clean before the next movie comes out. That's partly why I came on the cruise, to let all of you know first. You are the only family I've ever known, and your parents."

Gayle leaned forward and hugged her tightly. "God, Andy! You should have told me, us."

"Not everyone wants to know a woman who writes what some people like to call fluff, bodice rippers, smut, and porn and so on."

"That's bullshit! Does Jack know?" Gayle laughed, shaking her head.

Andy didn't question why her friend immediately wondered about Jack being in on the secret. She shook her head. "I plan on telling him tonight, if all goes well. I'm not sure how he'll take it."

"So, it really matters to you how Jack reacts?" Gayle asked quickly.

Andy nodded her head, which caused her hair on one side to swing forward. A few strands of hair caught in the soft pink lipstick she was wearing. Lifting her hand, she automatically tucked the hair behind her ear. Only now, it was too short to remain there and fell forward once more.

Gayle moved her hand this time, lifting the hair to see her friend's ear.

"Holy cow, Andy! Look at your ears! Didn't it hurt?"

Andy blushed as she replied. "Not nearly as much as the other two did." She let her gaze lower to Gayle's chest and back up. It took a few seconds and then recognition dawned on her friend's face.

"No way!" Her own gaze dropped and stayed on Andy's breasts as if glued. "You didn't…you couldn't…could you?" She lifted her hand, reaching towards Andy when a voice interrupted them.

"Now, this is delightful, and much better than I could have hoped for."

Andy turned her head, smiling at seeing the duke.

"Good evening, Your Grace," Andy said, standing to offer her hand. Beside her she was aware of Gayle sitting with her mouth agape.

Peter bowed over her proffered hand, kissing it lightly. "Please, mademoiselle, no formalities between friends. And who is your lovely companion this evening?"

"Oh, gosh, I'm sorry," Andy spoke quickly. "Peter Waldron, this is Gayle Green. We were roommates in college."

Gayle lifted her hand and watched in stunned surprise as Peter bent forward and kissed her knuckles.

"A pleasure to meet you, Ms. Green. The boys at your college were extremely lucky."

Andy felt her blush grow hotter and was relieved when she saw the usually unflappable Gayle was also flushed. What was it about dark-haired, attractive European men? Before she could think about anything more formative or conversational, Peter was looking at her again.

"I hoped to see you again, Andy. Would you please join me for dinner tomorrow evening? I'm having a small dinner party in my suite, and I would like it if you would be my dining companion."

Andy felt her heart stop. She couldn't believe this was happening to her...of all people! A real live duke was asking the ugly duckling to eat with him. She took a deep breath and "yes" came out on the exhalation.

"Delightful! Here is my card, and the suite information is on the back. Shall we say seven-thirty, for cocktails?"

Andy knew her head moved in agreement, and then she remembered something. "Clothing?" her voice was a bit screechy, and she hoped he didn't notice.

There was no missing the gleam in the duke's gaze as he smiled. "I'd love to say optional, but the Captain will be joining us. Unfortunately, more than this delightful concoction, but something like last night would be fine." He turned to Gayle and kissed her hand once more. "It's been a pleasure to meet you, Ms. Green. I hope you enjoy your cruise."

"Oh, uh, yes...uhm, thank you," Gayle stammered, looking at her hand after he released it.

Peter lifted Andy's hand, holding it between both of his. "I look forward to tomorrow evening." He kissed her hand once more, but to Andy it felt different, more intimate. "Adieu, ladies!"

Andy flopped down on the chair, feeling like a balloon that was suddenly deflated. Slowly, she looked at Gayle, who was still gazing at her hand.

Gayle finally glanced up. "Did you call him 'grace'?"

"Did I just agree to have dinner with him? Oh my God!"

"We've been looking all over for you two!"

Andy and Gayle both turned and saw Ray and Jack walking towards, up the aisle between the chairs until they were right behind them.

Ray, who had spoken, leaned over to kiss Gayle's cheek. He glanced down to where she was still holding her hand. "Did you hurt your hand, honey?"

Gayle looked from Ray to Andy. Almost on cue, they both started to laugh. It took a few seconds and then Gayle shook her head and replied, "No, Ray, I'm fine. I just got *duked*."

Andy started laughing again, until she met Jack's gaze. She knew instantly that he guessed what Gayle had meant. She looked away, suddenly feeling guilty, almost as if she'd cheated on Jack. Suddenly, she had trouble breathing and cursed her tendency towards panic attacks.

"Not now, damn it!" she muttered softly, trying to focus on her breathing. Behind her, she heard Jack talking.

"It looks like the ladies were visiting with a real live lord of the realm."

Ray looked confused, but sat in the chair behind Gayle's, which was still partially turned. "You lost me, dude."

Jack shook his head, sitting beside Ray. "The girls met the Duke of Claxonby, unless I'm mistaken."

"Oh, yeah. I've heard of him. He's on board!"

"Yes!" Gayle almost squealed her reply. "And Andy is dining with him tomorrow night, in his suite! I think I'm going to die!"

"No...but...I...am—" Andy gasped a moment later. She wasn't winning against the breathing thing and was starting to feel dizzy.

"Oh, crap! She's hyperventilating!" Gayle said beside her. She reached out and grabbed Andy's hands. "Come on, Andy, just focus on breathing. Breathe in for four counts. That's it. One. Two. Three. Four. Now out for eight. There you go, nice and slow."

Andy tried to focus on Gayle, but she couldn't get the image of Jack sitting behind her, wondering what he must think about her dinner with the duke. She took another hurried breath.

"Andy! You aren't focused. Listen to me and put everything else out of your mind. You can do this. It may be a few years since we did it together, but some things never change. Come on. Breathe in slow," Gayle encouraged her, beginning to count again.

Andy pushed thoughts of Jack and the duke out of her mind, for now.

Chapter Seven

"Good evening, Ladies and Gentlemen, Masters and Mistresses. Welcome to act two of our play, *The Castle of Dark Pleasure*. Tonight we find Mistress Danica handing over the slave she had tutored to her new Master. Let us begin!"

Jack was only half focused on the drama on the stage. His gaze kept returning to Andy, who sat directly in front of him. He couldn't decide if he was angry or aroused, or both. It had pissed him off to no end to hear she'd accepted a dinner invitation with another man. To learn it was with a well-known jetsetter and businessman had grated beyond his belief. Even if he had to give the other man his due, although reluctantly

Andy was his, damn it! Maybe he had not made it official, but in his mind he was coming to accept it as the truth. A good chance existed that he'd always known it, but he had been too immature to accept her the way she was in college. Or he'd been too scared. Seeing her again, and he was pretty sure it had nothing to do with the changes in her appearance, had made him realize Andy had been a big part of his college life. She had been the one who got his jokes all the time, not just some of the time, like the others. Many times, something would happen and he'd look over and find she was seeing the same humor in the situation as he. If only he had not made such stupid mistakes, had not listened to his friends, but instead gone with his heart and his soul.

He looked at the back of her head, which was tilted to one side, just a little bit. It surprised him still how sexy the back of her hair was, cut so short. If someone had questioned him, he would have said he preferred long hair to short. But he had gotten a sense of something, when he ran his fingers up, and then back down the soft pelt of hair, that Andy had been deeply affected. He wanted to rub his fingers over it again and feel its velvety softness. Even more he needed to verify her response to his touch once more. He had heard some women had an erogenous zone on the nape of their neck, but he'd never met one. Nor could he ever recall specifically touching the area and noting the woman's response.

Suddenly for no reason at all, he leaned forward as if to adjust his shoe. When he neared Andy, he blew softly towards her neck. Almost instantly he saw her stiffen and her head straighten. Just as he started to ponder her reaction, the action on stage drew his attention.

"I am quite sure you will find Magdalene to your liking, Count D'Orsi. She has been trained to the most stringent of disciplines you would find anywhere." Mistress Danica turned from the handsome, gray-haired man on stage. "Pierre, have Magdalene join us please."

Mistress Danica moved across the stage. "Would you like a drink, or perhaps an hors d'oeuvres?"

"No, Mistress Danica, I'm fine, thank you. I am looking forward to seeing what you've produced, of course."

"I'm sure you will be pleased." Danica turned towards the side of the stage. "Ah, here she comes now."

Magdalene entered onto the stage. This time, she was dressed in a black, tight-fitting dress, which covered her from neck to knees. It was very sexy in the way it molded her body. Her hair was pulled back into a French braid, and on her feet were four-inch heels. She walked slowly because of the narrow fit of the dress. She stopped the instant Danica held up her hand.

"Interesting choice in clothing," D'Orsi commented.

"Please, Count, be seated. Let me show you how obedient she can be."

Danica walked over to the younger woman. "Why are you dressed in such a fashion, Magdalene?"

"So I may appear in public and not embarrass my Master, Mistress Danica."

"Let's say you're riding in the car with your Master, and he wishes to play with your breasts. How do you accommodate him with ease?"

Magdalene reached up and with a few tugs, the entire center section of her bodice pulled free. Now, other than a black collar of material around her neck, her chest was naked to just below her breasts, which rested on a specially constructed platform to thrust her breasts together and upwards.

"Walk towards Count D'Orsi now, and kneel beside him so he may sample your wares."

With mincing steps, caused by the heels and tight skirt, Magdalene started over to the sofa. Each step set her breasts jiggling and bouncing and by the time she reached the sofa there was an appreciative spattering of applause from the audience.

Andy caught her breath as she watched this interaction on the stage. She couldn't say why but she identified with the Magdalene character. It was almost too easy to imagine what occurred onstage happening to her. Perhaps she had some submissive tendencies in her personality, or maybe she just liked the sexual play-acting. Whichever, she was getting aroused just observing it all.

As Magdalene came down onto her knees, D'Orsi's hands came forward and lightly patted and touched her breasts. His fingers rubbed back and forth on her nipples, finally pinching and pulling on them.

"Delightful," he told Mistress Danica. "And the other?"

"Just as you requested of course, completely shaved. Tell your master, Magdalene."

"Yes, Master, my pussy has been shaved and I will keep it that way for you."

"If you like, I can shave her head, as well," Mistress Danica offered. "It's a fairly new trend, but a lot of people seem to like it. It would be no trouble at all. Pierre rather enjoys shaving off a beautiful woman's hair. He likes to do it slowly, first cutting it off with a scissors, and then using the clippers to buzz it like a crew cut. Personally I don't see the attraction, but he gets off on it!" She laughed as she picked up her drink, sipping it slowly. "I'll have Pierre bring in the paddle and you can see how responsive she is to that."

Andy scooted around on her chair. She remembered the clippers running up her nape earlier that afternoon. It had felt very sensual, just those few short sweeps. Almost immediately, the touch of the buzzing clippers against her skull, and her pussy was wet. Strange, but it was as if the clippers acted like a vibrator against her clit rather than her scalp. By the time her hair was done, she almost a basket case!

"Get on all fours, Magdalene!"

The girl moved to the center of the stage, so her position would not be blocked by the coffee table. She then lowered her hands to the stage. Mistress Danica came up beside her and with a smooth movement, she removed the entire back section of Magdalene's skirt and left her ass completely bare, except for a slender G-string. It was quite a sight to see the bare ass and naked boobs of the beautiful woman.

D'Orsi accepted the paddle and began spanking Magdalene. On the fifth whack, the curtains closed.

* * * * *

Gayle stood, fanning herself, and looked at Ray. "If we hurry, I bet we can have one of the rooms for an hour."

Ray needed no further encouragement. He reached for Gayle's hand and they left at a near run to their cabin.

Jack noted that Andy was still seated and he scooted his chair closer so he was right behind her. Carefully, he lightly touched one arm and when she didn't jerk or pull away, he curved both his hands to rest on her shoulders. After a minute or so, he began lightly massaging her back with his thumbs. His face was close enough so he could either press it against the side of her neck, or the back of her head. He chose the latter, and lightly rubbed his cheek up and down the shorn nape.

"Ah!"

Even though it was quiet, Jack didn't miss the sigh that escaped Andy's lips. "It looks like that scene had quite an effect on Gayle, huh?"

Andy couldn't think with Jack's hands touching her. Then he rubbed his face against the back of her head and she almost slid down the chair. She was melting under his touch, just like butter on a hot knife. She heard Jack speaking but it was impossible to answer.

"When Mistress Danica jerked off the top of that girl's dress, I couldn't help but wonder if your little outfit has some hidden surprises as well." His voice lowered as he went on. "If I ripped off the top, would your lovely tits bounce out just like hers did? From what I've seen so far, yours are much prettier."

Andy couldn't move for a moment. Her body was trembling so intensely she was scared she'd fall down if she tried to stand. No doubt her knees would knock together! Watching the play, her mind had substituted the actors with Jack and herself. She was so aroused that she feared doing something stupid or inept. At least he didn't know about her books. If he did, he would most likely expect her to be more experienced. Little did he, or the majority of her readers, publisher and editor included, knew she relied on research to fill in the gaps of her imagination.

Slowly, she pressed one hand to her heart, knowing this was it. She was going to stand, turn and ask Jack to take her to bed. Finally and absolutely she wanted to—

"There you two are!" Ethan's voice interrupted her thoughts. "It's time for the party...the real party, anyway."

Behind her, she heard Jack laugh, albeit a slightly unsteady one. "Great! We're ready to party. Right, Andy?"

Reluctantly, Andy stood and nodded. Smiling until her cheeks ached, she turned around. "Sounds super!"

* * * * *

"Are you sure you are all right, Andy? You look a little pale. You know, you don't have to go through with this."

Andy shook her head, meeting Margrit's gaze in the mirror. Her friend had already prepared her outfit's transformation, and it consisted of lots of leather straps going in many directions. It looked complicated until Margrit showed her it was just a matter of pieces stitched in the right places, with the right kinds of closures. Her breasts were naked, perched on individual shelves, the nipple rings glinting.

Andy looked at her reflection, hoping she wasn't going to shock Jack too much. The entire top of her outfit was gone, down to the uplifting supports for her breasts. Below, the leather shorts had disappeared for a wide, black silk G-string, which left her ass cheeks bare. Her tattoo was visible since she was not wearing pantyhose but silk thigh-high stockings. Her skin shone slightly from the special ointment she'd been applying for post-tattoo care.

"Do they hurt?" Margrit asked, pointing towards Andy's newly pierced nipples.

She shrugged. "They are tender, but only when pushed."

Margrit smiled. "I remember the early days. You need to tell Jack and don't let anyone pull or tug, okay?"

Andy nodded her head. "Is there anything else I should do, or not do?"

"Well, the proper submissive will keep her head bent, looking at her Master only when directed. But tonight things will be much more relaxed. I'll point out things and people I see that I think you will find interesting. If you decide you want to leave, reach up and tug on your collar. I'll give Ethan the nudge. All right." Margrit took her hand. "Let's go!"

Inside the party, it took a few minutes to locate the men. Andy tried looking around, but she was intently aware that people might be looking at her.

Margrit touched her arm. "There they are, Andy. Let's go knock our men's socks off!" Threading her arm with Andy's, she tugged her forward.

Andy's gaze found Jack and Ethan when they were about fifteen feet away. The only difference from last evening was that neither had a drink in his hand. As they walked towards them, Andy was intensely aware of how much her breasts bounced and jiggled.

"Whoa!" Ethan elbowed Jack.

Jack turned in the direction Ethan gestured and his breath was literally stolen away. Andy walked towards him and she was half-naked! Damn! His gaze moved down her body and back up. The actress on stage couldn't hold a candle to his Andy, he realized with a start of surprise. Andy was a goddess! Hell, she was a goddess with—

Holy shit! Her nipples had been pierced! Gold rings adorned each distended bud and he couldn't pull his gaze away.

"The wait was more than worth it, ladies," Ethan spoke quickly. "Forgive me, Margrit, you look beautiful, as always. But hot damn, Andy!"

Margrit smiled and lightly elbowed her husband in his ribs. "I won't be offended by that comment. So, Jack, what do you think of Andy's surprise?"

Jack turned slowly to look at Margrit, dimly aware of what she'd said. "Uh, she looks good, uh, no, that's not right. She looks great."

Margrit and Ethan both laughed.

Jack could feel a flush moving up his neck. Before he could answer, Margrit handed something to Ethan. The older man attached the leather leash to Margrit's collar. He slipped it over his wrist, and there was plenty of slack.

Ethan must have noticed his curious glances because he explained a moment later. "We don't use the collar and leash as a denigration, but we've found that by my wearing the leash around my wrist, it alleviates a lot of problems for Margrit. The collar, in nearly every level of the lifestyle, indicates possession, or at the very least an established relationship. In some places, you will find a lot of eager young Doms, most with something to prove."

"And that is precisely why I got this for Andy today." Margrit quickly attached a black leather collar around Andy's neck. It already had a leash, which she then handed to Jack. "If she had been pierced previously, I would have gotten her a short gold chain in a Y-shape, attached to both nipple rings and then turned into a much longer chain. You must handle her with exquisite care tonight, and for the next few weeks, Jack. She is very fragile and delicate. After a few more days, there will be fewer worries, but for now, extra watchfulness is needed."

Ethan lightly slapped Jack on his back. "Don't fret, my friend. I remember my early days with Margrit's." He grinned and winked at his wife.

After that, Jack was afraid to move more than a step away from Andy. At one point, they went over and sat. Andy knelt at his side, the same as Margrit had with Ethan. Jack lowered his hand to make sure the slender leather strap didn't accidentally catch or rub against the rings.

Music played and people chatted all around them. Ethan and Margrit exchanged a few comments. Ethan pointed out several things he noted. Twice he was aware of Margrit leaning forward to say something to Andy. To be truthful, he was glad when the other couple announced they were tired and heading to bed. The party had been a blur to him from the moment he saw Andy. It only took a few moments and Andy was back, her chain tucked in, concealed by her cape.

Outside her suite door, she turned as if to bid him good night.

Jack shook his head with distinct determination, took her keycard and opened the door. He ushered her in and followed. As he moved into the room, he set the key on the bar top. "Where's Henderson?" Jack asked carefully, working hard to keep his emotions in check.

"I told him to stay in since I didn't know what time I'd be back here." Andy moved towards the sofa.

As he watched, her hands lifted to release the cape, but then fell back to her sides. Wasting no time, he crossed the room and turned her to face him. Without any warning, he released the cape and whipped it off her shoulders. "No need to play meek and embarrassed now, is there?"

He wasn't angry, but suddenly all the events and subsequent emotions came bubbling up inside of him.

Andy looked at Jack finally, embarrassed to be alone with him, half-naked. It was different now that they were alone. She couldn't read his thoughts, and after last night she wasn't sure what to do. She was very aware of the tenuous hold she had on her own emotions and actions. Earlier, she'd been ready to rip the clothes off his back. This was a situation fraught with sexual tension. She spoke quickly. "Are you angry?" she asked, taking a step backwards.

"Yes! No! Damn it all, Andy! I don't know." Jack walked away abruptly, shoving his hands through his hair, messing it up.

Andy felt something tug at her heartstrings. She remembered how he'd often done that when he'd studied, back in school. Finally, she'd got comfortable enough with him to just reach out and smooth it back down. Now, she wasn't so sure he would accept a gesture from her. Of course, the last time she'd done it she'd been wearing washed-out, stretched-out gray sweats. Now, she was bare-breasted—

Self-consciously, her hands lifted and crossed to conceal her breasts. It was silly, but she did it anyway.

Jack didn't notice until he turned back towards her. He didn't pause. Walking straight over, he pulled down her hands and replaced them with his own.

"There! That's what that guy did onstage, wasn't it? Sample the slave's wares." He paused as his hands tested the sweetness he'd worshipped from afar. Keeping his touch light, he curved his hands. "Much nicer than hers. Prettier. Bigger, for sure." To her surprise, he started to jiggle one and then the other. "That's lovely. Now, the nipples…that really shocked me. Granted you don't owe me anything, but I thought you might have mentioned it… Still, I had warning when you got the tattoo, you were acting outside the box."

Andy knew she could step away from him and he wouldn't pursue her. All she had to do was step back…but she didn't. Whatever she'd expected him to say, it wasn't this. His touch seemed to speak of gentleness and love. The words seemed colder, more remote. She wanted him, but she didn't think she could make love with him unless she knew that he cared for her, even a little. Reminding herself that time had passed and true emotions take time to develop, she took a ragged breath in, preparing to speak.

All of a sudden, it was as if Jack realized he was really standing there, caressing and holding Andy's breasts. And she wasn't pushing him off, nor had she run away. Andy watched as he slowly lifted his gaze to meet hers. She waited for him to say something. When he didn't, she spoke. "You should probably take the leash off, just in case."

Jack immediately went to work on unfastening the collar and leash. He dropped it onto the coffee table, and stood with his hands in midair.

Andy took a step forward and pressed her supersensitive breasts into his grip once more. Forcing another breath in, and then back out of her lungs, Andy told him softly, "You just have to be gentle. Maybe we should go upstairs."

Jack nodded. "Oh yeah, sure." He turned and started walking towards the stairs, not waiting for Andy.

Andy took a deep breath, grateful to know she wasn't the only nervous one. She walked over to the railing, grabbing hold of it. "Could you help me take these off?" she gestured to her feet. Within seconds, her boots were dispatched with and he reached for her hand. It seemed to take forever to reach the bedroom. Once there, she glanced around, sure it looked different. Then she realized she was only seeing it with changed eyes. She walked towards the bed and then sat on the edge.

Jack was still standing just inside the doorway.

She half expected him to be right behind her and naked. "Are you staying?" she asked softly a moment later.

Jack nodded, still holding her shoes. "Yeah, I'd like to."

Andy smiled. "Me too."

Her words seemed to act like a catapult. Jack dropped her shoes and started towards her. As he walked, his clothes dropped to the floor. He struggled a little over his shoes and socks. He finally stood in front of her, wearing only his shorts. As their gazes met once more, he spoke this time. "One of us is over-dressed, although not by much."

Andy giggled. She couldn't help it. "I was hoping for some help, but if not—"

Jack didn't let her finish. "Your wish is my command, princess." And he went down on one knee in front of her, his hands lifting to the top of her stocking. "I've spent most of the evening thinking about this."

Andy gasped as she felt his fingers against her inner thigh, curled under the silky material as he began pulling it down, and then off. He repeated his action on her other leg. His words sounded so gentle and tender that she wanted to pull him close. As his head lifted, Andy could tell the exact moment his gaze landed on her exposed breasts, directly in front of him. He lowered his other knee, and moved between her thighs. Her heart beat heavily in her chest as she watched him staring at her pierced nipples. A moment later, he touched the tip only of her right nipple with one finger as he spoke. "Why?"

"I can't say for sure. It's not like it was some deep, dark brooding secret. I saw Margrit's and I thought it looked daring, and sexy. I felt rebellious. I needed to do something defiant."

Jack nodded, but he still didn't look up. "What are you rebelling against?"

"That I've been boring for most of my life and never tried anything risky or dangerous."

Jack frowned, but instead of replying he lightly touched both nipples with his fingertips. He slid them around and around until they became even harder, poking out more than three-quarters of an inch. He paused to lift one ring very carefully, using his fingernail, and then letting it drop.

As she watched, Andy still wasn't sure if he thought it looked sexy. Taking a deep breath, she forced out the words. "Do you hate them?"

Jack looked up suddenly.

Immediately his expression shouted her confusion. "Hate them? How could you think that? God, Andy! You are so beautiful." He slipped his hands beneath each breast, lifting them. Lowering his head, he placed a kiss atop each snowy-white globe. "Perfection before and works of art after. I just hate the thought of you feeling the pain—"

Jack stopped as he shuddered. Andy lifted one hand to cup the side of his face. "It wasn't that bad, honest. The ears hurt worse. See?" Quickly, she scooped the hair back behind each ear. "I had them done, as well."

Jack smiled even as her hair was already falling back towards her face. "Are you sure this won't hurt you?"

"I don't think so. They said just nothing rough, and no sucking for a while."

Jack nodded and lowered his head.

Andy was prepared for the feel of his tongue slowly moving across the tip of her right breast. Lightly it began moving around the base of each areola, each circle making the nub even harder. She tried to lift her hands to caress him.

Jack pressed them back down, scarcely pausing. "Later," he told her. A few moments of discovery and he found the closures to the outfit. Soon he tossed it over his shoulder to land with his discarded clothing. He stood and encouraged her onto the bed.

She saw him toss aside his briefs before he joined her. In the dim light from the bathroom, she saw his hard, jutting manhood. She reached for him.

Once more he gently pushed her hands down. "If you touch me now, sweetheart, I'm afraid I will lose it."

Andy didn't question him. She was still nervous, but she had no doubts.

Jack shifted on the bed, moving down slightly. His mouth returned to her breast, this time he concentrated on the left.

Dimly, she was aware that he pulled down her panties, and she shifted to make it easier. When his hand caressed across her tummy, she parted her thighs in silent invitation.

Jack didn't need to be asked twice, and his hand arrowed straight down, over her pussy. His fingers wiggled between her folds and Andy felt her breath catch. A second later, he found her clit and her hips reacted instantly. As her body continued to respond to each caress, stroke and even light flickers, Jack lifted his head to watch her.

"What did you think during the play about the shaving?" Andy asked while Jack looked at her and continued to diddle her clit. She was beginning to wonder if he'd taken up playing a violin, he was so good.

"Are you asking me if I like a shaven puss?" Jack asked, grinning unrepentantly back.

Flushing at being seen through so easily, she nodded.

"I adore your smooth pussy, but please, don't shave your head."

Andy tried to laugh, but she knew *it* was coming. Without warning, she cried out as the first orgasm slammed through her body. She jerked wildly. Jack didn't wait for her to finish. He stroked and caressed her and before she knew it, two more orgasms tore through her. Dimly, she was aware as Jack moved above her when suddenly she remembered the other night.

"I'm not on the pill, Jack."

She knew he had heard and understood her whisper because of the way he stopped and held himself perfectly still. Quickly, she went on. "In the drawer...I bought some, just in case."

"Which drawer?"

She heard him groan and then pointed to the side nearest the bathroom.

"Okay, just a second."

As he moved away, Andy felt chilled for a moment, yet she knew that stopping him had been necessary. The last thing either of them needed would be a complication in their lives — the kind that would definitely bind them together, forever.

In the silence, she heard the foil package tear. Jack held her again only a few seconds later. She looked up at him. "I'm sorry. I should have said something sooner."

Jack shook his head, leaning down to kiss her lips for a moment. "No, my fault too. Now, where was I?"

Andy pointed to her breast. "I believe you were mucking about around here."

Jack grinned and growled at the same time. "Mucking about! I'll show you some real—"

The rest of his words were muffled against her warm skin as he buried his face between her breasts. Andy giggled for a few seconds, which changed as he returned his hand to the heated place at the apex of her thighs. Andy could feel his fingers moving around in her wetness, finding her clit, and—

"Oh God! Jack!" Andy cried out. Her body was still primed and eager for his touch. With his mouth lightly sucking on her skin, his fingers quickly brought her to orgasm once more. This time as he moved over her, she didn't stop him. In fact, she spread her thighs wide, welcoming him. She felt his cock brush against her, easing past and beyond her fleshy, swollen pussy. For a moment, she wished it were his bare flesh entering her body. And then, his hips moved and he thrust inside her completely.

Andy groaned as she felt him filling her body with his hardness. She kept her eyes closed, not sure why…maybe it was fear? A moment later, she felt Jack's lips at the side of her neck, kissing her, sucking on her skin gently. The slight growth of beard was oddly exciting and erotic. All the things she experienced overwhelmed her. Somehow, she guessed she should probably be doing something… Otherwise he would guess she had zip…zero…nada experience since the one and only time with him.

Lifting her gaze, her hands moved up his arms, over his shoulders, slowly absorbing the warmth of his flesh against her palms. Slipping one hand down, she curved her fingers inwards as her palm covered his taut nipple. Squeezing, she rubbed back and forth, wondering if his nipple would be as sensitive as hers. Moving her fingers, she began circling and then flicking back and forth across the tip.

Jack's groan told her he liked it, so she continued to bedevil the nipple, lastly rubbing the nub with her flattened fingers. She altered the speed and then used her fingernails.

"God! Yes!" Jack said hoarsely, and paused to ease away just enough to wiggle his fingertip onto her clit. "Come for me, Andy. I want to feel you squeezing...come on, baby. Let yourself go."

Andy was sure he almost said something more graphic. She wanted to feel her cunt sucking and squeezing his cock dry. But she didn't think she'd be able to tell him that. Sure, she'd written it plenty of times and said it in her mind. She flexed her hips and tightened her muscles. Jack's moan told her she'd been successful. A moment later, she didn't care.

Her hips jerked hard once, and before it happened again, Jack was thrusting in and out of her quickly, speeding up his motions as her contractions increased. Gasping, she closed her eyes, focusing on the fireworks going off inside. The wildfire rushed through her even as she felt Jack's cock filling her completely. Unbidden came the thought that she wondered what it would be like if he came inside her, without a condom.

God! She was turned on by the thought and acted instinctively. Lifting her thighs she wrapped them around Jack's and tilted her hips to meet his thrusts inside of her. Recalling some of her writing research, she tightened those Kegal muscles, which she'd assiduously tightened for years. Holding the constriction, she felt him pulling against the friction. A moment later, she heard a noise. It was something between a groan and a sigh, almost painful. Suddenly, he changed his movements, stiffening and pushing as deeply inside her as possible.

* * * * *

Jack shuddered as he lost control and climaxed within Andy's body. His hips jerked forward a few more times, and then he pulled free of her body and rolled to the side. He wanted to pull off the used rubber, but he was sure Andy was pretty much as inexperienced as when he'd last seen her. Turning his head, he saw her eyes were closed, so he murmured quietly as he moved off the bed. "I'll be right back, honey."

In the bathroom, he closed the door slightly and discarded the condom. Turning on the water in the sink, he peed standing at the toilet. Looking around, he noticed the marble room was beyond impressive. His family had always had money, so he was used to nice things. But this suite went beyond a nice stateroom for a cruise. In fact, he'd almost booked a stateroom for himself, but had decided against it, not sure how the other guys might take it. Or what he'd do when they asked if they could bring a woman back there for some privacy. The five of them would be a little crowded in the adjoining staterooms, but the travel agent had kept saying once on a cruise most people are rarely in their rooms.

Flushing the toilet, Jack moved over to the sink. He took a moment to wash up and then used a little of Andy's toothpaste on his finger. When he'd been buried inside the sweet inferno of her body, he'd realized he had not yet kissed her, not a really deep, soul-searching kiss. His one and only goal for the first night on board, other than talking and setting everything right between them. Well, he was a little behind schedule in some ways, and ahead in others.

Turning from the sink, he ran his fingers through his hair, smoothing it back. Her lips had been something he'd often thought about. She had a kissable mouth. Opening the door slowly, he anticipated stepping out of the light flowing from the bathroom, and looking at Andy's naked body, sprawled the way he'd left her. As he'd gotten out of the bed, he had looked back. Despite the dim light, he had seen the way her thighs were parted and her pussy lips were still puffy and slightly reddened. Her breasts, two truly magnificent mountains in his opinion, were definitely going to require infinite study and perusal.

Abruptly, he stopped. Stepping completely out of the light, he verified the bed was empty. Damn! Where had Andy gone? Glancing around, at first he didn't see anything until his eyes adjusted to the darkness. Then he noticed the sheer curtains covering the long bank of windows were now blowing gently. Moving quickly, he crossed the room. The sliding door was only open a few inches. Carefully, he slid it open all the way. At first he didn't see her, and then he realized her deck was a lot bigger than the one in the cabins he shared with the guys. Turning, he walked around the curve and saw Andy stood at the deck rail, naked.

Against the starry sky, she could have been a mermaid who'd just come ashore during high tide. There was a slight breeze and while it wasn't cold, he doubted few people would be walking on the observation decks without a light jacket or sweater.

"Did you never wonder why I stopped you that night, after letting things go so far? Or did you figure I was just being a tease?"

Jack was surprised because he thought that Andy hadn't heard him come out onto the deck. Of course he didn't have to ask her what night, but before he could reply, she went on.

"I forgot fat girls never get to flirt, so how could I possibly have learned to tease?"

Jack started towards her, speaking as he moved across the deck. "I knew you weren't teasing, sweetheart." Standing beside her at the railing, he hesitated touching her. "I figured I'd scared you."

"Ha!"

The last thing he expected was to hear her laugh.

Turning her head, she saw the surprise on his face. "Sorry, Jack."

"Maybe we should go back inside, sweetheart."

Andy shook her head. If she was going to say this, it had to be out here in the dark, where he wouldn't be able to see her face clearly. Taking a deep breath, she spoke again. "I heard you guys talking the night before you asked me on our one and only date."

Silence reigned between them for several long moments. Immediately, Andy guessed Jack would not have remembered that conversation because undoubtedly the guys had discussed the subject before. To him it wasn't anything special or life-altering, like it had been for her. Clearing her throat, she went on.

"Spring break, remember? Our last year in school and we stayed at your parents' house. We were all so excited to have eleven days away from school, campus and stress." Andy paused, taking a deep breath. "God! It was so beautiful there. Do you remember, Jack? The weather was perfect, almost as if it knew how important it was to us." Beside her, she felt Jack shift his feet.

Then he answered, "Yeah, I remember that vacation. We all had a hell of a time."

Andy laughed for a moment. "You guys were all sitting on the deck. I woke up and stumbled downstairs in the dark. I was just ready to call out or put on the light when I realized what you were talking about. I heard you volunteer to take the 'duffer' out." Andy looked towards Jack as she spoke the word "duffer". It took a few seconds and then she saw as he remembered. He might not remember the exact conversation that night, but he damn well recalled the meaning of that word.

"Andy," Jack started to speak.

She shook her head. "You don't have to say anything. I went out with you knowing why you'd asked me. I was ready to have sex with you, too, in spite of what I'd heard you all saying the previous night. Part of me was desperate to take whatever little crumbs you were willing to give me. Even though I knew I was the booby prize, or the 'duffer'. I was so confused and I had no one to talk to. My best friend was in on the con game, so I couldn't ask him for help."

A short sharp laugh escaped from her tight throat. "I often wondered what advice you would have given me, if I'd used a hypothetical situation. Would you have told me to have higher ideals or take what I could get? Translation—I'd be lucky to get anyone to fuck me. But then I realized I deserved better. That's why I stopped you."

"You mean better than me?"

Andy turned to face Jack, the hoarseness in his voice telling her that he quite possibly had not understood. "Not better than you, Jack, just better than being a duffer getting pity sex. I'm just sorry I let it get that far."

"Andy, I never thought of you like that."

She didn't want to hear him pretend he had cared for her back then. Nothing could change the past, and she had come to bury the past completely. Stirring up old emotions, or discovering something new which could open old wounds would only make it difficult to finally leave it all behind her. She reminded herself once more that finding happily ever after on a cruise only happened in romance novels or on *The Love Boat*. This was neither. It was just her sad, lonely life.

Damn it all! She rubbed her hands across her cheeks, trying to dry away the tears. As long as she knew he had used her for his own needs, or to help his friends, that night, she knew she could get through this. "We should probably go back inside. Perhaps I could find that brandy and offer you another drink."

Andy turned and walked back into the bedroom, leaving Jack to close the door behind them. Going into the bathroom, she splashed some water on her face and then looked at her reflection. Her eyes were the same, despite running mascara, but few people recognized her from the past. Inside, the fat girl still surfaced sometimes, but she'd worked very hard to expose and face her inner turmoil.

Quickly, she decided to take a shower. Walking to the bathroom door, she saw Henderson had hung one of the lovely negligee outfits she'd splurged on for the cruise. Smiling, she shouted out the door. "You can dress and go downstairs, Jack. I'll be down in a few minutes."

Jack had been gathering his clothes when Andy called out to him. Before he could answer, she closed the door. He only had time for one step towards the bathroom when he heard the key turning in the lock. His shoes fell from his hand as he dealt with the decisive way Andy dismissed him. Walking to the bed, he sat on the bench at the foot of it.

He had sensed when she'd spoken about offering him a drink she'd started to say something else. But now that she'd *told* him to dress and leave the bedroom, there was no doubt she wanted to leave. The sound of water caught his attention and he realized Andy was taking a shower. He smiled as he remembered the quick look he'd given at the shower. It had a built-in seat and easily Jack imagined walking into the bathroom and joining Andy.

He got hard as he mentally ran his hands over Andy's wet skin. Her new sassy, shorter haircut left her nape free. Closing his eyes, he could see his fingers rubbing up and down the super-short hairs, and then he could press kisses to her nape as he caressed his way down her back, gliding inwards at the curve of her waist before he cupped her ass cheeks. The water allowed his body to slide against her as he pulled her backwards. Andy would shift her thighs when he pressed his hard rod between her rounded fleshy globes. Turning them, he'd tell her lift one foot onto the seat. With one hand cupping her tit the other slipped down to cup her mound. Wiggling his fingers, he eased inside to find her clit.

Jack heard the water turning off and it ended his reverie. He could get in bed and demand she talk to him, or grab his clothes and finish dressing downstairs. That way, he might retain a little dignity. Quickly, he picked up the rest of his stuff and took the stairs two at a time. He'd barely finished buttoning his shirt when a noise caused him to turn his head. Since he'd turned on a few lights, he easily saw Andy as she descended the curving stairs.

Wearing a long nightgown and matching negligee in a golden chocolate color, he noticed how smoothly she moved.

Her hair was freshly combed, but he could see it was a little damp at the edges. She hadn't closed the negligee and it flowed backwards as she moved. The gown was all silky fabric except for the golden lace covering her breasts.

"Did you look for the brandy yet?" Andy asked with a smile as she reached the bottom step.

"Uh, no, not yet."

Andy wasn't sure if she was glad to find Jack still here. Suddenly, she was assailed with doubts over what had just happened. Maybe she should have just kept her mouth shut and never told him she knew about the past? But suddenly the past and the present were getting tangled and she found herself thinking about a future, one with Jack in it.

Sighing heavily, she walked over and sat on the sofa. "I should order some ice cream," she spoke quietly, half to herself.

Jack walked over. "What is the ice cream for?"

Andy looked up at him and felt really awful all of a sudden. Tears filled her eyes before she even realized she was going to cry. It was too late to do anything else, so she let the sob escape. At least, she'd washed off her makeup so it couldn't run, she thought, sniffling loudly. If anything would end this evening quickly, she had no doubt tears would have Jack running for the door.

A couple more seconds passed, she rubbed her eyes with her fingers. Sniffling real loud, she looked up, expecting to be alone.

Instead, Jack was still there, only he was now holding out a handful of tissues.

Gingerly, she accepted them. "Thank you."

"You're welcome, and I'm not leaving until we talk," he added.

She jerked her head back up to look at him.

Jack grinned. He ignored her sniffle and went on. "Yup. I'm not budging, Andy, until we talk this all out."

Andy tried to stand, but he was faster and pushed her back down.

"Hey!"

"You aren't running away this time."

Something in his words scared her. "Uhm, Jack—"

"Yes?" he asked, not moving an inch.

"You don't owe me anything."

"I know I don't."

Andy folded her arms across her stomach. "That means I don't expect you to hang around. I thought guys liked to leave after sex. Don't you want to go to sleep?"

"And am I to assume you are planning on staying up all night?"

"No, of course not. I just meant if you hadn't gotten up, I would have turned towards you to…you know, hug."

"Cuddle, you mean?"

"Well, yes. I assumed you didn't want to."

"I said I was coming right back. I know I wasn't gone more than three minutes, tops."

"Perhaps, but you still left."

Jack moved so fast, Andy gasped. He pulled her upright and held her tight against him. "I had to get rid of the damned condom." He shoved one hand into her hair, holding her face so she couldn't look away. "If I had come inside you, Andy, we'd still be in that bed. I would not have pulled out, but kept my cock buried in your hot, sweet pussy. I'd keep all my seed plugged up in your cunt for as long as possible. Only once it was too soft to stay there, would I pull away from you. Then I would lie at your side, sliding my hand down over your gorgeous bald mound, dipping my fingers into your honey pot. As our juices leaked out, I'd take a little and smear it over your sensitive little clit and slightly swollen pussy lips."

He slid one thigh between hers. "Just when your breathing finally slowed down, I'd play with your clit and pussy until you came again. When I was sure you were ready, I'd put my cock back inside you, and pump you full once more with my baby-making seed."

Andy gasped. She couldn't help it. His words were raising primal feelings deep inside her. She felt her womb contract almost as if it were accepting his seed, ready to nurture a child. Her knees were close to buckling.

"Now, should I go, or do you want to go back upstairs?"

Andy lifted her hand and pointed upwards with her index finger. She saw Jack grin as he turned her and they walked back upstairs.

Chapter Eight

Upstairs, Andy slipped off the robe and slid into bed wearing the negligee. Behind her, she heard Jack moving around, and scooted to the far side of the bed. She saw him walk to the bathroom, his naked backside highlighted for a few seconds until he turned out the light. She could tell he was doing something, but she wasn't sure what. Then the bed shifted as he eased in next to her. Since it was a queen-size bed, lying next to her still allowed some space between them. Jack reached over and scooped Andy towards him. He eased her into his arms, her head resting against his upper chest. His hand lightly caressed the upper part of her arm.

Neither spoke as they lay together. Andy listened to Jack's beating heart beneath her ear, calmed by it and the rhythmic movement of his chest. She hadn't really wanted him to leave and when he had spoken those sweetly erotic words downstairs—

She couldn't stop the restless movement of her legs, one of which bumped into his. Instead of stopping, she ran her foot up and down his shinbone, feeling the slight rasp of hair. Part of her wanted to spill her guts, and the other part told her to hold back and wait. What she did know was the need growing inside her had everything to do with the man beside her. Slowly, she twisted a little further over him and began lightly running her fingers across his left nipple. When he sighed, she pushed down so she could kiss the closest one.

Jack had figured some cuddle time was just what Andy needed to feel more comfortable with him and the change in their relationship. She might not realize it yet, but this was no "one-night stand" or a cruise fling. This wasn't going to be a memento for her to store away. She had crossed the line tonight.

Then he felt her moving around and next thing he knew, she tweaked his nipple! Didn't she know where this would lead? He guessed he would have to stop her and tell her a few facts of life. Pausing, he recalled that Andy wasn't the same woman he'd known in college. There was a good chance she'd had numerous sexual encounters since then. The way she looked there was a good chance she'd had more than he!

What the hell?

Andy kissed his other nipple now! *Wait*...she slowly licked it with her tongue. *Oh God!* She circled around and around, and then she sucked him into her mouth. She didn't bite, or just lightly move her lips...*hell no!* Her mouth pulled him inside, deeply, and then her tongue worked his nipple even as he felt the sucking coming from her cheeks. All thought of stopping her ended, and he slid his hand up to cup the back of her head.

Jack groaned at the feel of her foot moving up and down his leg, as she continued to suck his nipple.

"Holy shit, Andy!"

Her hand curled around his cock. No sooner had he stopped speaking and Andy was stroking and pulling, arousing him once again. His pre-cum was already easing her movements.

I'm going to stop her, he thought. *It's too soon —*

Andy released his nipple and slid down in the bed, shoving the covers out of the way.

Jack barely had time to lift his head off the pillow when he felt hot, wet heat surrounding his cock. Looking down, he saw Andy had taken his shaft in her hand, lifting it as she bent her head. As he watched, he felt the soft caress of her lips sliding up...down...*God!* She could drive him crazy.

Jack fell back onto the bed. His brain fogged as his body took over. His need was great...possibly even greater than earlier. Dimly, he was aware of Andy moving a little, but she continued to stroke and caress him while she kept him in her mouth. He could feel himself getting closer…his balls tensed up, getting ready to shoot another load of semen.

Suddenly, Andy was gone! Jerking up his head, he saw her pulling the nightgown up and over her head. A moment later, she straddled his thighs. He opened his mouth to say something, and then he felt the wet, soft and amazingly hot flesh against the head of his manhood. Her thighs relaxed and he entered her body as she pushed down.

"Unh!"

He heard her soft grunt as he filled her body. He wondered if she felt even fuller this way, than the other. It sure as hell felt like heaven to him! His hands lifted to curve over her hips. His gaze seemed to be glued to where his cock split her pussy lips. He forced himself to look upwards to where her breasts jutted out proudly with their new adornments. He imagined sucking her nipple, slowly, and when they healed, he would tug on the small ring with his lips. Not enough to hurt, though—

His gaze lifted to her head. The short wings of her hair fell forward, concealing most of her face. Now he saw how sexy the pert bob was. The sexy sides curling in drew attention to her lips. He remembered how her mouth had looked moments earlier, stretched around his cock.

"God, Andy! I don't think I can last much longer."

"You don't have to."

"I want you to come with me." Jack lowered one hand to stroke over her smooth mound. He delved between her lips and quickly found her clit. Wiggling his finger brought her quick response.

Andy felt her control slipping as Jack's finger slid around her clit. She couldn't stop the involuntary jerks and shudders of her hips. The regular rhythm kept getting changed. Then before she knew it, her body orgasmed. Muscles and nerves spasmed like crazy. She was dimly aware of Jack's hands again clutching her hips, holding her steady. A few seconds later, she realized he'd thrust up, inside her. The fire filled her from within as she felt his cock jerking deep within her contracting muscles. Over and over, his cock shot semen into her body.

Andy knew what she doing, in spite of her earlier doubts. She wanted this intimacy with Jack, even if nothing ever came of them being together. Her body spent, she fell limply forward. Sighing, she acknowledged that she trusted him more than any person she'd ever known, despite years passing since they'd seen each other. Then she blocked out her thoughts. Worries would come later. For now, she had no regrets.

Jack caught her easily, lowering her to rest on his chest. He was still hung up in the after effects of his climax. His cock quivered, nestled by the warm cocoon of Andy's body. Deep within her hot flesh, he could feel mini-muscular explosions taking place.

God! he thought in amazement. *This had been better than he had ever come up with in his dreams.*

He didn't move. He just savored the weight of her body on his and especially the feel of being inside Andy.

Hot damn! Eight long years had passed, but he was exactly where he had wanted to be that night before graduation. When he had finally figured out he was attracted to her it had been too late. But now, he had fucked Andy Bond! This was his Kilimanjaro, in a weird way.

When he heard Andy's deep, even breathing, he realized she'd gone to sleep. Knowing that she felt comfortable enough to go to sleep in this position filled him with warmth and a sense of…peace. As for him, closing his eyes, he was intently aware of the warm, soft pillows of her breasts on his chest. Of course, he was most aware of the way his cock slid slowly from her tight pussy. Jack did consider perhaps she was tight enough *his johnson* might not come out on its own. What he did feel was all the liquid leaking out around the seal he formed.

He had brought the waste can in from the bathroom and set out three condoms before he climbed into bed. His heart and mind had been in the right place. He could have slowed Andy down. Well, he probably could have slowed her down long enough to grab a condom. But he hadn't.

Taking slow deep breaths, Jack acknowledged a deep, dark desire. He wanted to bind Andy to him, ideally with love and commitment. But only a few days remained, and if he…his thoughts stumbled over the idea. Baby. Child. Andy. Saying the words gave him a warm feeling deep inside. It felt right. He already had a fairly good idea of what she would look like partway through her pregnancy. Unlike a lot of guys, that image didn't turn him off. In fact, he could recall the way she'd looked on that date—

It was the last night of spring break and they would have to leave midday tomorrow, Sunday, in order to get back in time for classes. And as agreed, Jack had asked Andy to go on a beach picnic. She hadn't looked at him, but she'd accepted. Of course, now he knew why. But that evening, he had just planned a nice beach campfire, food, and for them to just listen to the music of the ocean.

Love of the ocean was something he and Andy had in common. They both enjoyed listening to the waves. Everyone else always wanted the radio playing or the stereo on. Down on the beach, he had already set up a little campsite. He spread the blanket and invited her to sit while he got things going. Andy was never one to let people wait on her and she had started taking things out of the basket, setting up.

He easily got the fire started. All the food was ready and didn't require the fire. Soon they were eating the sandwiches, fruit and wine. He filled Andy's glass twice, thinking it was only red wine. Later, once they were back on campus, Tony and Danny confessed they spiked his wine with several different liquors. Each paper cupful had been at least one shot of hard liquor.

He had been feeling pretty relaxed he recalled as they stretched out on the blanket, looking up at the stars. For a while, they had played a game called "Name that Constellation", but Andy was much better than he. Jack suggested a game of forfeits. They could each ask the other a question, and if they got it wrong, then they had to pay.

It was fun at first, losing shoes, socks, and then he lost his jeans, followed by his sweatshirt. At least the night air was warm enough out so neither was chilled. Jack was in t-shirt and boxers when Andy lost her sweatshirt. He should have guessed by her startled reaction, first to losing, and then in her hesitation taking it off, but he hadn't. She didn't have anything on underneath it. If he'd known, he would have asked for her pants. Or at least, he argued he would have done the gentlemanly thing.

But Andy didn't voice her thoughts or emotions.

Jack knew he stared at her round, plump body, especially her lush, full breasts. Luckily, he answered his next one correctly, but Andy did not. There was nothing more in the world Jack wanted at that moment than to ask for her pants, instead he asked her to kiss him.

"Not a peck either. A real, up-close, personal kiss. With tongue," he added quickly, as an afterthought. He was sure she'd refuse.

"Okay," she whispered. "Uhm, how do you—?"

Jack didn't wait for her to ask more directions. He moved across the short distance and stretched out next to her. As he waited, he watched her nervously lick her lips, and that made him want to do the same. After what felt like an eternity, Andy moved closer and he felt the heat from her body.

She paused. "Should we sit up?"

Jack shook his head. "You lie back and I'll lean over, all right?"

Andy nodded and settled back on the blanket.

Jack took a moment to look at her lush, naked beauty and then he pressed against her. He didn't wait for her to initiate the kiss though. He found her mouth and delved right in. His tongue went searching and found hers. It took a little while, but he coaxed her tongue into his mouth.

God! How he had savored that moment.

Then he squirmed around a little and quickly cupped her farthest breast in his hand. She overflowed him and he loved it. Squeezing eagerly, he kissed her mouth once more and then headed south. Andy's squeal of surprise as he closed his mouth over her nipple told more than he had thought to ask. Moving swiftly, he wiggled around so he could kiss one breast while he squeezed and played with the other. He especially liked the way her nipples were getting longer as he sucked and teased them.

He was in heaven!

Soft little sighs told him Andy liked what he did and he made no effort to hide his raging hard-on. As he sucked one nipple, his hands were at her hips, dragging her sweats and panties down. In the moonlight, he saw her dark bush and smelled her arousal. It was mixed with scents of the ocean, the breeze and the surrounding trees and sand. Together, it was the most erotic thing he'd ever experienced.

Jack rarely lost control, until that night. He wanted Andy. Her thighs fell apart for him and his hand discovered her petal-soft, wet pussy. He nearly lost it. Quickly, he found her clit, and began working it feverishly to bring her to climax. It would be easier for her if she were relaxed as he entered her virgin—

"Hey! Jack! Are you guys down there?"

"We're back early!"

"Come up and let's play some poker!"

They both froze as they heard their friends' voices shouting out, carried on the wind. Jack moved away from Andy, afraid the others might come stumbling down here. Andy immediately scrambled for her clothes. She was dressed and standing before he could even move. He felt a little silly in just his underwear all of a sudden. And he was angry and frustrated.

"I'll be there in a few minutes. Deal me in!" Jack shouted back towards the house, and then turned to look at her. "Come on, Andy. We have time for a quickie. They'll never know."

He had seen a cloud come over her face and it was like a steel door shut.

She was already shaking her head. "No, you go back up now and I'll pack up and take care of the fire."

"No, I'll do that. After all, it was my idea."

"It's all right. This way maybe you can win some money and the whole evening won't have been a waste."

Jack remembered he'd gone back because he was pissed. And he needed to get rid of his hard-on before he saw the others. Several times he'd tried to talk to Andy about the incident, but she was too slick to pin down. Even now, he wasn't completely sure what had changed. Of course, now he knew she had known about the nickname and the forced date. In his eyes, it had not been like that. He volunteered because he wanted the chance…to what?

Good question. He would have bet money he had not planned to make it with Andy. She wasn't that kind of girl. None of the girls in their group fit the category, which was why the guys had been careful about getting involved with one of them. Ray and Gayle, on again, off again, had been the glue for four years. They had continued it since then, as well.

He wasn't a person to waste time on *what if* and *should have*. But he did wonder what might have happened if he had made love to Andy on the beach. Would they have ended up together?

Jack drifted to sleep on that thought.

* * * * *

Jack was pissed and at this point he didn't give a rat's ass who knew it. Very reluctantly, he agreed to come to dinner with the group. Both Ray and Gayle decided to sit on either side of him. He wasn't eating and he'd had two drinks before dinner. His humor wasn't improving.

Things had been bad since he had awakened this morning, quite late, and alone in Andy's bed. Assuming she was downstairs, he had jokingly put on the see-through peignoir she'd worn the previous night to go in search of her. Hard to know who was more shocked as he came down the staircase — Henderson or himself. Maintaining what he could of his dignity, he asked about Andy.

"Ms. Bond left for an appointment, sir. She did not say when she would be back, but she did leave instructions for which gown to prepare for tonight."

Jack did give Henderson his due in that not once did he smile, grin or even curl his lips. But he was still foggy from sleeping so late. "Dinner?"

"Yes, sir. Ms. Bond told me she is dining with the Duke in the Queen Anne Suite. Although, since he is occupying both suites this cruise, I guess it should be called the Queen Victoria-Anne Suite." Henderson had looked at Jack, as if anticipating an appreciative comment. When none was forthcoming, Andy's butler cleared his throat. "I understand the Captain will be dining with them as well. I hope Ms. Bond has a good time."

Jack didn't bother to add his good wishes. He still reeled under the fact Andy was going to dinner with that guy! What the hell was she thinking? Had last night meant nothing to her? Henderson's voice caught his attention.

"May I order you some breakfast, sir? Ms. Bond requested I get you anything you might require, as her guest."

Jack wouldn't have thought he could feel worse. He did. All of a sudden, he felt like her gigolo! Angrily he turned on the stairs, calling back over his shoulder. "Sure, order me up enough for two. Oh, and a friend of mine will be coming by in a bit."

Sleepy and his brain in a fog, Jack still sat on the bed ten minutes later when a chuckle drew him back to the present.

Ray stood just inside the bedroom. As Ray walked towards him, his friend held out a sack where he'd stuffed Jack's clothes and shoes. The closer he got, the less able he was to hold back his laughter.

"Go on, damn it! Get it over with!" Jack finally said.

Ray guffawed as Jack took the sack. "I must say your page caught the guys' attention."

"You didn't tell them anything, did you?"

"Uh, no. Just you needed a favor."

"Thanks. Where's Gayle?"

"She's with Andy. They are having a 'girls' day out' and warned me to be ready in time for dinner."

"So, that's where she is."

"Guess I don't have to ask how your night ended," Ray smiled as Jack started to the bathroom.

Jack turned, holding the sack in front of his crotch. "My night was better than my day."

Ray laughed again. "Don't tell me you went looking for Andy wearing that and found Henderson instead?"

Jack pointed a finger at Ray. "You can't tell anyone about this, no one!"

Ray groaned. "Not fair, man."

"You want me to tell Gayle about the belly dancer?" Jack threatened.

Ray deflated, defeated. "Okay, okay. Hurry and get dressed. Henderson said your breakfast would be here in a few minutes."

"I'll just take a quick shower and shave later."

Gayle touched his arm, drawing Jack's attention.

He had noticed her new haircut, a little longer than Andy's, but with the clipped back. Realizing she was talking, he tried to focus.

"I'm ordering you some dinner, Jack. You must eat something."

He considered arguing, but decided it wasn't worth his effort. "Okay, whatever you're having is fine."

Tony, who sat across from the three of them, reached across the table for a slice of bread. "We're planning on going to the dungeon party for a while tonight. Are you going to come, Jack?"

"Yeah, I will go to see what's happening." He saw no reason to elaborate he was only going to look for Andy. Exactly what he would do when he saw her, he was not altogether sure.

Danny set down his menu. "What was the favor you needed this morning, Jack? Ray didn't say before he took off."

Jack heard Ray, seated beside him, start coughing and then cover his mouth with his napkin. He looked at Danny as he spoke though. "Nothing too important."

"We were all gonna tag along, but then we decided to get some sun."

Ray coughed again.

Jack turned to glare at his friend. He had neglected to tell him he was almost surprised en masse. Wouldn't that have been a treat?

Just then, Ray glanced over and broke out in boisterous laughter. No doubt his so-called friend was imagining the same scenario.

"What's so funny, Ray?" Gayle asked, leaning forward.

The others were quick to pick up something was going on.

"Share the joke, man!"

"Now we're all curious. Come on, Ray, give over!"

Liz, who was seated across from Ray, looked from Ray to Jack. "I smell a mystery."

Jack saw Ray opening his mouth and he butted in quickly. "No mystery, just a little mix-up and I needed to be bailed out."

Gayle laughed. "Will I be able to tickle the truth out of Ray?"

Abruptly, Ray stopped laughing. "No, uh, honey. It's not important. Now, what is everyone having for dinner?"

Seeing Ray discomfited made him smile for the first time that day. Taking a deep breath, he tried once more to stop thinking about Andy and what she was doing right now, and with whom.

* * * * *

Andy had one formal gown. It was an iridescent material, which looked like black satin most of the time, but every so often, with a certain move or change of light, the dress became a beautiful emerald green. In her ears were emerald, straight-line dangles, and her neck was bare. The dress was mid-calf length, strapless, and where it dipped low between her breasts, she wore an emerald green pin. The pin had been a present from the woman she had worked for as a companion, and the earrings she had splurged on after she sold her first book.

Her knees were knocking together when she stood outside the Queen Anne Suite at precisely seven-thirty. The door was immediately opened by a middle-aged man, dressed more formally than Henderson usually was. His bow was perfect.

"Good evening, Ms. Bond. His Grace is waiting. We are delighted you could join us this evening."

"Thank you, Mr. uh—"

"This is Giles Fitzhugh, Andy. I call him Giles, but he is a stickler and prefers Fitzhugh."

Andy held out her hand to Giles, but he looked at her hand rather uncomfortably. After a moment, he shook her hand.

Peter came forward, joining them. He patted the older man's shoulder. "I'm convinced, Giles, that Ms. Bond is an American and used to a more relaxed way of doing things."

"Yes, Your Grace."

"I think that is a polite way of putting it. It is nice to meet you, Fitzhugh. Did you come with the suite like my Henderson did?"

Peter laughed, quickly coughing. "Giles has worked for my family for quite a few years."

"Oh, darn. I'm sorry."

"I take no offense, miss. Now, sir, if you will allow me, I will bring your cocktails and hors d'oeuvres." With another precise bow, Fitzhugh departed.

Andy looked at Peter. "Well, I feel stupid."

"Not at all, Andy. He's the stickler for protocols, not me. Come into the sitting room."

Andy gasped as she saw the wide vista of windows. "This is unreal. Are we at the front of the boat?"

"Yes, this is the ship's fore, and your suite is aft."

"That's probably why I keep getting lost. This suite seems awfully big though."

"I took both suites for this cruise. The dividing wall was removed, which gives the magnificent view. You should come back during the day when you can more fully appreciate it."

"Halfway across would be pretty cool, but this whole—" she paused and gestured with her hand from one side to the other.

"Your drinks, sir," Fitzhugh announced from behind them.

Andy turned and accepted one of the martini glasses. She took a sip and wrinkled her nose.

Peter took a sip and gave the butler a thumbs-up signal. "Perfection, as usual, Giles."

"Thank you, Your Grace, but I don't think Ms. Bond agrees."

Andy flushed, feeling surprised her expression had been noticed. "I'm not much of a drinker...of any kind of alcohol. I lean towards Long Island Iced Tea, because it tastes like tea. Oh, and Kahlua is good, too."

"Which would you like Giles to make for you?" Peter offered quickly.

"Please, don't go to any trouble for me. I'm happy with a glass of water."

The doorbell rang. Peter smiled, taking the cocktail serving tray from Giles. "You get the door, old boy. I'll serve the drinks." He added his glass to the tray.

Giles turned away to do his boss' command.

"Did he just roll his eyes?" she asked quickly, keeping her voice low.

Peter grinned. "Yeah. He really hates it when I reverse roles. When I really want to get under his skin, I go out to the kitchen and start rumbling around. Drives him crazy!"

"Can I help with something?" Andy offered, laughing at the idea of the Duke and a sink full of dishes.

"Yes." Peter nodded towards the glass he'd set back on the tray. "You can hold onto my glass while I serve the others."

Andy nodded, picking up the glass.

"Oh, one quick sip before I face the troops?"

Andy laughed and lifted the glass to his lips.

He took a sip. "Ah, sustenance at last. That Giles really does make a good martini. Do you think I should give him a raise?"

Giles had just reentered the room, preparing to introduce the next guests.

Andy saw him lift his eyebrow at hearing the Duke's question. She only took a moment to consider, but she winked at Giles across the room. "Yes, I really think you should. Double it even! He is most definitely worth his weight in gold."

Peter coughed, glancing over at Giles. "How much are you paying her?"

"Obviously, the lady is not only bright and intelligent, she comes from good breeding, as well," Giles replied, his family barely revealing the humor enjoyed exchanging with his employer.

Peter laughed, nodding his head. "On that point, we agree. Welcome, one and all!"

The doorbell sounded again, and Giles turned to answer it.

"Hello, John, Marisa. I'm glad you could join us tonight. Would you care for one of Giles' delightful martinis?"

After that, Andy found it hard to keep up with arrivals, but finally she was sure all of the Duke's guests had arrived. Peter returned and set her glass down and retrieved his. He offered his arm and took her around the room, introducing her to everyone. The Captain was very polite and quite dapper in his white uniform. She quickly learned his wife was traveling this time, since the date covered their wedding anniversary.

Andy was very happy to discover the Williams had been invited to the dinner as well. There was a lot of chitchat before dinner, but eventually Giles announced it was served.

Andy had never seen so many courses to a meal. She found the experience fun, strange and delightful. She kept making mental notes about certain things she wanted to remember for use in a future story. Only once did she reach for the wrong fork, but Peter, who was seated at the head of the table on her left, cleared his throat and picked up the correct one for her to see. She felt her cheeks flush, but he only shrugged.

After dinner, Peter announced they were having a traditional English evening. The ladies were to retire to the sitting room and the gentlemen would linger for a glass of port and a fine cigar. As Andy and the other women stood, Peter smiled and promised they would be brief.

In the sitting room, Andy ended up on the sofa in between Margrit and the Captain's wife, Carol. She was surprised to find Carol was quite down to earth, and a grandmother. Right before the men returned, the Captain's wife leaned over and invited both Andy and Margrit to attend the private anniversary party on the sixth night of the cruise. After they agreed, in less than two seconds, Carol told them they would receive the party particulars at their suites.

About thirty minutes later, the party broke up, with Ethan and Margrit staying behind at Peter's request. Together they decided to walk to the Dungeon Party. Once inside, Andy knew she'd see Jack before too much longer. Suddenly, she knew her avoidance technique all day long might have worked during the daylight hours. But now she was going to have to face him, and she wanted to run in the other direction. Her excuses for accepting this dinner invitation with Peter suddenly seemed less important. The fact that it was an experience that most likely would never be repeated and served as great research only worked if Jack knew about her career. Now she regretted not revealing all to him.

Leaving wasn't an option since she'd have to face him eventually anyway. More importantly, she tried to live her life facing her problems, rather than running away, or burying them under food and fat. Stiffening her spine, she walked with the other three people for a short time, and then she excused herself. After refusing an escort, she hurried back to her suite.

Henderson arrived a few minutes after she did, to see if she needed anything.

"I'm stuffed," she mumbled, half-seated, half-lying on the long sofa.

"Did you have a good time?" he asked, casually picking up the shoes she'd kicked off on her way to the sofa.

"I was Alice down the rabbit hole. I stuck my foot in my mouth a few times, but I only picked up the wrong fork once."

Henderson chuckled. "I'm sure you did fine. I'll take your shoes up for you. I've pulled down the bed and laid out a fresh gown."

Andy saw a smile curl his lips, and then it was quickly gone. "Is something wrong?" she asked.

Henderson shook his head. "No, miss, not at all. Would you like me to draw your bath?"

"No, but you are spoiling me. How will I function back home?"

"Quite well, I am sure."

Andy stood and took her shoes from Henderson. "You can go. I'm going to take that bath."

"Do you want a wake-up call in the morning?"

"No, I'm going to sleep in. I'll probably skip breakfast."

"Very well, Ms. Bond. I'll tidy up down here before I go."

Andy smiled and started up the stairs. "Thank you, Rick. You really are a doll."

"Thank you, I guess. And if you get hungry, I've left a few surprises in the refrigerator."

"Ooh, now that sounds interesting."

* * * * *

Rick moved about the downstairs, straightening cushions and making sure everything was in its intended spot. He checked his watch. From here, he was going to meet Amalie for a late snack. They were both signing over to the desk for the night so they could have some uninterrupted time together. It had been a long time since they had both been this busy on a cruise. He was nearly ready to go when the doorbell rang.

Opening the door, he found it hard to not smile. "Good evening, sir," Rick murmured.

Jack glared, walking past him into the suite. "I think we've passed the usual pleasantries."

"Yeah." Rick agreed as he closed the door, turning to look at the other man. "Ms. Bond didn't tell me she was expecting company."

Jack stopped halfway towards the stairs. "She forgot. Did she ask for a wake-up call?"

Rick shook his head. He had two choices. He could try and stop the man determined to reach the woman upstairs. There was a chance he would win, but they both would end up hurting and bruised. And if ever he'd seen a man in love, this guy was it.

"No, no wake-up call. And there is some food in the refrigerator, if anyone gets hungry."

"Thanks for not making this day from hell any worse," Jack told him as he started up the stairs.

"I had a few days like that before Amalie straightened me out. Good night, Jack."

Chapter Nine

Jack had removed his jacket by the time he reached the top of the stairs. As he entered the open bedroom, he could hear sounds coming from the bathroom. Water stopped running, and he heard the sound of the jets starting. It sounded like Andy must be using that great tub, which overlooked her deck. As he rounded the corner, he had shed the rest of his clothes and saw the bathroom was lit with a few candles.

Andy was already in the tub, her head back and eyes closed.

As quietly as possible, he crossed the room. For a minute he considered climbing in, but then he decided to sit on the side, facing her. Once he was seated, he made a soft whispering sound.

Slowly, as if waking from a sleep, Andy opened her eyes.

Even in the dim light, he could see she had not removed her makeup, which had run down her cheeks because she was crying. "Damn, honey! Are you okay? Did something happen?"

Andy shook her head, sniffling loudly and then gulping a little. "No…I-I'm fine." She stopped as she started crying again.

Jack slid into the tub, pulling Andy into his arms.

"No…no…you shouldn't do that." She resisted, pushing against him, but weakly.

Jack shook his head. "Of course I should, sweetheart. Uhm, I am a little worried about that goop getting in your eyes. Do you have some kind of remover for it?"

Andy nodded. "Yeah." She twisted away and grabbed a small jar. Taking some out she passed it back to him to close.

Quickly, she smeared it all over her face. "You've probably forgotten what I look like without all the war paint."

"No, I still remember."

"You have to admit it's an improvement." She continued to work her fingers all over her face.

"No, I don't have to admit that, Andy." He knew immediately he had her attention by the way her fingers stopped moving.

"Don't be silly, Jack. I thought men liked a pretty, made-up face." Her voice was a little shaky when she replied.

He noticed she had not opened her eyes, or bothered to rinse yet either. "I disagree, Andy. A little makeup is okay, and for special occasions a lot seems to be required. But in general, and personally speaking, I like kissing a clean face." Slowly he reached out with both hands and started to touch her face, removing the cream. Grabbing a washcloth, he wet it and gently dabbed at her eyes, working it all off carefully. Finally, he was done and her face was clean.

"As far as being silly, you will have to promise me you won't tell a soul about this," he paused, knowing she would open her eyes out of curiosity. She did a few seconds later, nodding her head in agreement. "Very well. I reached the height of silly this morning. When I woke up and you weren't in bed, I thought I would be funny...well, I assumed you were downstairs. I put on your see-through robe, the golden one."

Andy covered her mouth with her hand.

Jack could see the laughter starting to bubble over. He went on deliberately, knowing this would break down any barriers she had built during the day.

"I came sailing down those stairs, anticipating surprising you—"

The laughter came out. "Oh no! Oh my God, Jack! I'm so sorry."

He held up his hand. "It would be hard to say who was more surprised. Needless to say, I'm sure *that* is why Henderson took pity on me tonight when I came banging on your door."

"That's awful. I am sorry," Andy said again.

"It wasn't your fault and it gets worse. I came back up here and called Ray to bring me some clothes so I wouldn't have to walk through the halls…well, you get the idea. He got here faster than I thought, or I was daydreaming. Anyway, Ray came barreling up those stairs and found me…in my golden morning splendor."

Andy shook her head, still chuckling. "You better have a big, bad secret to hold over his head or he is going to tell everyone."

"It came close tonight at dinner, but he remembered at the last minute. Gayle was threatening to tickle it out of him. Ray won't say a word."

Andy moved back to sit beside Jack in the bubbling tub. As she leaned back, she thought she should warn him. "I hope you aren't holding the belly dancer story as the threat." By the way Jack started, she knew she'd guessed correctly. Turning to smile at him, she shook her head. Her hair fell forward and with wet hands, she scraped it all straight back, off her face.

"Gayle already knows that one, but Ray doesn't know that she knows. And, she doesn't want him to know that she knows."

"Wait, this is too complicated. I figured she'd be pissed."

Andy shook her head. "I can't tell you why because then I'd have to kill you. And if Ray breaks down, Gayle won't talk."

"How do you know that?"

"Because she doesn't want Ray to know…this is confusing. You promise you won't say a word?"

Jack held up three fingers.

"All right. We heard about the surprise for Ray's birthday, and we set up you guys. I got Tony to call the number to arrange a dancer. A big guy I knew from Chemistry lab went as her bouncer and protector."

"She thought she'd need someone to protect her from us?"

"You didn't know it was Gayle. Anyway, that's why."

Jack cleared his throat. "Did she tell you what happened?"

"Just that she danced. She and I had taken an exotic dance class one semester together, and—"

"You know how to dance like that?" Jack knew his voice went up a notch, but he couldn't help it. He didn't recall a whole lot of the dance but he did suddenly have a recollection of veils dropping. Arousal shot through him. This time when he spoke, his voice was much deeper and husky. "I would have liked to have seen that."

Andy glanced at him. "Uh, you did see it. You were there."

He saw her confused look as she spoke. Jack reached out and pulled Andy around to face him. As if she knew what he wanted, her legs parted and he eased her forward onto his lap. He shook his head as he pressed her against his hard cock. "No, Andy. I meant I would have liked to see you perform the same dance, back then."

He saw the look in her eyes—doubt, arousal and then fear.

She pushed against him but he refused to let her move even a millimeter. She looked away as she stopped struggling. "Please don't say things like that."

"Why not, Andy? I'm not lying."

"I heard all of you that night. I know what you thought."

Jack threaded his fingers through her hair and tipped up her face. Finally, she lifted her gaze to meet his. "I've thought a lot about what you said, Andy. I've tried to recall that conversation, but other than bits and pieces, I can't. I do know I volunteered to ask you out on the last night, Andy. I didn't lose the draw, or anything else."

"Pity," she whispered.

"That's not what I was feeling on the beach."

She looked away, unable to hold his gaze.

He released the hold he had on her head, moving his hands down her back, stroking up and down, rubbing and caressing. "Whose idea was it to lose a piece of clothing?" he asked a few seconds later.

"Yours," she mumbled.

"Who lost the most clothes?"

"You did because you didn't know the answers."

"Funny that, huh. The guy who scored sixteen-hundred on his SATs?" Jack answered slowly. He could feel the effect his words were having. Slowly, he felt the tension leaving her body. "I had no idea you didn't have a bra on that night."

Her head moved up and down, almost like a bobble-head doll. "That was a dumb idea, huh?"

"I couldn't believe how the fortune gods suddenly favored me. I picked the hardest question I knew, pretty damned sure you wouldn't know the answer. I wanted to feel you next to me, Andy. I wanted to kiss you, but I knew if I made the first move you would bolt." His arms moved to pull her closer and his mouth lowered to kiss her neck. Slowly, he rubbed his chest back and forth against her breasts.

"If I close my eyes, Andy, I can still feel how wonderfully warm and soft your breasts felt against me. When I finally held you in my hands, God! You felt better than I had imagined...yes, Andy! I had thought about you like that. I just couldn't accept it."

"Because I was fat!"

"No, because you were my friend. You so easily supplanted Ray, it was eerie at times. I told you all my personal shit. I was so stupid to tell you about that one girl...hell! I can't even remember her name—"

"Helen."

"See? That's how little she meant. I admit I let the pressure of my peers guide my judgments in the earlier years, but senior year was different, damn it! And then you became Miss Invisible after spring break."

"I was too embarrassed. I was afraid you were only kissing me out of pity."

"Pity? God, no, Andy! Didn't you feel how hard I was for you that night?"

Andy flushed brightly. She remembered very well how he'd felt — to her anyway. "Yes," she replied, choking up a little bit. "I hated the thought you might have told the others about what almost happened, and you were all laughing at me."

"Andy, sweetheart, I would never have done that. I'm just sorry you felt like you didn't know me well enough to believe it," Jack told her a moment later.

She glanced up, shaking her head.

"And if anyone should be worried, it's me," he added.

Andy shook her head. "What do you have to be worried about?"

"Because you have a gorgeous body now and I work sixty hours a week sometimes. I also skip some workouts and don't eat right all the time."

Andy slid her hands down Jack's sides. There was only a little bit there to pinch.

"Hey!" Jack objected quickly.

"Something to hold onto," Andy told him quickly, lowering her head and pressing kisses to the side of his neck. A moment later she shrieked in surprise as Jack showed her what he could hang onto. Then she groaned as Jack proceeded to squeeze her breasts, gently.

"I can just imagine you, Andy, swiveling, shimmying and sashaying around, dropping veil after veil. Slowly, you reveal one more luscious curve or valley. When I put my hand between your thighs that night, Andy —" Jack groaned loudly. "I knew I had to be inside you. It hurt like hell, getting interrupted."

Andy remembered every single second of that night. Suddenly, she spoke from her heart. "I wanted to stay, Jack. I was so angry they came back early."

"So, why did you give me the cold shoulder? I tried to ask you out again."

Andy shook her head. "You said something on the beach, right after we heard the others."

"What? What did I say, Andy? I've replayed that night countless times and I don't know what happened to change—"

"You said 'they will know'."

"Yeah, if we'd gone up there half-dressed."

"You didn't want them to know. You were afraid to have them know we'd almost made—" Her voice broke, but she forced herself to go on. "You were ashamed the guys would know you'd made out with the duffer."

Silence followed her accusation and she felt him tense. She'd known all along she was right, and this was obviously proof—

"You're wrong, Andy. I said we had time for a quickie, and then I said 'they'll never know'. You see, I've replayed that time more than once myself. Look at me, Andy."

Reluctantly, she lifted her head and met his steely-eyed gaze.

"I was hard as hell, frustrated and angry at being interrupted. I hadn't had sex for well over a year and I was lying half-naked with my hand on your pussy, which I might add was dripping wet." Jack paused as he saw a blush spread across her cheeks.

"God, Andy! I was a horny kid. I was with *you*, damn it! I wanted you. But I didn't want to share what we had with anyone else. I knew what they would say and how they would look at you afterwards. And I knew if I didn't think fast, the decision would be out of my hands. I'm sorry. You have no idea how many times I wish I'd driven us to another beach, away from the house."

Andy could feel her stomach twisting into knots. *They will know*. It did sound completely different from *they'll never know*. And she had wished so many times he'd picked a different spot, or that their friends had come home later. Slowly, she opened her mouth to reply. "Me too, Jack. I wished the same thing. But afterwards, I was sure you were ashamed of what had happened and didn't want the others to know. Even though logically I knew you weren't like that, I couldn't shake the idea."

"What about the night before graduation? At the party?" Jack swallowed hard. It was his turn for some answers.

"The one where you got me drunk and were about to have your wild college boy way with me?"

"Don't tell me…that's Gayle's description of the events, after the fact. Do you remember anything?"

"I'm not sure. I remember drinking tea, and then I thought we were sitting on your bed."

"I tried to find out your plans for after graduation, like where you were going, grad school, work? You hadn't told anyone…or at least none of the guys knew. I asked Ruthie, but she clammed up, and Gayle pretty much refused to talk to me for the next year or so."

"I do recall one thing."

Jack felt his stomach clench again, wondering what she did remember. "What is it, sweetheart?"

"I know I wanted you to touch me, when we were sitting on your bed. I imagined you pressing me back onto the mattress. You pushed my shirt up and out of the way. It was hot that day, and you had already stripped off your tank top. I wanted to feel your body against mine, even if it was only one time. I desperately hoped you would put your hand between my legs again—"

Andy buried her face in his shoulder. A moment later, she continued. "I didn't fully understand what I needed. I was so naïve back then."

Mlyn Hurn

Jack felt his heart pounding hard and fast in his chest. His voice sounded hoarse as he spoke. "Tell me what you wanted me to do, Andy. How did you want to be touched?"

"I wanted to feel you holding my breasts again. Your hands—" Her voice broke.

Jack ran his hands up and down her back, holding her closer.

"When you held me…my breasts, Jack, for the first time in my life I felt…I—"

"Pretty? Beautiful? You were all that to me, Andy, and so very much more. I was just an asshole back then." He could feel shudders going through her body. "Is this too much, honey? We don't have to talk about it anymore for now. We are probably looking like a couple of prunes anyway."

Andy sniffled a few times and then nodded her head. She slid away and came to her feet, stepping out of the tub first.

He followed her, reaching for a couple of towels. As he turned, he saw her leaning over to turn off the tub jets. Her reflection in the mirror was sideways. Her breasts hung heavily from her body and he remembered another fantasy starring Andy he'd frequently enjoyed. As she straightened, he placed a towel around her shoulders, bringing the edges together in the front. Once she took it from him, he wrapped another around his waist.

"What do you want to do?" he asked her quietly.

"I thought I might be very naughty again and step outside to dry off."

Jack chuckled. "I'm game if you are."

Andy smiled and started towards the balcony. She opened the sliding glass door and stepped out onto the deck. "Hmm, it is just a tad cool, without clothes."

Jack stopped since she had paused. Suddenly, she turned to face him, dropping her towel. His gaze traveled down and back, just in time to see her hand grab the knot in his covering. One second later, he was as naked as she. His erection sprang

178

forward. Andy's smile, which flashed briefly, forewarned him of what was to come.

"I wouldn't want to freeze off the family jewels." Her voice was low and husky. When she glanced back up, she licked her lower lip.

He couldn't be sure, but he was sure she'd done it deliberately. Taking a deep breath, he was pleased she'd been checking him out. He groaned loudly when he felt her hand curl around his cock, tugging on it, squeezing firmly, as she spoke.

"Good thing I know of a warm place to put them."

"God, Andy!" Jack pulled her close, kissing her hotly. When he released her mouth, he muttered, "To hell with drying off, come here!"

They reached the bed and Andy pushed him back to sit on the edge. Before he knew what she would do next, she dropped to her knees in front of him. Her hands busily stroked and caressed, gradually increasing the pressure and pull. He leaned back on his elbows, breathing deeply.

"Andy, you don't need to—" He should make a token protest.

He heard her mutter a reply, in between kisses and licks. "I know." Then she took him into her mouth.

Jack stopped thinking. He was dimly aware of Andy kissing and sucking on his cock. Each time her lips caught and pulled over the rim, he groaned. Then her hand started fondling and squeezing his balls. One voice in his head told him to stop her and the other said *SHUT THE FUCK UP*!

Finally, he moved his hands to her head, cradling it gently. His fingers wove between the silky strands and the tips rested against the short hairs of her nape. He started rubbing the soft pelt and was immediately rewarded by her sudden shiver. He opened his mouth to speak.

Andy beat him to the punch. "I would like to shave you, Jack. May I?"

Her words were the most erotic thing he'd ever heard. Without thinking it through, he nodded his head. "Sure." And then he thought about Andy touching him, holding him and pulling things tight—

"Oh God!" Jack yelled as he climaxed like a volcano. His hips jerked upwards and felt Andy's mouth still surrounding him. He fell back onto the bed, more than spent, in every sense of the word.

Time passed, yet he had no idea if it was seconds or minutes before he became aware of Andy, still ministering lovingly to his cock, licking gently, as soft as a butterfly's kiss. He finally sat up and gently took hold of her upper arms.

She lifted her face towards him.

Jack tried to read her thoughts but couldn't. He urged her to stand, pulling her between his thighs. Her arms looped over his shoulders and he looked up at her.

"Thank you, Andy…Andrea. I think it's a little odd to be thanking an 'Andy' for the best oral sex I've had."

Andy laughed. "You're welcome."

Jack lowered his gaze and naturally stopped at her breasts. His hands slid down to curve over her hips bones, now easing them up slowly. He stopped just below, not quite touching them yet. Deliberately, he blew across her right nipple.

She shivered.

He watched as the bud tightened and the nipple ring was moved ever so slightly. Right then Jack knew that he longed for the day she was properly healed and he could suck and play with that saucy nipple ring with his tongue! He cleared his throat and then asked her, "Do you know what I wanted to do to you that night, Andy?"

* * * * *

Andy was still feeling dizzy from just giving her first blowjob ever. She was aroused, but felt uncomfortable coming right out with what she wanted. Sure, she could write about it, but when it came to doing it, she felt like her tongue had the ring rather than her nipple! She knew it didn't make sense she could walk half-naked in front of strangers, like she had yesterday evening, and still have trouble discussing sex with Jack. But that was how it was for her. Being with Jack seemed more intimate and revealing than a room full of strangers.

From a distance, she shivered as air rushed across her nipple, tightening it. Wait…it was warm. That meant Jack had deliberately…then he spoke.

"Do you know what I wanted to do to you that night in my room, Andy?"

As if it came from a distance, and beyond her control, she heard herself reply. "What?"

"First, I'd kick myself for not locking the door."

Andy giggled because she had wondered that as well a few times. "Go on."

"You are lying back on my bed—a place I've imagined you many times—and I shoved up your shirt. You don't have on a bra because that is how I see you, since that first time. Right in front of me are the most beautiful, big—" Jack paused and cupped Andy's breasts. "Tits."

Andy felt a shock go through her as he said the word. Obviously, here was another example of writing it and living it being different. She shivered as he squeezed her ever so gently.

"Yes, Andy," Jack went on deliberately.

She could hear it in his voice, as if he now had a key to see inside of her, what made her tick and what aroused her.

"Big, round boobs," he told her softly. "I dreamed about them all the time. In class, I'd have to be careful because I found myself doodling drawings. When I was eating, I wondered how this nipple would look covered in whipped cream. And then, naturally of course, I could visualize myself…" he paused. His tongue came out and licked her right nipple, long and slow. Yet, he seemed to be very conscious and careful not to hurt her.

Andy's knees nearly buckled and she held onto his shoulders.

Jack started talking again. "On this other nipple, I often saw myself just dribbling chocolate sauce all over it. I watch the delicious topping as it slid down mountain peaks, to the valley in between. There I was, all the time wishing I was sucking your mouthwatering tits, letting my tongue lap up chocolate rivers."

Jack moved swiftly, which was good as Andy's legs gave way. He turned them, so she now lay flat on the bed.

Andy looked up. Her legs were widely splayed, and the roughness of his leg hair against her inner thighs was an erotic signal he was between them. She saw his gaze had dropped below her waist.

"At night, I'd dream of sleeping on your luscious pillows. I would be your slave and beg you to allow me to plump your pillows." He spoke again.

Andy giggled, shaking her head.

"Oh, yes indeed. What I really wanted was below deck, hidden from all prying eyes. I knew what awaited me because I'd sampled it but once. Yet, I really wanted the feast."

Andy tensed in anticipation. His words promised intent and delight. She could barely wait for it to begin.

Jack knelt beside the bed. He hooked his arms around her legs and pulled her to the edge of the bed.

"Jack, you don't need to—" Andy spoke hastily. *This* was much more than she had hoped for.

"I want to, my lady, which is the difference. This is the feast."

Andy dropped her hands to the bed in acquiescence and nervous anticipation. All the words she'd ever written suddenly dropped away in burnt ashes as Jack's fingers spread her folds and delved between. A few flicks of his fingertips and her hips moved without her volition. Then his tongue replaced the fingers and she knew what a truly amazing object the human tongue really was.

One, then two fingers slipped inside, moving all around. She guessed what he was looking for but she wasn't at all sure she had—

"Jack!"

Andy cried out in surprise. His fingers busily pressed and rubbed the whole time his tongue continued to conduct a symphony on her clit. And then her body released everything at once. The dam broke and Jack lapped the essence quickly as her hips jerked and shook. Andy lay quivering on the bed.

Jack got to his feet slowly, and then he lay down beside her. Staying on his side, he covered her pussy with his hand, and slipped two fingers back inside her. He sighed heavily as he still felt her internal contractions.

God!

His brain had difficulty forming the thought. He felt proud like a rooster knowing he'd given her pleasure, to that depth.

What a night!

* * * * *

Jack pulled the empty chair back for Andy. Joining their friends for breakfast had seemed like a good idea when they hurried to his cabin for a change of clothes.

At first no one seemed to notice them as they took the two empty chairs at the end of the table. Andy looked at Jack and he must have seen the nervousness in her face because he covered her hand where it rested on the table with his.

"Don't worry, sweetheart. Everything will be fine," Jack murmured and then winked at her.

That was when Gayle saw them. She knew immediately. If ever two people had spent the previous night fucking each other's brains out, this was it. Quickly, she kicked Ray under the table.

"Ow! What are you doing?" he growled, dropping his fork.

Sitting across from him, Gayle tried to tell him to look at the far end of the table with just her eye movements. She then tried gesturing with small jerks of her head towards Jack and Andy.

"What the hell? Why did you kick me? What's that weird thing you are doing with your eyes?" Ray glared.

Jack spoke up. "Good morning. Sorry we're a little late."

Gayle watched as they all turned to look at Jack and Andy. She remained steadfastly quiet, loath to cause a scene.

"Did you two oversleep?" Danny asked cheerfully amidst the greetings.

Ray must have moved his legs because Gayle's two kicks didn't land until Danny yelled out a few seconds later. "Ouch! What the hell! Who kicked me?"

Andy shook her head. "No, we've been up almost since dawn."

Gayle stared in disbelief at the two slow-witted men across the table when Ray winked at Andy.

"Early morning calisthenics, huh?" Ray's suggestive wink said it all.

Gayle's roll bounced off the side of his head.

Jack broke out laughing when Ray looked affronted and confused.

Andy hoped no one could see her chagrin as everyone started talking once more. Many mornings in college she had listened as they joked similarly about the others, but this was a first for her.

Ruthie, who was seated across the table with Mark, smiled with encouragement. "We were trying to decide what we all wanted to do today," she told them quickly. "Have you made any plans, Andy?"

Andy glanced at Jack. She realized she didn't have any plans for the day, after all. Shaking her head, she turned from

Jack and looked at Ruthie, and then down the table at Gayle. "No, I haven't. What were you guys thinking about?"

Tony had an opened paper beside his plate. "Here is a program I think Ray and Gayle need to attend."

Ray and Mark both asked what it was.

Grinning, Tony read from the paper. "The Dominant Woman and the submissive man in today's world — Fun in the home with everyday household items."

Everyone but Ray laughed.

Gayle quickly asked, "What time does it start?"

"Very funny, Tony." Ray glared at him. He grabbed the paper and started reading.

"I'll sign Tony up for this one — Humiliation, Objectification and Degradation. Or perhaps you could find a date at The Spanking Group. They are presenting 'The Slow, Sensual Spank'. Maybe you could find a big Swedish girl there who would handle you."

"A tall, buxom blonde? Now that sounds good," Tony joked with his friend.

Jack asked Ray, "What else is listed?"

"'Dominant Men and submissive women — Why ask why?' Also, under the same heading is 'Lustful Letters, Wistful Wishes and Festive Fantasies'. In other words, how to perk up your boring holidays. Is that what you and Andy are looking into?"

Before Jack could answer, Gayle leaned across the table and shoved a roll into Ray's mouth. Silence followed her action for a moment.

Then Andy spoke loud enough for everyone to hear. "Actually, I need to attend the lecture about S and M throughout the Middle Ages."

Everyone stopped talking and eating to look at her. Immediately, she flushed in embarrassment. She wasn't used to having everyone's attention all at once.

"Well, that sounds like fun," Danny commented a few long moments later, breaking the silence.

Ruthie shook her head. "It's for work, right?" As soon as she said the words, she covered her mouth with her hand. She added, "Oops."

Andy wished she'd taken the time to tell Jack sooner, but she didn't think there was any way to backpedal from this faux pas. Quickly, she looked at Jack, not surprised to see the confused look on his face.

"Work?" he asked her softly.

Silently, she mouthed the words *I'm sorry*, and then turned to look at the others. "When my publisher heard about the cruise, they wanted me to use this opportunity to research a new book. They were partially responsible for the suite upgrade, so I could work. I'm ashamed to say I haven't done much work at all."

"Book? Is this your first?" Mark asked quickly.

"Uhm, no. I've had several books come out already."

Danny looked from Ruthie to Andy. "How come Ruthie knew? Did anyone else know?"

"I did," Jack replied quietly. "But I was waiting for Andy to decide when to tell the group."

Andy jerked her head towards him, but he continued to look at Danny. She suddenly felt cold and couldn't stop the shiver that went through her.

Gayle held her hand up, and then started to speak. "I only found out fairly recently."

Andy saw Liz looking from Ruthie, to Gayle and finally towards at her. She wasn't sure what to say, and then she felt Jack's hand cover her knee, squeezing it gently. Her breath rushed out and she was stunned to discover she'd been holding it. Warmth rushed through her and tears welled up. She blinked quickly.

"Oh, Andy, it's okay," Liz spoke reassuringly, smiling at her friend.

Ruthie spoke before Andy could open her mouth to reply. "The only reason I know is because Andy needed an attorney when the second book involved a movie deal."

Like déjà vu, everyone turned from Ruthie to Andy once more.

Tony broke the silence. "Do you publish under your name, Andy? What are the names of the books you've written?"

Ray leaned over. "More importantly, what was the movie?"

Might as well tell them her pseudonym, and go on from there. "My nom de plume is Emeraude."

"Wait a minute!" Danny pointed at Andy across the table. "My mom has all *her* books. They're all over the house. Holy Cow! Mom will just shit when I tell her."

Andy smiled. "If you'll give me her home address, I'll send her a signed copy of the new release due out next month."

"I'm in love!" Danny announced. "Oops, sorry, honey." He winked at Ruthie.

Tony interrupted. "Yeah, but what's the movie?"

Andy felt her cheeks flooding with color, hoping they had forgotten. Sometimes she still felt like the *fat girl who hated being the center of attention*. "*Blood Dream*," she answered them, her voice catching.

"The vampire movie, with the twist," Liz added, smiling. "I liked it. Didn't I just read about another one?"

"Two more, actually," Ruthie put in promptly. "As her attorney, I am *very* happy."

Andy laughed nervously, staring down at her plate. This wasn't how she would have done this, but she was glad the subject of her writing was out in the open. She took a deep breath, which changed abruptly as she felt Jack's hand moving up her thigh. Quickly, she covered his hand with hers, stopping him. Sexual tension, along with her already scattered emotions, seemed too much suddenly.

He met her gaze with a bland smile. He spoke softly. "Since this is a buffet, perhaps we should get started. Keep eating everyone. We'll be back in a minute." Jack stood and pulled Andy's chair out for her to stand. With his hand lightly gripping her elbow, he started towards the hot foods first. When they reached the long warming table, he handed her a plate.

"I'm sorry, Jack," she spoke quickly as he took a plate. "I started to tell you a couple of times, but I couldn't think of how to bring it up. I mean once I didn't let you know right away, it seemed to get harder each time I thought about it."

Jack pointed for her to precede him in the procession.

Reluctantly, she started down the line. She stopped at the eggs, turning to face him. "I mean there were a few times that would have been good, but I wasn't sure what you would think."

Jack put eggs on his plate and then gently pushed it at Andy.

She took the dish and let him take her plate in exchange.

"Move along, honey." He filled that plate with some eggs.

Andy was stopped at the meats. "You know at first I wasn't going to tell anyone and that is probably what colored my thoughts the first few days."

"Uh-huh." Jack handed her his plate that now contained an assortment of bacon, sausage links and ham. Again, he took her plate and duplicated the procedure. "This looks good," Jack said and added some hash browns to the plate. "Let's go over here, this looks interesting." He gently steered her to the table with rolls, coffee cake and muffins. He put one of each on the plate he held and then exchanged dishes with Andy again.

"I know you are angry with me, Jack, and I don't blame you. I should have told you as soon as I saw things were getting...uhm—"

"Involved? Serious?" Jack offered as he walked to the juice area.

Andy trailed behind him, frustrated at his placid attitude. Surely he should be getting upset. "Well, yes. But I wasn't prepared for things to…to…uhm—"

Jack handed Andy a glass of orange juice. "Escalate? Skyrocket? Turn volcanic?"

Andy laughed. "Yeah." She turned and started back to the table. She had set her food down and was just sitting as Jack returned.

"Wow, Andy! That's quite an appetite you have there, girl!"

Silence followed his words until Jack added, "I filled both plates so I wouldn't have to go back for seconds."

"Yeah, that's what Gayle always says in the buffet line about her plate," Ray added with a grin at the woman across the table from him.

Laughter followed and soon they were all chatting back and forth once more. Andy was struck by how much it resembled their days on campus. She suddenly turned to look at Jack and found he watched her. Slowly, he smiled and once again she found breathing difficult.

As if he knew, he winked, but kept on eating.

A thought kept running around the back of her brain, every time he looked at her in a special way. But she wasn't ready to face it just yet.

* * * * *

The next two days were idyllic. Andy spent time with her girlfriends, the whole group together, and Jack. Margrit joined them for "girl-time" and they all had fun. The morning of the anniversary party, Andy went to Ethan and Margrit's suite to get the older woman for their spa date.

Amalie opened the door after the second time she knocked.

"Oh no, Amalie!" Andy cried out seeing tears on the other woman's cheeks. "What's wrong? Are you all right?"

From deeper in the suite Andy heard Margrit call out. "Is that Andy?"

"Yes, it's me, Margrit. Are you all right?"

Margrit appeared a few seconds later and she was crying, as well.

Andy looked from one teary woman to the other. "Did you peel an onion?"

"No," Margrit laughed while Amalie shook her head. "I wanted to wait and tell Ethan, but I can't. It's his fault for getting up early to meet Jack and the guys for racquetball, this morning of all the others."

"What's going on?" Andy stomped her foot.

Margrit slowly lifted a white stick.

Andy immediately saw the blue in the middle. She pointed towards it as she spoke. "You've been trying?"

Margrit nodded. "Almost since we got married. We did the testing, everything was normal, and we just needed to relax."

Andy laughed. "Maybe you can get a discount on your next sailing to be used as advertising."

Margrit joined in the laughter. "I can just see me, swollen belly, posing sideways for photos."

"Too tense?" Andy volunteered. "Cruise us."

Amalie clapped her hands. "Can I steal that? I'll turn it in to the cruise line."

Andy shrugged, but gestured to Margrit.

Margrit nodded. "Sure. I'm cheap enough to go for the discount but Ethan hates publicity."

"Maybe they'll give you something special for Rick and your honeymoon," Andy suggested.

Amalie held up her hands. "Not so fast!"

"Okay, okay. Now what?" Andy asked.

"Well, the steam room and the hot tub are off my spa list," Margrit told her. "Let me get my purse and we can go."

Margrit tried keeping her news a secret, but it came out when Gayle confided that as soon as she and Ray were married, she wanted to get pregnant.

Andy looked at Margrit and she giggled.

The happy news just spilled out, and hugs, laughter and tears followed.

Andy reached out and pulled Margrit aside finally. "It's none of my business, but before the whole ship finds out—"

"You're right. I better go find my husband."

"We can help with that." Andy turned around, looking at her friends. "Who has their beeper?"

Ruthie held her hand up sheepishly. While all the guys carried theirs everywhere, it seemed easy for each woman to forget hers. Everyone except Ruthie, who was as much a techno-geek as the men.

"Page Jack and we'll see where they are."

The men were having a drink at the Regatta Bar on deck thirteen. Without revealing their intention, the women decided they would meet the men. Hopefully, the fact that Margrit pulled Ethan aside would be less obvious amidst the mingling of the eleven people. As they walked to the bar, Margrit spoke softly, "This sounds like a good plan."

As they rode the elevator to the upper deck, they were all quiet. Andy couldn't help but think about babies. That led her to remember the one time she and Jack had made love without the condom. Would she feel the same unbridled joy as Margrit if she were to discover she was suddenly pregnant? At least one thing was sure...she could afford to raise a child alone. This didn't mean she wanted to—

The doors swished open and they all trailed out, looking around.

Ruthie pointed out, "The sign says we have to circle back around past the sports center."

It was easy to spot the men, but they were unprepared to be suddenly deluged with women.

"Hey! What's going on?" Ray asked, who saw the women first.

All the men stood. Andy hung back for a moment, as everyone started talking. She was anxious to see how Ethan reacted to the news. But even more important, she wanted to see how Jack responded when the couple revealed their news to everyone else.

Ethan left the table and came over to where Margrit stood, which was next to Andy. "Hello, sweetheart. What a nice surprise!" Ethan kissed his wife's cheek.

Andy thought Margrit looked a little stiff, especially in the smile she gave her husband.

Before Margrit could reply, Ethan was speaking again. "Why don't you join us, if you can stand all these sweaty men?"

Liz overheard him. "We love testosterone."

"Sometimes," Gayle pointed out.

Soon they were all seated around three round tables, shoved hastily together.

Andy wasn't surprised to find herself seated beside Jack, and Margrit on her other side. Talk was lively and nonstop for at least half an hour as drinks were ordered or replenished. Andy kept looking at Margrit, even though she tried not to. It got worse when she saw Gayle, Liz and Ruthie also looking over at Margrit. No doubt, she wasn't sure how to get him away from the table now that everyone was seated and having such a good time. Andy gave the older woman a questioning look.

Margrit shrugged and appeared as if she was at a loss.

Andy winked and cleared her throat. "Ethan?" When he looked her way, she went on. "Could I speak to you privately for a moment?"

The surprise on his face was obvious, but he was the perfect gentleman as he nodded. "Of course, Andy. We can step over there."

"Perfect," Andy murmured. She made a show of picking up her purse, pulling something out, and then setting it in Margrit's lap. "Count to ten and then come over with a frown on your face. The men will think you are jealous."

Andy walked with Ethan a short distance away where they now stood at the railing.

"What's on your mind, Andy? Is there something I could help you with?"

Andy nodded, silently counting in her head. *Nine, ten…eleven…twelve…thirteen… fourteen…damn it! Where is she?*

"Andy, are you all right?"

Andy looked up at Ethan. She hadn't considered what she could say if Margrit got delayed. Confused, she scratched the top of her head. Honesty was usually the best policy. "Well, I had a plan."

"A plan. Now that sounds interesting." Ethan grinned, leaning against the rail with one hip.

"Yeah, but you know what they say about the best-laid plans." Andy shrugged, realizing that any plan would have been better than having Margrit just count. Perhaps someone at the table had held her up.

Ethan shook his head. "Possibly, but I would have to say it depends upon what conditions one tries to put the plan into action."

Andy started to say something and then stopped, considering her words. "That's true. You can't control everything."

"Are you trying to control something?" Ethan lifted one eyebrow in query.

"I'm here." Margrit rushed up, bumping into Andy and breathless.

Andy saw the odd look Ethan gave his wife. Still, her relief was so great she didn't care. She winked at the older woman and thanked Ethan before walking back to the table. With relief she sat down, fanning herself.

"Is something wrong?" Jack asked her softly.

"Oh, no, everything is fine." She leaned over and picked up her glass to sip her tea.

"Good. Margrit was acting strange. I tried to talk to her after you left, but she seemed agitated and I swear she was counting on her fingers."

Andy couldn't help it. She laughed, choked and sprayed tea. Everyone offered her napkins.

"Hurray!"

Andy twisted in her chair and saw Ethan lifting Margrit in his arms, swinging her around in a circle. The moment was so romantic, in spite of her initial bungling. She grinned as she turned back towards the table and found Jack staring at her. The look on his face revealed his curiosity.

Before she could say anything, Ethan and Margrit returned to the table. As if he were born to be a proud papa, Ethan made the announcement. "We're having a baby!"

The rest of the morning was spent celebrating, with juice only for the mother-to-be!

Chapter Ten

Andy spent some intensive time researching the topic she'd been sent here to learn about. One of the things she heard during different sessions had to deal with training of a slave, or a submissive. The course teacher had stated.

"The first step in training the sensual submissive, or slave, is to understand what triggers passion, and desire in you."

He talked about the importance of knowing yourself, and studying your own fantasies, to find the common thread that runs through them all.

In the end, Andy knew some things were hitting a little too close to home for her to be entirely comfortable. When she did her self-discovery while losing weight, her sexuality had not really been a topic for discussion. Now it was unavoidable. She was uncomfortable with some of the things she saw and often how they made her feel.

In the beginning, she had been so sure she wanted nothing to do with this whole scene. She discovered there were so many sides to it and you couldn't just pigeonhole the whole thing. Pain was one part of it, but it certainly didn't seem to be the overruling theme she once thought it was.

She found some of the aspects arousing. Like never in a million years would she have seen herself with pierced nipples, or a tattoo. Both had seemed too far beyond what she had considered normal. Now, she began to wonder what her *normal* truly was.

Many displays and seminars she'd seen the last few days had her thinking about doing or trying some with Jack. She knew the idea of being restrained excited her, and the idea of tying Jack up and having her way with him got her wet each time she thought of it.

She wondered if Jack would like the notion of playacting. Her mind kept going back to the scenes they'd witnessed at the party. It excited her to imagine Jack's fingers ripping away her bodice. And several times she wondered what he would do if she smacked his butt.

There was also the idea of jewelry, and she'd discovered it went far beyond her simple piercing. The places she learned that people pierced didn't shock or surprise her so much as that she shuddered in thoughts of the pain. The worst had been the Prince Albert —

Andy shivered again.

So many things to consider and now confusion was beginning to dominate her every waking minute. The future would most likely take care of itself. The real question was no longer how far she was willing to go?

How far would Jack ask her?

* * * * *

The Captain's Anniversary Party was a cocktail party, and while she enjoyed attending, Andy had much more fun with her friends when they all met together for dinner. Sitting around the large table, just the nine of them because Tony still had not hooked up with anyone, it turned into a pretty raucous event.

Andy explained some of the activities she had researched thus far, and the one that caught the men's attention was when she talked about polygyny versus polyamory.

"That's what I need — a harem," Tony said with a big grin, sipping his wine.

Ruthie, seated across the table from him, scoffed. "You haven't even been able to get one girl, let alone enough to qualify as a harem."

"His mouth has always been making promises and claims his body can't keep," Gayle jested.

Ray held up his hand. "I'm confused, Andy. I thought the term was polygamy. What did you say?"

"I got confused, too," Andy told him with a smile. "Luckily, they had handouts. Polygamy is one person married to more than one person at one time. Then specifically, broken down as to gender, polygyny is when one man has many wives, or at least more than one. And then there is polyandry, which is one woman with many husbands."

Tony grinned as he spoke. "I should hope sex comes into the picture."

Liz rubbed her hands together. "And they all look like Fabio!"

"Brad Pitt!" Gayle said quickly.

Ruthie shook her head. "No...Pierce Brosnan. Give me the Bond man!"

Silence followed for a few seconds and Andy realized her girlfriends were staring at her, waiting for an answer. "Uhm, George Clooney."

"Ooh, yeah!" Ruthie and Liz concurred.

Gayle spoke quickly. "If I get two, then my second choice is Hugh Jackman. I'll have one blond and one brunette."

"We get a second choice?" Liz whined.

Ray interrupted. "I protest!"

"It's been proven through time it needs to be one man with several women. That's how it works in the wild," Mark added, folding his arms across his chest.

Andy shook her head. "I beg to differ, Mark. I watch the nature shows all the time, and it is often one female and all the males come to her, when the time is right. Often they must perform elaborate mating dances to attract her attention, or battle to determine who has the best genes. That is the one she mates with."

Jack shook his head. "Explain the other one before this gets nasty."

"Polyamory works in an ethical environment, where all opportunities are afforded equally to all parties, regardless of sex."

"Put it that way, Andy, and no one would be interested!" Danny pointed out, in between bites of salad.

"All members of a relationship have equal rights," Andy laughed, shaking her head. "It's not about collecting women for your harem, Tony. Instead it focuses on sharing, a part of your life and your love, with more than one person. And your lovers share a part of his or herself with other people. There is no 'ownership'. If there is a primary relationship, then they will establish their own boundaries and rules. In a polyfidelity relationship, the people within it work out their interpersonal dynamic relationships, and problems, among themselves. The focus is not who is sleeping with whom, but who is in love with whom. Polyamory relationships are about love and romance."

"I don't imagine anyone here is interested—" Tony started.

"No!"

"No!"

"No way!"

"I don't think so, Tony!"

All four women answered at the same time.

The men were laughing as Tony flushed, but he added quickly. "Lucky for you ladies my ego isn't too sensitive."

While they were all still laughing, Gayle interrupted, "Well, I did a little studying myself." She paused and pulled out a piece of paper. "Don't laugh. I didn't want to mess this up, so shush. Now, the main problem submissive women encounter is non-dominant males pretending to be Dominants. The men are back-lashing against the feminist movement and searching for a submissive, but what they really want is a woman who they believe is 'begging to be abused'. And the guy is looking for something where he doesn't have to think, to understand, to be skillful beyond the act of meeting genitals, or to feel or experience any degree of intimacy that one would find in a true relationship."

Andy leaned forward to look at Gayle. "Could I borrow your notes?"

"Sure, sweetie, no problem."

Jack touched her hand a moment later.

Andy turned to look at him, wondering if he had an opinion on all of this. He had been fairly quiet throughout most of the conversation. "Yes?"

"What did you want to do tonight?" Jack asked her quietly.

Andy had to lean closer to hear him. "Oh, I thought it might be fun to go to the slave auction. It's being held in the back room of the dungeon party. The proceeds go to charity."

"Did you sign up to be auctioned off?" he asked quickly.

"No. I didn't want to get that close to the action."

"I'll make a donation and you can be my slave. How long is the contract for?"

Andy was intensely aware of Jack continuing to watch her. "Oh, it ends tomorrow evening, before the last party, so people can get ready."

"Are you game?"

Andy felt her heart trip and then begin racing. This was the moment she had been waiting for, right? Now she would know the truth about herself...and Jack. "How do I know that you'll know what to do? Maybe you are some vanilla male—" She deliberately used one of the catch phrases she'd picked up.

"Trust me, Andy. I know what goes where, and why," Jack told her with a slow wink of an eye.

Andy suddenly felt hot. Had someone turned off the air conditioning? Perhaps she'd had too much to drink.

Jack interrupted her thoughts. "They'll probably have a contract for people to use and, of course, there are safe words."

Butterflies were dive-bombing in her stomach. "All right," she spoke quickly before she could change her mind. "I'll do it."

"Hey, what are you two talking about?"

It didn't take long for the other three couples to agree.

* * * * *

After the auction, all the slaves, even those bought in private agreements, of which there appeared to have been quite a few, were brought up on the stage. Each Master, and then each slave, or sub, were called. The Master, or Mistress, had been given the opportunity to buy a collar, and at this point the sub was "collared" and chained, to be led off the stage. Off-stage the contract was signed by both parties, during which a safe word was decided upon and added to the contract.

Andy stood with her three friends, waiting for their names to be called. There had been a moment when Peter had approached her, bemoaning the fact he could not bid, but was very polite and gracious.

"Gayle G."

The girls stopped talking when Gayle was called forward.

Ray was there waiting, and he grinned the whole time he put a narrow black collar around her neck and then attached a silver link chain woven with black velvet ribbon.

Liz turned and smiled. "The black velvet was a nice touch."

Gayle's outfit was a black vest and trousers. With her dark hair, she looked good.

Liz had her dark auburn hair pulled back into a high ponytail, with curls spilling down. She had gone to one of the shops and purchased an outfit. It was red leather, sleeveless and laced down the sides, but showed a gap of several inches of skin on the sides. The skirt was tight to her knees and slit straight up the front, just shy of indecent.

Mark's eyes almost popped out of his head when he first saw the usually quiet, sedate chemistry professor.

Danny, Tony and Jack had all expressed their surprise and appreciation, as well. They also applauded the other women's outfits as well, but Andy's won hands down. She was wearing a leather bustier, with a leather thong, black lace-top stockings, of which the right one boasted a small red rose, and black high heels. Her breasts were mounded up high, resting on a special shelf inside the bustier. When the breakaway was removed, her breasts were displayed as if placed on a tray because sewn into the edge of the shelf, was black lace.

Ruthie rented a French maid's outfit and Danny had not been able to take his eyes off her. She was called next and received a collar that was black velvet with a miniscule white lace edging. Her leash was black silk ribbons.

Liz was called next and received a beautiful red leather collar and silver chain link leash. Mark swung her around before they reached the table where they signed the contract and sent her giggling.

When Andy's name was called and she started walking towards Jack, there were a number of "whoops" and catcalls, along with people applauding. Obviously, Andy decided, they liked her outfit. Reaching Jack, she smiled, waiting for her collar.

He pulled something from his suit pocket. He didn't show it to her first as the other guys had, but instead he fastened the thick gold herringbone chain around her neck, fastening it in front, where it clicked shut with a tiny lock. The key hung down the front from a small, fine chain. There was a small circlet, where he hooked the thick gold curb-link chain.

Jack turned, without saying a word, and led the way to the contract. The safe word was set, and they both received a copy of the contract. They joined their friends.

"Now what?" Ray asked.

"There's a party...ow!" Andy stopped abruptly. A light smack on one cheek caught her attention.

"My submissive only speaks with permission," Jack told her softly.

Andy felt something inside of her twitch. It surprised her how quickly Jack had gotten into this. "Ja—" she stopped abruptly. "Master, may I speak?" she finished her question softly.

"Yes, Andrea, you may."

Andy froze at the sound of her full name being spoken by Jack. It sounded so much sexier than her nickname. She swallowed quickly. "There is a party for all owners and slaves."

At the party, Andy got her first real glance at the inside. Nearly all the slaves, or subs, were either standing behind their Master, or kneeling at their feet. Many had part of their outfits removed to bare their breasts. As soon as Andy saw that, she wondered if Jack would remember the way her bustier could be broken down. She didn't fancy that!

Jack sent her off to fetch him a drink as they all stood, watching the comings and goings of the others. She and Gayle went together, and when they returned, Ray and Jack led them to a quiet corner where two comfortable chairs were arranged side by side. Jack took the silk pillow from his chair and tossed it down. Pointing to it, he directed her. "You may sit there."

Andy started to sit when the leash tightened. She saw him lift one eyebrow and she realized she'd forgotten something. "Thank you, Master," she murmured, sitting next to his chair.

Ray duplicated Jack's actions, flushing a little as he did so.

Andy glanced at Gayle, who now sat on the same side as she. Her friend appeared a little miffed at the experience. She could imagine that being submissive was something her friend, as a physician, had rarely encountered, if ever.

As for herself, she wasn't altogether sure how she felt. She remembered what she'd heard in one of the lectures about submissive service. Her role in public was to be attentive to her Dominant's needs and desires. She had a joyful task to demonstrate, through her attitude and demeanor, and that was to ensure the Dom's needs came first.

But some considered the private appearance equally, if not more important. Frowning, she recalled one woman had said the ability to "take a heavy beating" and reach arousal, or not break, did not prove you were a good sub. Instead, what mattered was whether you could say you were as good a slave to your Dom during the quiet moments as when he was giving you what you craved?

The whole idea of pain and punishment made her cringe, or she believed it did. She'd never experienced pain intended to arouse, and its culmination was in a climax. Of course, that was the private stuff, or in a pre-orchestrated scene. In her mind though, the private stuff was very important, if you were thinking about long-term.

Andy stiffened. Where the hell had that idea come from? Long-term? Nobody here had talked anything beyond this cruise. The next day, she'd be saying goodbye to all of them once more. This had all been fun and she couldn't deny that. But none of this echoed her normal life, not in any way. More importantly, could Jack possibly be in her future? She'd never imagined it in her wildest daydreams regarding this cruise. Perhaps the fat girl still lived inside her, and she'd only been fooling herself all this time. Was her subconscious beginning to think long-term, with Jack?

It was possible, she guessed. They were both single, and unattached. Sexually, they certainly sparked. In college they had talked about everything, up until the spring break incident. Jack had been her best friend. Would he want to be her lover upon their return?

After all, there were still the times she reached for the ice cream. She couldn't forget that fact. No matter how much talking it through with a therapist, journaling her thoughts and emotions, and making changes in her life and eating patterns, sometimes the little fat girl remained.

Gentle as a kiss, she felt Jack's hand touch her hair. As she felt the caress across the back of her head, she was just as aware as if it were her skin he stroked. His hand moved down the back of her head until he reached the velvety super-short pelt at the back. That's when everything changed. His fingers began rubbing up, the opposite direction the hair grew, and all her nerve endings flared like firecrackers. Her body shook visibly, and she knew that with this touch — he controlled her.

A moment later, she knew he had felt it as well when his fingers paused until the shiver stopped. As soon as she was in control, he began the sensual tease once more. Andy could feel her pussy flooding as her passion shot forth, like superheated lava from an erupting volcano.

God!

She needed —

Jack's hand moved away. "I don't think you saw the interesting thing about Andy's costume, Ray."

Andy jerked her head around to stare at Jack. She pleaded with him silently, yet she also knew one of the primary things about submissiveness was feeling embarrassed and sometimes even humiliated, while in public. She did wonder if this was payback for her not telling about her writing…and going to dinner with the Duke of Claxonby.

"Andrea. Please remove the special inserts on your top and pass them to me." Jack held out his hand.

By his action, Andy guessed he had no doubt he would be disobeyed. She couldn't stop her erratic breathing, partly due to nervousness, but also she knew some of it was excitement. Looking down at her already burgeoning bosoms, she pulled them off together, guessing that was how he would prefer it, more dramatic, she thought. Immediately, her breasts sprang free, the lightweight gold chain between the gold rings wiggled wildly.

"Holy shit!"

"Oh my God, Andy!"

Jack touched her hair again. "Andy, I want you to readjust your breasts, so they are propped on the shelf to show them off better."

Andy paused for a moment. His words reminded her that she had wanted to try some of different activities with him—

"Andy! If you refuse, it will go into your punishment book."

She stiffened and then brought up her hands. Andy lifted one breast and then slid it more fully onto the small piece of leather, which extended from the bottom of the bodice. Its slightly bowed convex shape pushed her breast higher. She heard Ray gasp as she completed the second side more quickly.

"Wow!" A second later, "Ow!" Ray leaned over and was rubbing his right lower leg.

Andy glanced at Gayle and even though the other woman was looking down, there was a smile on her face. Andy almost laughed. Most likely, it should have been Ray receiving a collar tonight, instead of Gayle. She wondered if this exercise would change her friends' relationship. Abruptly, her thoughts stopped as she felt Jack's hand resume its slow stroking over her clipped nape. With only a few caresses, her body reacted once more. The shiver that shook her this time caused her breasts to jiggle enough to set the little chain swinging.

Gayle stood abruptly, pulling Ray up with her hand. As if she were making him speak, Ray grimaced as he opened his mouth. "Well, I guess we are leaving for the night. Good night, Jack...oh, good night, Andy."

Silence followed their friends' departure. Andy knew according to the contract, she had to ask permission to speak. She wasn't completely sure what to say.

"I think the wrong slave is on the leash." Jack's fingers paused as he murmured a few moments later.

Andy laughed. Technically, it was probably wrong, but she couldn't stop it. Bubbling up from inside, it showed their thoughts truly were "simpatico!"

Seconds later, Jack's fingers tangled in her hair and tilted her head backwards. A smile slowly curved his lips upwards and Andy knew without one doubt left in her body, mind or soul, she loved Jack. The feelings—love, passion, friendship—had always been there, but she had denied them for so long that she had not recognized it, until now. This was why she had butterflies in her stomach, and everything didn't make much sense.

His hand moved around her head until it cupped her jaw. His thumb rubbed back and forth across her lower lip.

Andy did what felt right—she kissed his thumb on its fleshy pad before taking it inside to suck on it. The look on his face revealed that she'd startled him, but she didn't stop. For a moment, though, she thought he was ready to stand and lead her out of there.

"Well, well, well," a cultured, British accent interrupted them.

Andy immediately saw the pleasant look on Jack's face fade as he undoubtedly recognized the voice of the Duke.

He pulled his thumb from her mouth.

She watched as he turned to look at the other man.

"Hello, Waldron," Jack said.

"Good evening, Riley, isn't it? I wondered if you were familiar with some of the standard practices within certain clubs."

Andy glanced at Jack and saw his jaw tense and a muscle started to flicker. A moment later, she understood.

"Yes, I am," Jack replied.

"May I sample the wares of your new possession?"

Andy gasped as she realized what the two men were talking about. During her study and research, she had learned at these gatherings, other Masters and some Mistresses commonly chose to sample of another Dom's slave or sub. Common practice called for the Master to say yes, but also to retain the right to stop the sampling at whatever point he chose. A sign of good training, and reflective on the Master, was how the submissive responded. Understood, of course, was that the sub would accept the attention. What was questionable was whether the sub should respond or not?

She wasn't sure what she needed to do. On the one hand, she had come to the realization Jack might be the one of their group with prior knowledge about this lifestyle, and perhaps it was he who had suggested the cruise. The ramifications of that were almost overwhelming at this moment. If she rebelled, would he see this as a rejection of something to which he might be committed wholeheartedly? Or would her acceptance of this appear as her silent commitment? And there was always the chance her acceptance might appear that she wanted to be felt up by Peter.

Oh hell! I can't win!

"Yes, you may," Jack finally replied. "Stand, Andy."

She got to her feet, but she was shaking so much she almost stumbled. Peter's quick hand to her upper arms stopped her from tumbling back down. "Thank you, sir."

"You are most welcome, Andy."

Andy didn't look up as she waited to see what he might do. In the classes, she had found stories that told about such encounters. The non-owning Master would often begin by holding one or both breasts. Usually, he would kiss one or both breasts, sometimes taking long enough to suck on each. After that, the man would almost always reach down to explore her pussy.

She stiffened and unconsciously stepped backwards as Peter reached towards her, but all he did was take her hand in his.

"Little one," Peter spoke softly to her.

Andy looked up, surprised that he spoke.

"You have no idea how difficult it is to do this," he whispered hoarsely as he bent to kiss her fingers. "Good night and goodbye, but I shall leave my contact numbers with your publisher, just in case you become free again." He turned and walked away.

Jack had heard enough. He reached out and grabbed Andy's other hand. "Come on! We're getting out of here, now!"

He was so angry that he was walking as fast as he possibly could.

"Master! Please, stop! I can't walk this fast!"

Jack stopped abruptly, hearing Andy's pleading. He felt guilty immediately at not realizing what he'd been doing. Then hearing her staying within the role only deepened the guilt. He shrugged off his tuxedo jacket and had her slip it on. Without saying anything else, he removed the gold chain. Taking a deep breath, he was careful in detaching it from her neck. The temptation to touch her was overwhelming. Abruptly, he tucked the slender gold leash into his shirt pocket. Curling his hand around her elbow, he began walking much slower, keeping pace with her.

He led the way to her cabin suite, opening the door with her keycard. Henderson appeared just as he finished pulling the card from the slot.

"Good evening, miss, sir." Henderson greeted them with a warm smile.

Jack muttered something and walked over to the sofa. He had plopped down when he remembered Andy. Surely, she wasn't going to continue this scene in front of her butler?

"Master, may I explain to Henderson?"

Jack nodded, surprised at her continued willingness to progress with the scene. He had been ready for her to object when Waldron asked for inspection privileges in that obtuse way. No doubt he'd done it that way so as to not alert Andy beforehand. Had she known what the Duke had almost done?

Damn!

Hell, Jack realized that he hadn't thought about that. Perhaps Andy had wanted Waldron to manhandle her.

"Henderson, my Master—" Andy gestured towards him. " — And I are participating in one of those scenes from the cruise. You can take the rest of the night off and we'll call for you in the morning."

He bowed. "Of course, Miss Bond. I'll await your call. Good night, miss, sir." Henderson left quickly, but Jack was sure he saw a grin on the other man's face as he got on the elevator.

The lights turning out around the living room of the suite drew his attention. Turning his head, he saw Andy had removed the tuxedo jacket and stood at the bar. She poured a drink and began walking to him. His gaze moved to the sexy bouncing of her breasts and the wildly wiggling chain between the nipple rings. When she reached the sofa, she knelt, bent her head and then offered him the drink.

"Thank you, Andy."

"You're welcome, Master. May I ask a question please, Master?" Andy questioned in a soft, almost sibilant voice.

"Of course, Andy," Jack replied, wondering what she wanted to know. He wouldn't be the least bit surprised if she asked him if they could end this thing now.

"Are you ready to chain your slave again, Master?"

Jack coughed as he swallowed the wrong way. That was pretty much the last thing he expected her to ask. "We can stop all this if you want, Andy. I had no idea things might go in that direction. I assumed most of the people would be novices—"

"What does my Master have planned for his new submissive this evening?"

Jack felt his heart jump and his breath catch in surprise. Already, his cock was hard and he had to clear his throat to speak. "I guess it depends on how far my sub is willing to go with all this."

Andy glanced up at him through her eyelashes.

As far as looks went, it wasn't the sexiest ever. But combined with their situation, the tilt of her head and the look in her eyes...well, he felt his rod twitch in aroused reaction.

"I trust in my Master's judgment to do what is right for his possession," Andy told him softly, looking down once again.

Jack reached into his shirt pocket and pulled out the gold chain. He hoped Andy didn't see how his hands shook as he attached it once again. "Let's go upstairs." He stood, but stopped when she did not. "What is it, Andy?"

"I've heard that most slaves crawl on their hands and knees in their Master's presence. Is that what you wish me to do?"

"No, Andy. We'll walk upstairs." Holding the chain loosely, he led the way with Andy following close behind.

Chapter Eleven

Andy remembered about the folded hands and crossed them quickly at her back. In the dim light from the bathroom, which Henderson had probably left on for her to find her way, she could see the surprise on Jack's face as he turned around to face her. She saw the way his eyes dropped to her breasts, which were now forced even further up and out from the position of her hands and arms. It also set the chain to swinging again.

Jack came towards her and she saw him smiling. "Andy?"

"Yes, Master? I await your command." Since she still looked down after sneaking a peek when he called her name, she felt the unsteady breath he exhaled. Could he be as nervous and unsure as she was? But she thought she discerned his uncertainty on how to proceed.

He surprised her when he walked over and sat on the side of the bed.

She couldn't resist and glanced up quickly to see what he was doing. His shirt was unbuttoned and his tie hung loose around his neck. He kicked off his shoes and then eased back onto the bed until he was propped against the headboard.

"I want you to slowly remove your clothes, Andrea. Work your way towards me as you do so, leaving your discarded clothes in a trail behind you."

Andy nodded and then remembered to reply correctly. "Yes, Master." She started to remove her heels.

Jack stopped her. "Leave your socks and shoes on until I say otherwise."

Her eyes closed and she shivered at his command. She had no idea why, but she was getting more turned on with each passing moment. Her fingers fumbled as she struggled with the fastening of the bustier, but finally it was done. She had to struggle to hold it in place at the last minute because she'd forgotten to detach the chain first. Once the leather corset was removed, she reattached the chain. For all intents and purposes, she was naked. Still, she hooked her thumbs into the waistband and dragged the thong down and off, stepping out of it.

"Come closer."

Andy walked until she was at the side of the bed. With each step, she'd been intently aware of how much the bustier encouraged her breasts into jiggling. And the high heels only made it worse.

"Has my submissive been a bad girl? Does she need some discipline for her wicked, naughty thoughts?"

Andy gasped. This was the question she'd been avoiding in her head and dreading. Now she was out of time…what should she do? Before she knew the answer, she heard herself speaking. "I am here to pleasure my Master." Her heart knew to trust him.

"I see," Jack replied very quietly and she had to lean forward to hear. "Come onto the bed and lay across my lap, on your stomach."

Okay, no more delaying, Andy! She eased one knee onto the bed.

"You can take off the shoes now."

Andy got on her hands and knees, kicking off both shoes. She crawled to Jack, lowering herself to lie on his lap. Butterflies were going crazy in her stomach, waiting to see what he would do. *God! What will I do if he spanks me?*

Andy felt the heat of his hand and realized it hovered over her left ass cheek. She took a quick breath, trying to mentally and physically prepare herself for this. No doubt this could be the "sticking point" for her future…and that unnerved her terribly.

"You have a beautiful ass, Andy."

Andy's breath caught in her chest. Praise wasn't what she'd expected. Then his hand lowered to rest on the closest cheek. For a few seconds, there was no action, but then it began to move around in circles, caressing, massaging and finally squeezing.

"Very nice, lovely to look at and even nicer to hold. So sexy, and with the cutest jiggle. I am reminded of a plump, succulent peach."

Andy was at a loss so she murmured her reply, "Thank you, sir."

"Have you thought about what it might feel like to be spanked?"

She could lie, but that wasn't her. "Yes, Master, I have, and I'm not sure how I will react."

"Does that mean if I raise my hand—" Jack's hand lifted from her ass.

She immediately noted the cooler air with its absence.

"You would have to wonder if I am going to bring my hand down forcefully, connecting my palm and fingers with your tender, slightly tanned perfect cheek. At the same time you feel the pain, there is the sound of flesh against flesh, and lastly you experience the heat. Now, you must decide whether you stay right where you are, or do you…wait! My hand isn't off somewhere in the business office. No, I believe my fingers are between your thighs. Yes! I have discovered your sweet, hot pussy is tight, and more than eager in its quivering and jumping in anticipation."

There was no way to hide her gasp of surprise. She'd been so focused on his words, and waiting to feel his slap, the fact of her arousal had slipped past her conscious. She felt his fingers slipping along her wet lips, dipping in and flicking her clit once, twice.

"Oh! Oh God!" Andy cried out, her response shocking her in its intensity.

"Uh-oh. It appears my submissive has forgotten she is not to speak without permission. I guess she must be punished, after all." His hand came to rest again on her closest ass cheek.

"Forgive me, Master," Andy stammered as quickly as she could.

"I'm thinking you are hoping because you've apologized, I won't discipline you. Isn't that correct?"

"Yes, Master."

"Well, that goes against the laws of discipline. Once an infraction has occurred, it must be dealt with. Now many Masters keep a punishment book on their slaves and record transgressions there."

Andy felt Jack's hand moving in erotic, hypnotic circles as he spoke. Each one made it more difficult to hear what he said.

"Of course, the punishments have usually been detailed in advance so the miscreant knows in advance what she will earn if she disobeys. For example, speaking out of turn or without permission would earn one slap, first occurrence. Do you deserve one slap?"

"Sort of, Master," she added quickly at the end. She still wasn't sure if she knew what she wanted or how she'd react.

"Usually the Master decides these things, which relieves the slave of the confusing feelings," Jack explained patiently.

"Confusing, sir?"

"Yes, indeed. If the slave asks for the punishment, knowing she will gain enjoyment, she could feel guilty for seeking her own satiation before her Master's. She could also ask for it, enjoy it and feel as if she has betrayed not only herself but her female sisterhood."

Andy was having more and more trouble following his words. *His hand wouldn't stop moving, damn it!*

SLAP!

Andy gasped in surprise. Jack had slapped her. Only once and not a hard one, but it stung a little nonetheless. And even as she felt the heat following the ease of the tingle, there was an undeniable rush of liquid heat between her thighs. "Aah," she exhaled in embarrassment. Before she could formulate something to say, Jack's fingers were back.

"Hmm, look what I've discovered. It seems my sweet sub has a very sensitive bottom, besides it being a curvy one." His fingers slipped inside her folds once more. While she felt his thumb easing forward to her clit, the other two fingers were inside her. He was working the music of passion with her tissue and nerves, even as he spoke once more. "By my removing the decision, you are free to feel whatever it is that your body dictates, be it pain, anger, retaliation and even arousal."

"Aah...uh...yes, Master," Andy managed to stumble past a reply. Her hips were starting to hunch against his fingers, moving more rapidly towards her climax.

"It usually goes without saying the sub must ask her Master before she comes. It is required."

Andy tried to hold off, but Jack had very clever hands, exceptionally dexterous fingers, and words sweet enough to seduce a vestal virgin!

"But I must confess, Andy," he added after a few more seconds.

Andy gasped, trying to focus, because he had not yet given her permission. What did he have to say now!

"I've wanted to do this for a very long time. I can't tell you how many times I thought about putting you over my knee when we were in school and yanking down those damned sweats. I knew just one smack would put me in heaven. I always watched you walk away from me just to see your jiggle."

Andy couldn't help it. Her whole body jerked forward, just once, but it meant she was losing out on the whole control issue. His fingers were busily moving around, finding her g-spot and massaging it.

"I would spend hours imagining how each cheek would look with just one slap, then two. A pretty, flushed pink hand mark. Very sexy, incredibly hot and arousing. Sometimes just one look was enough to—" Jack broke off abruptly.

Andy guessed he'd said enough. She was pretty sure she knew where the sentence had been headed. Thinking about it she realized it aroused her even more to know he'd gotten so turned on just thinking about her...well, just her. She couldn't wait. "Master?"

Jack cleared his throat. "Yes, Andy? What is it?"

"Fuck me, please, Jack! Now!"

Not a word was said about proper speech. Andy thought she was flying through the air for a minute, and then she was flat on her back.

Jack loomed over her, smiling. She heard his zipper sliding open as he spoke.

"With pleasure, Ms. Bond!" He thrust into her hot, wet flesh lickety-split!

Andy gasped at his forceful entrance. It was just what she needed. Her orgasm was so strong it surprised her. While her hips jerked and her body writhed, she realized Jack had reached his peak and was coming inside her. For a brief moment in time, she imagined they were making a baby. She knew she wanted Jack's child, even if she would never have him in her life.

The image of a baby flashed into her mind and while it didn't make sense, she came once more. That's when she knew it was meant to be.

* * * * *

Jack held Andy in his arms. After they had made love, he rearranged them in the bed, moving Andy's limp body easily. He removed her chains after he stripped off his clothes, setting the gold on the bedside table on his side.

Lying with her now, he admitted the strength of his response surprised him. He'd had a few D/s encounters, and not once had he lost control like tonight with Andy.

When they started this charade, he'd made a simple plan in his head. If Andy were agreeable, he'd proceed, explaining different submissive expectations, and subsequent disciplines if disobeyed or ignored. But then that damned Waldron had shown up, asking for inspection privileges. He had been ready to spit, and then fight. As a gentleman, he agreed. A part of him wanted Andy to refuse, but she had not. At the time, he wondered if she completely understood how far it could go, but a look into her face, and he had guessed that she did. God only knew what he would have done if the Duke had touched her intimately.

Hell! The minute he had her remove the breastplates of her outfit, he had regretted it. Maybe at some point he might be willing to share her beauty with others, but not now.

Then when it had come time to actually strike Andy, he'd been torn. If he spanked her, and she hated it, there was a good chance she'd reject him, as well. There was also the risk that she'd love it and want even more. The truth was he'd never been into the pain thing so much as the role-playing and mind game. But when it came down to it being Andy on his lap, everything had suddenly changed and taken on a new meaning.

When he'd entered her, he had almost stopped to grab a condom. Then he had thought that perhaps if she did get pregnant, they would stay together, and he had come to realize this is what he wanted. Andy in his life would complete his world. A pregnant Andy, while occurring a little sooner than what would fit his plan, he would accept wholeheartedly. He liked the idea of her belly growing round and her hips widening once more.

Closing his eyes, he merged the old image of Andy, soft and plump, with a newer ideal, where she had a round belly and full breasts. In fact, it turned him on to think about making love to her. It would almost be like loving her back in college, which he'd longed to do so many times. Of course, the fantasy of taking her doggie style got him hard again.

Baby?

Daddy?

For the first time in his life, it felt right. He didn't feel the need to run away. Instead he imagined holding a baby in his arms. It was even easier to see Andy breastfeeding his child. A few moments passed before he realized that in his fantasy, Andy was plump like she used to be. Pausing, he considered it, but he knew he loved her, regardless of her size. Now that he had her in his life, none of it mattered. What did was how they were going to find a way to be together? He was willing to do just about anything to be with her.

Anything short of murder or a crime, anyway. It always surprised him in books and movies how people would do just those things to be with someone. Don't they get it? The cops always win, what with DNA and all the forensic stuff these days. So, they'll never be together anyway!

With a big grin, Jack settled further down in the bed. It wasn't too long before he fell asleep.

* * * * *

Jack was up early, which surprised him. He showered, shaved and Andy still slept. Going downstairs in the trousers from his tuxedo, he called Henderson to arrange a sumptuous breakfast for them. He went out on the balcony to wait for the butler to arrive with the food. As long as Andy slept, he'd let her go. Then he would tell her the slave thing was over and it was time to discuss the future. They had only one night to go on the cruise, and then it was over. He couldn't let her walk down the gangplank and back out of his life.

"Good morning, sir," Henderson called out from the living room. "Would you like breakfast out there, or in here?"

"It's a little breezy, so we should probably stay inside."

"Very good, sir."

Jack watched as Henderson set the food on the small table. He was just deciding to have a cup of coffee before he woke

Andy when Henderson turned to hand him a cup of hot, steaming black coffee.

"Would you like cream or sugar, sir?" Henderson asked.

"No, thanks. Black is perfect."

"Coffee, coffee, coffee! Whatever happened to good old tea?"

Both men turned to see Andy coming down the stairs as she shared her opinion. "Good morning, gentlemen," she added, greeting them both.

"Good morning, Andy! I was going to let you sleep a little longer." Jack came towards her, shifting his cup so he could hug her. She had pulled on a black and white nightgown and dressy robe. Jack thought she looked like an actress out of an old movie from the thirties.

"Thank you, but I don't want to sleep away the last day. Hello, Henderson! How are you today?" Andy asked as she took the chair Henderson had pulled out from the table.

"I am quite fine, miss, and good morning to you, as well. I included a pot of tea for you, just in case." Henderson poured her tea into a porcelain cup.

"How am I going to survive without you, Rick?" Andy asked, laughing softly.

"I'll make tea for you the first morning," Jack told her softly. He waited, wondering how Andy would reply. He was nervous about their future, and this was testing the way...quite possibly for both of them.

"Sure, that's just the first! I'm worried about the next hundred." Andy put a bite of eggs into her mouth.

"I'll contract for the next ten thousand," Jack offered, raising his voice enough to be sure she heard him. He knew she did by the way her fork paused on its return trip to her mouth.

Her hand shook and the fork dropped the bite of egg upon it.

Henderson set a plate in front of him, but Jack waited to see what Andy was going to do. Henderson added more coffee to Jack's cup, and then unnecessarily added more tea to Andy's. He made a disgusted sound and finally spoke. "The conversational ball is in your court, Andy, answer him!"

Andy laughed. "Thank you, Henderson, and you can go, hopefully without any further comments."

"Obviously, they would not have the needed effect!" The elevator doors slid shut on Henderson's last comment.

Jack continued to stare at her, waiting for her to look at him. Surely, she would say something. She'd have to respond...right?

Andy speared the dropped piece of egg with her fork, eating it quickly.

"Andy? I want to talk about tomorrow." Jack reached across the table and caught her hand in his before she could refill her fork.

"You mean when we disembark? I hadn't thought about it actually. I assumed everyone would be catching his or her own flight to wherever. Of course, we can exchange emails and phone numbers."

Jack released her hand slowly. "You're joking, right?"

"Well, relationships can develop under unusual circumstances, but they can't survive in the normal world where the people live everyday. It just happens," Andy finished, staring at her plate.

"Sounds to me like you have everything all planned. What about today?" Jack prompted impatiently. "Your slave contract."

"Uh, yes. If you still want to, we can do that today."

Andy's reply pissed him off even more.

"You make it sound like I'm your dog, and you'll play with me because you have nothing better to do," Jack pointed out immediately. His anger was boiling over.

"No, Jack. I just wasn't sure if you still wanted to...to—" She paused, struggling for the right words.

Jack interrupted. "Fool around? Play little games?"

"Yes...no! That is not what I thought. You are confusing me, Jack!"

"Forgive me!" Jack shoved back his chair as his impatience and anger got the best of him. He stared for several long moments. Turning, he walked across the room towards the suite's entrance. He grabbed his tuxedo jacket as he did so. Only as he opened the door did he speak again. "I'll see you later, Andy."

Andy continued to eat her eggs and only realized she had tears on her cheeks when a drop landed on the table. Sniffling loudly, she wiped her nose on the back of her hand because she wasn't going to use a linen napkin to do it! Standing, she walked over to where a tissue box was discreetly concealed. Blowing her nose loudly, she had no idea why she had reacted to Jack like she had. The only reason she could come up with was fear. Maybe she was afraid that he'd been kidding, and later would come the "gotcha".

The fat girl inside told her that this could not continue. Jack would return to his perfect world, as would all the others. She had her own little life to resume, she reminded herself. But it didn't make her smile. In disgust, she went upstairs and got ready for her last day on this amazing cruise ship.

* * * * *

Andy filled her day with so many activities she didn't leave herself time to think. Tonight was the buffet dinner and costume party. Any type of costume was allowed and she decided to go shopping for one. First, she spent time over lunch with "the girls" to find out what they had planned.

Gayle revealed Jack was playing racquetball with the others, which included lunch for them, as well. "Ray is reveling in all this 'male' time. He'll probably want to continue it when we get back."

Margrit laughed as she sipped her lemonade. "I'm confused. Is there a problem with them spending time together?"

Liz and Ruthie added their laughter. "When these men get together, too often, they turn into little boys. There is a long history."

Liz nodded in agreement to what Ruthie said, but leaned over to pat Margrit's hand. "Since you live in New York City, as well, I wouldn't be surprised if our 'frat' boys don't adopt Ethan."

Margrit looked at the other women. "And you all still live in the city?"

Ruthie nodded. "Pretty much, or nearby."

Margrit turned to Andy, who was on her right side. "And you as well, Andy?"

"Yes." Andy quickly decided to change the topic. "What is everyone wearing tonight? I still need to come up with a costume."

Liz grinned. "Well, Tony is going as Don Juan. Mark and I are going as chemistry professors."

"Unique! Not!"

"Did you put your creativity on hold there, Liz?"

Liz held up her hands. "Mark thought putting a tuxedo on was over the top. At least with this costume, he'll be comfortable. I made sure he packed a clean, white lab coat."

Ruthie patted her friend's hand. "I guess you're forgiven. Danny wasn't that much better, but I told him he had no choice...not if he wanted any chance of...you know. Anyway, I rented us clown costumes and brought them along."

"I love clowns," Margrit smiled. "Ethan and I are going as Master and slave. We have some rather elaborate leather costumes."

Liz clapped her hands. "Sounds like our table is going to be very interesting. What about you, Gayle?"

"Ray talked to Mark before we left," Gayle added with a frown. "He and I are going as interns. We've got green scrubs and stethoscopes and so on."

"I'm sure it will be great."

Ruthie nodded. "You and Ethan are still sharing our table, aren't you?"

"Yes, we are. So, Andy, what did you have in mind for a costume?" Margrit asked softly.

"None! I have no ideas at all." Andy sighed heavily, feeling depressed at the way the morning had gone. "I made an appointment at the costumers."

"Hopefully, they'll still have something," Liz added.

Ruthie nodded, and then turned to look at Andy. "What is Jack wearing?"

Andy tried to hide her reaction to the question. It hurt to have listened to her friends all talking about their "guys" and what kinds of costumes they'd all worked out together. It was jealousy, she knew, but even more it was the pain of not being connected with Jack. Silly to care about something as small as costumes, but she did. It wasn't easy, but she held back the tears that desperately wanted to fall. "I don't know what Jack has planned. He hasn't said."

"Do you want me to find out?" Gayle offered a moment later. "I'll call Ray and have him see if he can do some snooping."

"I don't think so, Gayle, but thanks. I'll find something." Andy forced a grin to her lips, hoping it convinced her friends.

"Do you want company while you look?" Liz offered. "I could cancel my body wrap."

"No, don't bother. I'll find something, and this way I can surprise all of you."

* * * * *

Andy hurried towards the Queen's restaurant on deck three. All of the normal dining had been converted for the costume dinner and dance tonight. Walking in this outfit she'd found wasn't easy, but there was no doubt it would get attention. The truth was that the only attention she really wanted was Jack's. Tonight, she was determined to lay all of her cards, her intentions, on the table. If he rejected her, so be it. She wore her gold collar, and had the leash attached. It didn't drag on the floor, but was tucked quite obviously into the top of her outfit.

Jack sat at the table with his friends. He felt it couldn't be more obvious the only empty chair was next to him. No Andy.

Of course, they had so much "interest" at their table it was hard to even notice one empty chair, unless you were seated by it. As far as his costume, he'd relied on Ethan to bail him out. He wore a pair of his own black leather pants and boots. His top consisted of black leather straps, crisscrossing his chest, and had a scabbard across the back, which held a wicked-looking, twelve-foot long whip.

Upon his arrival, he had quickly learned no one knew what Andy was wearing. He was more than curious. It had been tempting to bring a blanket just in case he felt the need to cover her body. Logic told him that was stupid, but he seemed to be operating on emotion ever since he set foot on this damned ship.

"Is that Andy?" Gayle's screech brought all of their attention towards the figure coming towards them.

Jack felt his stomach sink and his shaft went rock-hard. Coming towards them was a woman, dressed all in white, with gold and pink trim. White boots came above her knees. She had on a white bustier and white bikini bottom, with the high French-cut sides. Above the elbow gloves, which left her fingers free, added to the pretty look. As she came closer, he saw she wore a wig, cut into a long, stylish Mohawk shape, and was a silvery white, with a long fall down her back, as if it resembled —

Holy Crap!

Suddenly, Jack jumped to his feet. He knew exactly what Andy's costume was. "I should have brought that freakin' blanket," he muttered quietly as she neared.

Gayle had gotten out of her chair, running forward. She hugged Andy, and then made her turn around.

The rest of the table gasped but Jack knew what Gayle had just seen — a gleaming, silvery white three-foot long horse's tail. It was held in place by the bustier and leather straps that circled her body and upper thighs. Atop her head was a headdress composed of sheer white material, gold and aqua accents and a full, one-foot long feather. Andy was the epitome of a high-class, well-cared for "pony girl".

All the men stood as she approached.

Jack saw the faint flush of color that tinted her cheeks as she sat beside him.

"Sorry I'm late, everyone," Andy murmured, smiling.

Tony whistled, leaning forward to get Mark's attention. "Hey, Mark! Change places with me!"

"No way," Liz answered for him.

Margrit leaned forward, looking around Jack next to whom she was seated. "Brava, Andrea! You look fabulous!"

"Indeed! I must agree, Andy," Ethan added, smiling. "You make the prettiest pony girl I've ever seen."

"Thank you, but I drew the line at the bit," Andy replied. "I wanted to eat tonight."

"The buffet looks fabulous!" Ruthie spoke quickly. "I took a bathroom break so I could scope out the tables and see what I wanted to eat first."

Danny put his arm around Ruthie. "It's time to stop eating for two, Ruthie. Margrit is taking over that role. Oow!" He stopped to rub his newly bruised side.

Ethan was already laughing. "Margrit started before we found out," Ethan hurriedly scooted his chair back as evidenced by the scraping noise.

"Well, I don't care who is eating for whom," Andy interrupted, pushing her chair back. "I'm going to eat now."

Immediately, everyone stood and moved towards the buffet tables. Andy didn't move, which hemmed Jack in, or he could climb over five chairs. As soon as they were alone, Andy pulled her chain from the bodice and passed it silently to Jack.

Jack took the chain, looping it around his hand. Gently, he pulled it until Andy stepped close. "What does this mean, Andy?"

Andy took a deep breath and Jack watched as her breasts swelled from the bustier's tight compression. He waited until her gaze lifted before he pressed her again. "I owe you an apology for this morning," he told her quietly. His hand was now looped enough in the chain to rub against the soft skin of her cleavage. Taking advantage of the position, his knuckles lightly rubbed over the top of her mounded bosom.

"I am sorry, Jack. I wanted so much—" Andy stopped as her voice broke.

"Shh, sweetheart, it's okay. How long do you want to stay here tonight?" Jack asked her, fighting the lump forming in his throat.

"I want to talk to you and I want to spend time with our friends." Andy shrugged her shoulders.

"Come on, Andy." Jack gently pushed her away from the table. Without another word, he led her from the room. They walked up the outer stairs to the observation deck one level up.

The entire deck was empty, which wasn't surprising considering this was their last night on board. Jack led her to two deck chairs, helping her keep her tail from getting crushed as she sat. Quickly he pulled the other chair around to face her, their knees touching.

"I'm putting my cards on the table, Andy. I love you. I was an idiot when we were in school. I was stupid and I've spent the last years regretting what I didn't do. I did try and find you. Gayle refused to speak to me for a year or so. I soon figured out Liz and Ruthie didn't know."

"Ruthie didn't know until the last few years, when I needed a lawyer."

Jack nodded. "The only way I'll let you walk away from tomorrow is if you say there is no chance in hell for us."

Andy couldn't breathe. Surely, she had not heard what Jack just said. He loved her? No. She misheard him. "You love me?" She unconsciously voiced her doubts.

Jack's hand touching her cheek drew her gaze to his. "Yes, Andrea, I love you. I want to marry you, but if that isn't what you want, then I'm willing to work on defining a relationship the way you want."

"Are you sure, Jack? This person you've met on this cruise…me…well, I'm not like this normally."

"None of us are, Andy. This cruise is like a one-time deal. We've all had our grown-up clothes on. After tomorrow, we all get back to normal. I want you in my normal life, from now on." Jack put his hands on her knees, rubbing in small circles.

Andy was intensely aware of the heat coming from his slow, gently caress. She forced a deep breath. "You don't know me."

"We all have things to learn about one another, Andy."

"This is bigger than that. I've lied to you since you knew me. Gayle was the only one who knew the truth about me, and then Ruthie found out, when she became my attorney." Andy took a deep breath.

"Just tell me, sweetheart," Jack slid his hands up, curving his hands over her thighs. "I think we've learned a lot about each other so far."

"I don't have the family I always talked about. I spent most of my life in foster homes, and then I met Gayle in high school. Her family took me in. I was at school on scholarship and hardship grant money. I was very lucky, I know. But at the end of four years, I had nowhere to go. No job and I refused to sponge off Gayle's parents any longer. That's why I just took off. I didn't want anyone's pity."

"Oh, Andy, honey!" Jack lifted his hand and rubbed the back of his fingers against the side of her face. "What did you do? Where did you go?"

"To the city, New York City. I checked the want ads and looked for apartments. Again, I got lucky and met this wonderful woman who needed a companion. I had free time and I started to write. She encouraged me to submit to a publisher." Andy paused and took a deep breath. After so many years of silence, she had to get the truth told as quickly as possible.

"I live next door to a wonderful elderly gentleman. He was the one who sent me the champagne and further upgraded my cabin to the suite. And before you have time to think any nasty thoughts, he cooks and has me over for dinner. I do his shopping, run errands for him and take out his garbage."

Jack nodded. "Sounds like a great setup. Is there room in the apartment for two?"

Andy was trying to catch her breath after spilling her guts. *Wait! What did Jack just say? Did he ask her a question?*

"Is there room at your place for both of us? I don't mean we have to live together right away, but I want to spend as much time with you as possible. I have a place, but it sounds like your place is more of a home. I had my place professionally decorated and while it looks a magazine layout, it's not comfortable. And I'm not really on close terms with any of my neighbors."

"Live together?" Andy was having trouble taking it all in.

"Yes, darling. I want to live with you. I want to marry you." Jack leaned forward and put his hand flat on her belly. "I want to have a baby with you. If you don't want kids—"

Andy put her hand over Jack's mouth. "I do. I want your baby, Jack. I love you…so much. I don't know how good I'll be at this stuff." She paused to flick her hand at the feather on her head, meaning the outfit, and all it represented.

"This stuff is icing, fluff. Like electronic toys…fun if you can afford them. It's piqued my interest over the years, and if you want to pursue it, we will. Otherwise, I'm perfectly happy with a deck of cards and you." Jack smiled.

Suddenly, Andy pressed her hand to her heart. Jack had just referenced to a time they'd spent most of a day together, just the two of them, playing card games. Tears suddenly filled her eyes. Sniffling loudly, she had to ask him the all-important question. "What if I gain weight, Jack? Like with a baby, or something? It wasn't easy to lose it, and I may not be able to lose it all again, or maybe just some of it."

"So what if you do? I wanted you back in college, Andy. I was a fool. If you gain weight, I'll help you lose it, if you wish. We will take walks with the baby and get some workout equipment for the apartment. But if you do or don't, you are still my Andy, the woman I love. Every sweet, soft inch of you." Jack reached into his pocket, pulling out something.

Andy recognized it as a ring box the minute his hand turned it over. "Oh, my God!"

"It's amazing what a person can buy on a big ship like this," Jack said quietly. "I hope you like it. If not, we can return it in the morning and we'll pick one out when we get home." He opened the lid, showing her the ring.

"Oh, Jack!" She lifted her left hand, extending it towards him.

Jack grinned. "I take it this means yes," He laughed and slipped the diamond ring onto her ring finger. "I love you, Andy Bond. Will you marry me and end my misery?"

"Yes, Jack. I love you, too. I think I've always loved you!" Andy threw her arms around Jack as he stood up. She kissed him quickly, pressing her lips against his.

"I love you, my sweet Andy. Shall we go back and tell our friends?"

She had no doubt their friends would be surprised, but they would certainly share in their joy. Andy nodded and she practically skipped back to the party, more than ready and eager to start her new life with Jack.

Epilogue

Andy laughed as she danced for the third time with her dear friend and next-door neighbor, Mr. Edwards.

"Yes, my dear, you make me feel like a young man. You have indeed enriched my life, Andrea." Emerson Henry Edwards smiled.

Andy noted once more how dapper he looked in the traditional morning suit he and Jack both wore for the wedding. Only the three men were in the small wedding. Since their reunion cruise nearly eighteen months earlier, she'd been in each of her friends' weddings. After talking to her college friends, and learning they were all pretty much "wedding drunk", Andy asked Margrit to be her matron of honor. Ray served as Jack's best man. That's where the small quality about everything ended.

"I'm not letting you claim all the benefits, Mr. Edwards. I've adored living next to you all these years, as well. You were always cooking me healthy meals and reminding me to eat." Andy protested with more laughter.

"We'll call it a draw. But I will fully understand, as I've told you before, if you choose to move." The elderly gentleman reminded her in the middle of executing a complicated dance step. As he finished, with Andy gasping in his wake and merely following as best she could, friends and family on the dance floor stopped to applaud. Quite graciously, Henry gestured to Andy, bowing towards her.

She shook her head first, and then her finger at the older man. She had to raise her voice to reply. "We're very happy! You will have to evict us." Andy paused to rub her obviously pregnant belly beneath her white wedding dress. "And what kind of mean condo owner would evict a pregnant woman?"

Henry held up his hands. "Very well, my dear. I accept you are happy, as is your new hubby, who gave me the same answer when I approached him earlier. And soon we'll have a new baby to make us all laugh."

Andy walked with Henry back to the main table where they were seated. "I hope you will still feel like this when the baby is crying at one in the morning and then again at four."

"Of course I *will*, Andy, my dear. I've received one of those sound machines as a wedding gift," Henry told his neighbor with a big grin on his face.

"Who gave you a present on my wedding day?" Andy asked, frowning at the older man's comment.

"Your husband, actually. He told me that he got the idea from his father. Me? I am just grateful for his thoughtfulness and generosity. Now, is there a honeymoon?" Henry asked, just as they reached the table.

Jack, seated at the table, stood to hold Andy's chair. "I've been trying to keep that a secret, Henry. I hoped we could sneak away at some point this evening, when everyone is distracted with food and dancing."

Henry nodded. "That sounds like a plan."

Jack leaned over to whisper to Henry, "I have to be careful, after what I and the others did at the three weddings we've attended since we've been back…let's just say retribution could be hell."

Henry took the chair beside Andy. "Those would be the weddings of your college friends?"

Andy looked at Jack, seeing him flush around his neck. "They were very bad boys, to say the least," she told Henry.

"I'm hoping to get out of here before my friends can formulate a plan," Jack explained with a grimace.

"They tried to rope me into the plan, but I begged off, citing that the baby comes first," Ethan added with a grin.

Margrit shook her head. Seated next to her husband, she explained, "He keeps claiming the baby, but I've yet to see him nurse her even one time."

Everyone laughed.

Ethan grimaced as he added, "I tried once, but she didn't care for it!"

Jack joined in the laughter, patting Andy's belly. "I'll keep that in mind, Ethan. Thanks."

"Of course, that means you have to get up, change the diaper and bring the baby back for feedings," Ethan pointed out a moment later.

Jack shrugged though. "I won't complain for the first four."

Henry chuckled. "The first four weeks you mean?"

"I meant the first four kids," Jack clarified with a laugh and kiss on Andy's cheek.

Andy saw Margrit looking almost cross-eyed as she mouthed the word "four". Andy shook her head, and held up two fingers. As the evening wore on, dancing with her college friends distracted her.

At ten, she tossed her bouquet, followed by Jack removing her lacy garter. She thought they were staying the night, but when she went upstairs to use the bathroom in the suite, Margrit followed with the news she was to change her clothes quickly. Jack would meet her at the front door in twenty minutes. She was stunned the whole time Margrit helped her get dressed. Dimly she heard her questions, but had no idea if or what she answered.

Once she reached the rental car, Jack and Ethan were standing beside it, idly chatting as they waited. Both men smiled as the women approached. Hugs were exchanged and as Andy got into the front seat beside Jack, she overheard Margrit speaking to Jack.

"You be good to her, Jack Riley."

"I've been waiting a long time to do just that, Margrit." Jack smiled gently at the other woman.

Ethan grinned as he wrapped his arm around his wife, pulling her close. "I'll wait until people start asking where you are, which will probably be about thirty minutes. Then I'll spill the beans about the honeymoon escape. Have fun, you two, and we'll see you back here in a week!"

Andy waved as Jack started the car forward. "Where are we going?"

"I thought you might enjoy a relaxing cruise, before the baby comes. After that, it could be a number of years before we can get away," Jack answered.

"Oh, Jack! That is so sweet! I love the idea." Andy reached over and caressed Jack's leg. "Wait! Clothes?"

"Margrit, with Henry's help on the timing, packed a bag for you. We fly out tonight and embark tomorrow. We will cruise the Hawaiian Islands."

"I love it, Jack. It sounds perfect! I love you so much. Thank you for thinking of this."

He kissed her cheek, quickly returning his attention to the drive.

Andy found it difficult, but she managed to barely feed the curiosity that bubbled over inside. On the plane, they put away the armrest between their first-class seats. After takeoff, followed by the seat belt lecture, they were treated to a glass of champagne. Her friends, after Margrit let them in on the truth when she needed some help, arranged the expensive champagne. A congratulation note accompanied the bottle, as well as permission from her obstetrician.

When the "fasten seat belt" sign darkened, Andy heard Jack sigh heavily. She turned to look at him. "That sounded like you had doubts we were going to make it."

Jack shook his head. "Never!"

Andy laughed. "Well, I am impressed. I was afraid we were going to end up either with a bed filled with condoms or a car dragging God-knows-what down the street."

"I had hoped to avoid that, as well, and hopefully I have."

"I'm sorry you didn't get a chance to change clothes though, Jack."

"Don't fret, Andy. I've got casual stuff in my carry-on. I'm going to change in a few minutes after I talk to them about the dinners I ordered."

"They don't serve food on these late flights, Jack."

"Normally, no, sweetheart, but they have taken pity on the runaway bride and groom."

A stewardess stopped by Jack's aisle seat. "Good evening, Mr. and Mrs. Riley. Congratulations!"

Jack smiled. "Thank you."

"Yes, thank you very much," Andy added.

"I'm preparing your dinners and they'll be ready in about five minutes." The stewardess offered another glass of champagne.

"No, thanks," Jack paused, looking at the nametag. "Ms. Phillips. My wife's obstetrician limited us both to just one glass."

The stewardess laughed. "How sweet! I'm telling my husband that one."

"I'm going to change my clothes, if there's time," Jack told her.

"I'll make the time, Mr. Riley."

* * * * *

Andy and Jack followed the directions to their suite. They walked around the living room, and out onto the deck, which featured a table, chairs and two lounge chairs.

"I like it, Jack," Andy told him as she went back inside.

He followed, sliding the screen closed. "It's not as big as your suite was, but this one is the best they had on this ship."

"It's beautiful. Now, is this the bedroom?" Andy walked into the next room. "Ooh, Jack! Look at this bathroom!"

Jack followed her, but then he turned her to look in the other direction. "Just go past the bed, and you'll see," he prompted her.

Just beyond wall, through the glass door, she found a semi-concealed deck, which had a lounge chair on one side, and on the other was a Jacuzzi, which opened up to a fantastic view of the ocean. As she turned around, Jack stepped out as well. "I've had them turn down the heat on the tub, but we'll check it for sure before we use it."

"How do you manage to think of this stuff?" Andy asked, walking back into the bedroom. She sat on the silky down bedcover.

Jack shrugged, closing the glass partition behind him. Their bags still needed to be delivered. Otherwise, there was nothing to do until then. "It's easy. I have a book and two doctors on call."

Andy looked at her watch. "What do you want to do? Do we have time to…uhm?"

Jack grinned. "No, unfortunately, we don't have enough time for that, Andy. The bags could be delivered at any time. Also, we have butler service with this suite. I'd hate to get caught in your robe again."

Andy giggled and lay back on the bed, kicking off her shoes. "That one doesn't fit at the moment, so I hope Margrit didn't pack it."

"I have the credit cards in case there is anything you need and don't have." Jack sat down beside Andy.

"I thought honeymoon couples don't usually leave their room," she suggested, and then winked at Jack.

"Well, I guess we'll just do what the mood tells us." Jack replied as he kicked off his shoes, and then removed the jacket, tossing it onto the small stool in front of the mirror on the wall opposite the Jacuzzi. He swung his legs around and stretched out beside her. Reaching up, he pulled down pillows.

Andy took one of the pillows and scooted closer to Jack. "You know what I really want to do, Jack?"

"Well, if it is what I need to do—"

"Sleep?" Andy asked, glancing up at her new husband. "I sound terribly boring, don't I?"

"No, darling, because that is precisely what I need. We just need to recharge our batteries," Jack added.

Andy felt his hand lightly stroking her hair. "I love you, Jack."

"I love you too, Andy. And I think we should do whatever we damn well want while we still can. Soon we'll have another person to direct our lives, and I can't begin to tell you how much I'm looking forward to that day."

Andy snuggled even closer. Very quietly, she murmured, "Thank you, God."

A few seconds later, she felt Jack press his lips to her forehead, kissing her. "Yes, indeed, Andy. I've been thanking him every day since I saw you on our last cruise. I've been blessed in many ways since then. Let's snooze for a bit so we can at least not fall asleep in our salads later!"

Andy chuckled, but she promptly obeyed her husband.

Enjoy this excerpt from

Submissive Passion
© Copyright Mlyn Hurn 2003

All Rights Reserved, Ellora's Cave Publishing, Inc.

Chapter 1

John had watched her for a very long time, before he ever approached her. They had been working in the same office for over a year. He had been there much longer, having worked his way up through the brokerage house, after getting his master's degree from Yale. He was forty, graying at the temples, and had never been married. He was past that age when people played matchmaker for him.

All of his friends assumed he was a confirmed bachelor. And even though he was considered devastatingly attractive by all of the females he had known over the years, no one had ever suspected—no one who knew him, anyway—had ever questioned his sexuality. He had always preferred women since he had first played doctor at the age of six with Susie Flanagan, who had lived next door. He'd had plenty of dates over the years, and several relationships. One of these had progressed to the point of them living together for a brief while, and then had ended amicably.

But as he grew older, he had learned things about himself that he had not faced in his earlier, less introspective years. He had come to realize that he needed a different kind of relationship to be happy, to feel satisfied and fulfilled. He had started investigating things that interested him, reading about things that aroused him, and finally facing his personal reality.

He was a Master, a "Dom" in search of a "sub," a slave, or a submissive. He wanted the kind of total, trusting relationship that would allow this degree of trust, acceptance and love between two people. He wanted the freedom to be himself with his partner, and for her to feel the same. He wanted it "24/7" or as much as possible.

He had gone with the group from the office the last few outings, when he had learned that *she* was going as well. He had watched her in the beginning, wondering about her, listening to her participate in the conversations, the activities, and only doing so himself when he had to. He had decided that he needed to find out whether she would be interested in a relationship. If his instincts were correct, he would need to proceed carefully.

* * * * *

Maggie enjoyed her work at the brokerage firm. She was an administrative assistant to the junior Vice President, Mike Waters. He was a happily married man, in his late forties with four children, and had not shown the slightest intention of doing any "chasing around the desk."

Maggie was a beautiful woman. A natural beauty because she didn't wear any makeup to work; her skin was always clean, shining, and flawless, barring the occasional blemish that dared to pop up. But she just ignored it, knowing it would go away, and saw little reason to cover it up. She had left her last three jobs because of "chasers" who wouldn't listen to reason. She was really enjoying this job and didn't want to have to leave it.

Maggie thought of herself as only average height and average weight. She wore her waist-length auburn hair in a bun or low ponytail at the base of her neck. Her suits were always simple and loose fitting, never hinting at her curves beneath. She'd always believed this was necessary, because it was her curves beneath that usually caused the chasing to start. Her eyes were a hazel-green, with dark brown lashes, and lighter colored eyebrows. Her mouth was full, curved usually in a near smile.

It had taken her friends about two months to convince her to start participating in the twice-monthly outings that people from the office would plan. They were usually for bowling, drinks after work, or an occasional birthday dinner for someone. She had reluctantly joined in, and soon began having a great deal of fun. All the people involved were single or divorced.

There had been an occasional drop-in from the other office people, who were on their own for an evening while their spouses, or significant others, had been out or unavailable also. There had been a few who, while separated, had joined in to stave off the loneliness. But all in all, they were all very friendly and gregarious, and she had never had any problems with any of the men. She always made sure she sat with a female friend on either side, though, or the wall, or an escape route on the other side if two of her friends were tied up.

There were a few of the group who were looking for more than just a friendly outing, but they either "got into the groove" of the group or dropped out. The people here were interested in long-term relationships—either a committed one or a friendly one. Just last week, the women had all thrown a luncheon bridal shower for one of their set, who was getting married to a young man in the group.

Everyone was quite happy for them. Next weekend was the wedding and against her better judgment, Maggie had been persuaded to be one of her bridesmaids. A very sophisticated wedding was planned and it was an all-weekend event, being held at her fiancé's parents', who were very wealthy people and had an estate in upper New York.

But about six months ago, John Ford had begun joining their outings. Maggie had been aware of him since she had seen him on her second day on the job. Mike had had some special papers for her to deliver to a senior Vice President's office, and when she arrived there, the senior VP had been standing at his assistant's desk.

Maggie had felt a jolt deep inside her the very first time she had seen John. He was a very attractive man, but the feeling had gone deeper than that. It had seemed to pull at something inside of her, like she recognized something in him and in herself. His assistant, Carlie, had introduced them. Carlie Smith was very friendly and had met Maggie her very first day and had taken her under her protective wing, so to speak. Maggie had returned to Mike's office, but all the way there, she had felt as if someone was watching her.

If she had looked back, she would have seen that she was quite correct. John watched her the whole way, until she was out of sight. He had felt the jolt and the connection also. And from that point on, he had been watching Maggie silently…waiting and wondering. Several times he had been very close to asking her out, but he had quickly learned that Maggie was as slippery as an eel. She managed to never be alone with him or any other man, he had noticed. That was the only reason he had started joining in on the group outings, when he had learned that she was attending them also. At least there he had gotten closer to her than before.

* * * * *

Maggie had learned quickly from Carlie that John's joining their social group was a "really big deal." No other member from the senior level joined the casual outings, even though they were free to do so. Of course, John was the only single man at the senior level. Maggie had also learned from her friend that John had asked who all the members were in their group, and then he had asked to join in.

Maggie had at first suspected that maybe it was because of her, but she had quickly disabused herself of that notion for he had never made any attempt to catch her alone, either at work, or on their outings. Of course, there had been a few times that they had been alone, but they had been accidental times. So Maggie had calmed her foolish heart and her worries, and reminded herself that if a man was interested, he didn't beat about the bush…so to speak. He came out with it, and moved things along rapidly.

So the time they had ended up dancing together, the only slow dance of the evening, she had put down to accident. It just happened he was at her side when the music had started, and he had turned to her.

"Care to dance?" John asked softly.

From somewhere deep inside, she murmured, "Yes."

His movements were clean and smooth, as if he'd had professional lessons. Of course, the feeling of his arms around her, his hard body pressed against her soft one, soon had her heart racing madly. She was desperately short of breath by the time the dance finally ended, and jerked away from him, out of fear of her own reactions to him.

"Is something wrong?"

His voice had been like velvet and even now she could hear it in her daydreams. Dear God! His arms around her, the scent of him, and the feel of his hard, muscular body against hers had caused her body to respond as a woman. The dampness between her upper thighs, her racing heart and difficult breathing, had scared her. Most importantly, it had made her realize that her feelings were out of control. And that was something she didn't allow to happen, because in the past, her feelings had usually gotten her into trouble.

She'd gone back to the table and when he managed to sit next to her, she spent the rest of the night squirming in her seat. She was hot and needy for him; her womanly wetness had come unbidden. She felt her face flush when she saw his gaze on her one time, and that had only made things worse.

From that time on, she had worked hard at always keeping her female friends close at hand. She had done very well, except for the last week. The group had gone out to a movie and there had not been enough seats together, the place had been so packed. She was unaware that John had worked hard at maneuvering her to be with him at the end, so they had to sit a couple of rows back from everyone else.

He didn't touch her, but she smelled his male scent mingled with his aftershave and felt his body heat. With each passing minute she just got hotter and wetter. Finally, the movie came to an incredibly hot love scene and two things happened. The scene had involved some light bondage to the woman, followed by the man possessing her lovingly and completely.

At the end of the scene, Maggie had been sitting there tense, both from the scene itself, its subject, which was a bit of a surprise to her, and the proximity of John.

"I rather think that wasn't just acting on their part. It looked like they were having too much fun."

John's soft whisper teased her and the side of her face. The fact that he had echoed her own thoughts was unnerving and she gasped in surprise and agreement. When she turned to look at him, there was a fire burning deep inside him and it sent a message from his inner being to hers. She wanted to break eye contact with him, but she could not. Then it was John, something on the screen capturing his attention, who turned away first. Maggie had wanted to escape to the bathroom, but she'd been afraid that her rubbery legs would not support her. So she had sat through the rest of the movie trying to calm her breathing, her heart, and her racing desires to a semblance of normal.

After the movie, they had all gone out to a nearby bar for drinks and a light dinner. Maggie had grabbed Carlie and told her she had to sit with her. She knew her friend had looked at her strangely, but she had agreed. Even though there were nine other people at the table, Maggie had felt at times when her eyes would stray to John, that they were alone. And she admitted to herself for the very first time that she *wished* they were alone. The danger of involvement at work be damned!

* * * * *

John had watched her all the while she listened to others talk, smiling slightly here and there. He had a feeling that she had been as affected as he had by the hot bondage love scene. He had seen the fires deep inside her that she worked so hard to contain. He had been sorely tempted to grab her and storm out of the theater, and show her just how they could duplicate that scene at his apartment. But the thin veneer of modern propriety had stopped him. So he had sat there through the movie and in the bar afterwards, harder than a rock, wanting nothing more than to be alone with Maggie and explore the bounds of love, trust and sex.

John had arranged it so that he was driving Carlie, her live-in boyfriend, Max, and Maggie to the wedding party this weekend. Maggie had arranged to ride with Carlie and Max, and John had called Max and suggested that he drive. His Jaguar was bigger than Max's economy Hyundai, and that way they could all be more comfortable. Max had eagerly agreed. He liked Carlie's boss and when John had suggested that Max and he could share the driving...well, there had been no more questions in Max's mind. The opportunity to drive a Jag was just too damned good to pass up...in his opinion, anyway.

Maggie wouldn't find out until they picked her up at her apartment. John wasn't sure what would happen this weekend, but he was determined to make something happen.

About the author:

Mlyn lives in Indiana, USA. She worked as a Registered Nurse for 23 years in Pediatrics. Reading Barbara Cartland and Harlequin romance novels in high school spurred her to start writing. She did technical writing for her employers until she started writing erotica four years ago. She began her own website for people to view her stories. Mlyn is single and lives with her cranky cat Georgia, whom she named after her favorite artist for inspiration, Georgia O'Keeffe.

Mlyn welcomes mail from readers. You can write to her c/o Ellora's Cave Publishing at 1056 Home Avenue, Akron OH 44310-3502.

Why an electronic book?

We live in the Information Age—an exciting time in the history of human civilization in which technology rules supreme and continues to progress in leaps and bounds every minute of every hour of every day. For a multitude of reasons, more and more avid literary fans are opting to purchase e-books instead of paperbacks. The question to those not yet initiated to the world of electronic reading is simply: *why?*

1. *Price.* An electronic title at Ellora's Cave Publishing and Cerridwen Press runs anywhere from 40-75% less than the cover price of the <u>exact same title</u> in paperback format. Why? Cold mathematics. It is less expensive to publish an e-book than it is to publish a paperback, so the savings are passed along to the consumer.

2. *Space.* Running out of room to house your paperback books? That is one worry you will never have with electronic novels. For a low one-time cost, you can purchase a handheld computer designed specifically for e-reading purposes. Many e-readers are larger than the average handheld, giving you plenty of screen room. Better yet, hundreds of titles can be stored within your new library—a single microchip. (Please note that Ellora's Cave and Cerridwen Press does not endorse any specific brands. You can check our website at www.ellorascave.com or

www.cerridwenpress.com for customer recommendations we make available to new consumers.)

3. *Mobility.* Because your new library now consists of only a microchip, your entire cache of books can be taken with you wherever you go.

4. *Personal preferences are accounted for.* Are the words you are currently reading too small? Too large? Too...**ANNOYING**? Paperback books cannot be modified according to personal preferences, but e-books can.

5. *Instant gratification.* Is it the middle of the night and all the bookstores are closed? Are you tired of waiting days—sometimes weeks—for online and offline bookstores to ship the novels you bought? Ellora's Cave Publishing sells instantaneous downloads 24 hours a day, 7 days a week, 365 days a year. Our e-book delivery system is 100% automated, meaning your order is filled as soon as you pay for it.

Those are a few of the top reasons why electronic novels are displacing paperbacks for many an avid reader. As always, Ellora's Cave and Cerridwen Press welcomes your questions and comments. We invite you to email us at service@ellorascave.com, service@cerridwenpress.com or write to us directly at: 1056 Home Ave. Akron OH 44310-3502.

THE
☥ ELLORA'S CAVE ☥
LIBRARY

Stay up to date with Ellora's Cave Titles in
Print with our Quarterly Catalog.

To recieve a catalog,
send an email with your name
and mailing address to:

CATALOG@ELLORASCAVE.COM

OR SEND A LETTER OR POSTCARD
WITH YOUR MAILING ADDRESS TO:

Catalog Request
c/o Ellora's Cave Publishing, Inc.
1056 Home Avenue
Akron, Ohio 44310-3502

ELLORA'S
CAVEMEN
LEGENDARY TAILS

Try an e-book for your immediate
reading pleasure or order these titles in print from

WWW.ELLORASCAVE.COM

ELLORA'S CAVE
THE BEST IN TODAY'S ROMANTICA™

Discover for yourself why readers can't get enough of
the multiple award-winning publisher
Ellora's Cave.
Whether you prefer e-books or paperbacks,
be sure to visit EC on the web at
www.ellorascave.com
for an erotic reading experience that will leave you
breathless.